All the way in.
No way out.

Kyle A. Medlam

ISBN-13: 979-8-218-41488-7

Intro:

They say dead men tell no tales. The interesting thing about dead men is they in fact have a lot to say. If you look closely and listen carefully, they will tell you exactly who killed them. When you spend your lifetime experiencing murder and death, you get a deeper understanding of not only how to kill people, but how to read those who have been killed. Death's whisper is much more than a few words, it's a story. It was obvious with what just happened that Death and I needed to have a conversation. It was also clear I was going to have to start writing a lot more stories for Death to tell.

Acknowledgements

"For from Him and through Him and to Him are all things. To Him be the glory forever. Amen."

Romans 11:36

A special thank you to Ashley Ceselski & Alexis Jackson for being my read-as-I-write critics. Having your trusted opinion, insight, & support made this so much easier. My confidence was steady & I was completely secure in my work because of your participation in helping me make a life-long aspiration become a reality. Also, a big thank you to my son Rayce Medlam for the photo he took that became part of the cover art! I love y'all forever!

Chapter 1

The Meet and Greet I never wanted

This morning felt like any other normal day. Wake up, workout, eat, shower, get dressed, and head out to check on business. However, some people had other ideas for my day. They were not ideas I liked at all either.

As I walked out the door everything immediately felt off. I slowed my pace heading down the steps off my porch I began to notice a lot. It all happened so quickly I was caught off guard when a very angry looking man in fatigues stepped into my path and stopped me dead in my tracks. My brain was running one thousand miles an hour. Did I grab my gun? What the fuck are all these cars everywhere? Who the fuck is this guy?

That guy: *"Well good morning Mr. Ingerham. You and I have a lot to talk about."*

Kyl: (Pronounced Kel) *"I don't have a fucking clue who you are and as far as I'm concerned, we have nothing to talk about."*

That guy: *"Oh, but I know so much about you now, your name came up multiple times this morning. I'm Agent Hague with the DEA and this is Agent Lewis with the ATF. I'm the lead investigator on this case."*

I barely noticed the short douchebag looking man that had joined the taller douchebag who's name I'd already forgotten.

Kyl: *"Look, that's a great intro, well thought out, and I bet your mom tells you just how proud of you she is every morning when she hands you your lunch. But I'm busy and I don't have time for whatever story I know you and you're oompa loompa looking pal are dying to tell me."*

1

Rule One of any situation, never let them see you look caught off guard and always shift into a smooth calm demeanor layered with a couple great insults to shift the power back to yourself. I needed to see what this guy was made of quick.

Agent Hague: *"Look here asshole you're not funny and you will listen..."*

Got him, now to keep him off balance.

Kyl: *"I'm sorry, what was your name again? Agent Gag, right?"*

Ooh that one did it. He was as red as a tomato now.

Agent Hague: *"It's HAGUE. H-A-G-U-E. HAGUE."*

Kyl: *"Cool name bud. Have a wonderful day!"*
As I walked past him, he made a mistake that most men in this world knew not to ever make. He grabbed my arm and attempted to spin me back towards him. I felt his grip lighten quickly when he realized he hadn't budged me at all.
Deep breath Kyl, keep the lead here.
I slowly looked down at his hand and turned slightly towards him...

Kyl: *"You can let go of my arm, Agent. Now."*

As quickly as he had grabbed me, he let me go. As I turned all the way towards him, I noticed his partner position his hand on this gun. Agent Hague was as pale as a ghost. He swallowed hard and tried to speak with confidence again, but he was shaken, his voice cracked as he spoke sounding like some pubescent little shit. I wanted to hit him. I knew better though.

Agent Hague: (Stuttering) *"Y-you listen to me mother fucker. We've been after you for a long time, and we are getting closer to nailing your ass and I'm going to be one to do it. I will see you rot in prison for life. You fucking wait."*

The smile that creased my lips unnerved him even more.

Kyl: *"That's a lovely story Agent whatever your name was. I love your passion, but unfortunately, I have no idea what you're talking about, and I don't need to be a part of your little meet and greet. I run a construction and real estate company. I purchase land for development to build houses and buildings. Whatever you think in your head is going to happen, is never going to happen bud. Now, as I already said once, have a great day."*

As I turned and walked to my car, I quickly took in everything around me. I barely heard anything Agent Gag was saying except "I'll be seeing you again", as he yelled across the yard at me. As I got into my car it finally dawned on me that all this was because they had raided the house four doors down, Mikey's place. I fucking warned those idiots not to do any business where they lived and not to bring heat to our neighborhood. As I drove away, I spotted the two tails pull out and keep their distance. Great. Did Mikey, Shane, and Jeremiah really have the balls to speak on me? My brain started ticking away even faster. What did they know that they could have said? Did I keep them distanced enough to not have much information? This was a real issue. Why had my fucking name ever come out of their mouths? As my thoughts shifted to who I was going to task with silencing them forever, it hit me. Like a fucking truck, it hit me. These were my boys. My fucking people. Guys I had known my whole life. Did I really just consider having them whacked? There are rules though...But these are my people. I hadn't noticed the light turn red and almost ran into the intersection. I slammed on the brakes and slid to stop. Good one Kyl.
This was not how my day was supposed to start. I'm so fucking pissed.

I needed to clear my head, but today was a vital day for things to appear absolutely normal and in order. I would just have to deal with things as I moved through my day as if nothing were wrong. Damn, this is not a spot I considered I'd actually be in. I had done everything so carefully. Meticulous even. Not a single detail left unmanaged. Or so I thought. I mean, I'm not an idiot. You don't get to where I am and not know the feds have your name. It's a matter of what they can do with your name that's important. How much do they really know?

Son of a bitch. Mikey. Shane. Jeremiah. You mother fuckers. These three stooges that I loved, like brothers, may have broken the rules and upset the balance of everything. For what? For fucking what!? I needed Luka asap. Cell phones were out of the question, never speak business on a phone. Any kind. Not at all. I needed to make a stop and get a message out. I pulled off into the gas station. It was one of my properties. When you do certain things, you need a lot of things to cover for it. I had six different completely legitimate businesses. Not including rental properties. It got deeper than that, though. Some of my businesses owned businesses, and some of those businesses paid other businesses. It was a logistical nightmare for any accountant or IRS auditor. I had it all in my head, though, and Pete, my business manager, knew it like the back of his hand.

I shifted into park and took a deep breath. Come on Kyl, slow down, think, be rational. Sometimes easier said than done. I'm not known for putting up with bullshit. I'm better these days than in previous years. I'm not as reactive as I am proactive. Violence has always come so easily. That is until Luka came into the picture. I was one of the most, if not the most violent kids you ever met. Honestly, thinking back, I couldn't even really tell you why. I had a pretty decent childhood. It was strict. My parents were all business. That's all they knew, and they ruled our home and lives with an iron fist. I actually hated them more than I loved them. But, in my defense, they didn't do a fantastic job of showing the affection most parents do. I remember discipline, hard work, and reward for hard work. Anyways, welcome to my brain. I'm in the middle of potentially the most dangerous situation to my empire and freedom and I'm sitting here fucking reminiscing on my childhood. Focus Kyl. Luka.

As I got out of the car, I casually glanced over my shoulder to get eyes on my tail. Yep, still there. Shake it off, not the first you've been tailed Kyl. As I walked inside the young clerk behind the counter lit up like a scoreboard. Amy was her name, one of the most loyal women I'd ever know. Typical sad story, broken home, piece of shit dad, and addict mom. So why would she be so loyal to me? I may be a lot of things, but human trafficking is disgusting to me. If you hurt a child and I find out, you won't have many breaths left before your last. Amy's mom had given her up to the dope man to pay her debt

4

and get her next fix. Still makes my stomach turn. I had heard through one of my many ears that this piece of shit dealer was selling off this young girl for sex and had been abusing her himself. I walked into his house and beat him as close to death and you can be. I let him live because I knew I had crippled him, and I turned his testicles into a sack of mush after stomping on them repeatedly. I let him live so he had to suffer the rest of his miserable existence for what he'd done. I took Amy from that place and gave her a new life. She never looked back, and she vowed her life to me. She's never wavered in that for all these years.

Amy: *"Well looky there, it's the magnificent Mr. Ingerham! Welcome to my little slice of heaven, what brings you in today?!"*

She knows I don't require such a formal greeting from her. But it always gets a smile out of me, and she just beams. I would never take that away from her.

Kyl: *"Good morning, Amy, I'm grabbing a water and I need you to page Luka a zero two four please."*

Her smile faded a little, and she tensed. Zero two four is the pager code for "Going to the beach".

Which had nothing at all to do with actually going to the beach. It was an emergency code for shits gone sideways, meet me at the quarry.

Amy: *"Yes sir. Right away."*

Her eyes searched mine for some sort of sign the world wasn't about to burn down. I simply smiled and winked at her.

Amy: *"All good to go, have a wonderful day, Kyl."*

Kyl: *"You too Amy."*

Pagers were fairly outdated by this point but still used in early two thousand. They were virtually untraceable, and you could create your own codes and leave anyone to guess what they meant. Whatever Luka was doing, I could guarantee he was on high alert and already on his way. I still had to make a few stops at jobsites to sort out the three stooges being absent from their posts. Luckily, I keep a lot of good talent around that I knew I could count on. But I still needed to check in and get things organized. Luka knew to be there and wait. It was something I knew I never had to question with him

Chapter 2

Excuse me sir, you can die now.

Luka Blazevic. No one in this world will ever know the depth of
friendship and loyalty that flows between the two of us. It's
something most will never come close to understanding.
Luka was born in the former Yugoslavia. In the 80's and 90's,
Yugoslavia experienced a period of intense political and economic
crisis. Which led to a very violent collapse of Yugoslavia in what is
known as the Yugoslav Wars. The part of the country that Luka was
born in became what's now Croatia. A lot of families embraced the
opportunity to create and fight for a land now their own. Others,
however, fled to America. Unfortunately for most, that violence
followed them here. I met Luka in the most unfortunate of
circumstances. To be honest, I'm not really sure why I chose to turn
around and go back that day. Maybe it was just the mood I was in
after the day I'd had. Something in that kid's eyes as he looked at me
while five Serbian teens and men stomped and kicked him caught my
attention. I turned back and watched for a few seconds.

They were beating him to death and not once did he give up. He kept
giving them hell. I saw one of the men pull out a knife and stab him
slowly several times. In my head I knew this was none of my
business. But my heart spoke and said this should stop now, how
weak of five people to beat one person and then torture him. I had
made my decision and there was no turning back now. I walked up to
the man with the knife and said, *"Excuse me sir, you can die now"*,
and shot him point blank in the head. As the others scrambled to get
away, I shot them too. One of the teens was crawling to get away as I
stood over him ready to fire again, this badly beaten kid reaches out
and stops me. He picks up the knife and carves this kid's eyes out
then slices his throat ear to ear. I watched him put those eyes in his
pocket. I helped him drag all the bodies to the dumpster and heave
them in. He didn't really speak English, but he said he was Luka. He
gave me a nod and started to walk away. Men like this were an asset
and I knew I couldn't let him leave. He had killed one of those guys

to make us equal in that moment. Guilty of the same. I yelled after him and motioned for him to follow me. What the fuck was I going to do at seventeen years old with a fourteen-year-old non-English speaking Croatian with a set of fucking eyes in his pocket? We'll get those after while, don't worry.

I pulled into the quarry, Luka was waiting by his truck. Same stoic face as always but I could read him better than anyone. I saw the worry in his eyes as I parked. Luka was like a brother to me, even though I was older and slightly bigger, most of the time I felt like the little brother.

As I got out, he met me with our usual bro hug and then paused to try and read the situation in my eyes. I'm not an open book. I could stand behind a counter bleeding to death, with one leg laying on the floor and you'd never know it.

Luka: *"I heard Mikey, Shane, and Jeremiah got popped. It's already on the streets."*

Kyl: *"Ya, lovely way to start my morning. I had a douchebag Fed in my face claiming he knew all about me blah, blah, blah, and that my name had come up several times that morning. Said he was coming after me."*

Luka: *"You think they spoke on you?"*

Kyl: *"Man...."*

I had to choose my words carefully here. Luka was his own man and the only man who didn't follow my orders like the others. He had this way about him that made him the most dangerous person you could have at your side.

Kyl: *"I don't want to jump to conclusions Luka. I want to sort this one okay. I'm going to be honest and just say it doesn't look good. They broke code, they defied my orders, and something with this fed rubs me wrong."*

Luka took a deep breath. I knew exactly what he was thinking. He already didn't like the boys; this was not going to help. He kicked at a rock and stared off into the distance for a couple of moments before he turned to me.

Luka: *"I know they're your longtime friends. But you know the rules. We wrote them together and we're where we are today because of those rules Kyl."*

He was right. I knew where this was going.

Luka: *"We need to be extra cautious here, I'll respect your wishes and we'll take this one slow. But we decide together on this one. Ya?"*

Kyl: *"Deal. Look, I know where this is going Luka. I just need to be sure. Got it?"*

Luka: *"Understood. I've already started getting my ears and eyes in place. They're downtown in the county building. Interrogation rooms. No charges yet."*

Kyl: *"Do we know what they were holding?"*

Luka: *"Spilz said they've been working with Russ and his people. Couple pounds of heroin, cutting supplies, and apparently, they ended up with a couple of the burner AK's."*

Kyl: *"Mother fuckers. So, they're the ones who stole those. You're sure it's Russ and his people?"*

Luka: *"100%"*

Russel Kessler is the degenerate son of Phillip Kessler, one the three crime families in this state. We have a non-competitive agreement, and we don't handle anything in the streets. We settle our disputes like business. Everything is a gentleman's agreement and we've kept it that way for a substantial number of years now. This is a direct violation and a bad one. On both sides. I could spit fire right now I'm so angry.

Kyl: *"I'm going to Kessler. I need you to get to the bottom of this quickly but be careful using our people on the inside. Feds are a different animal, and I don't want any of our people burned."*

Luka: *"Got it, you sure you don't want me coming with you?"*

Kyl: *"No, I need you focused on this thing. If it makes you feel better, you can send Quiz to camp out in the corner."*

Luka smirked, he knows I'm not fond of Quiz, but he's Luka's ace. The guy is a former professor from Armenian who ended up collaborating with mercenaries to fight the extremists during the wars in Yugoslavia. Extremely intelligent and even more dangerous. The most unassuming man that you could imagine, and you'd never think he could hurt a fly. Drives me up the wall because he talks constantly and wants to tell you every stupid fact known to man. I can't hear myself think when he's around. I do appreciate his skill though; just wish he were mute.

Kyl: *"Stop smiling. I'm only agreeing to that, so you won't worry yourself to death.*
Tell him to keep a low profile."

Luka: *"You got it boss. I'll see you at Rocky's at seven then?"*

Rocky's was one of the bars I owned.

Kyl: *"Ya, keep everything moving on the business side like usual. It's important we look unbothered."*

Luka nodded and walked off to get things underway. I knew he was tense and annoyed to have to playthings out this way. People don't make mistakes under Luka's watch. They just know better and the ones who do fuck up, well, they always seem to move away. Usually don't hear from them ever again either.
It was only 11am and I already needed a drink. Suppose I'd have one

with Kessler, in his book there was never a bad time of the day for a drink. He was going to need one after this conversation. The three families all had different agreements and arrangements. Kessler's deal was chop shops, heroin, and Prostitution. I don't fuck with heroin. Not that it's any better than the others but in my eyes, it was the bottom of the barrel shit. I fought for a long time to keep it off the streets and out of my neighborhoods. The Kessler's had brought it in during the mid 90's when the Asian culture started to grow here. Their drug of choice apparently. After some negotiations, we came to an agreement on where they could push their products and where it was absolutely not allowed. The fact that my three idiot friends were working with Russ to peddle heroin not only in my area but on my fucking block in my own neighborhood presented a whole separate set of issues. I'm going to take the high road on this and guess the old man had no idea. Doesn't make it better though. I took a deep breath and hit the call button. He must've been waiting, think it rang once.

Kessler: *"Good morning, Kyl, to what do I owe the honor of your call?"*

Kyl: *"Cut the shit Kessler, I'm not in the fucking mood. Natoli's, noon. See you there."*

I didn't even give him the opportunity to respond. I just hung up. In the pecking order I didn't need a response. If I call, you show up. It's that simple.
I remembered that I had left the house without my gun. Which was fine today, couldn't take it in Natoli's anyway. The Natoli family had been around longer than the town itself and in the oldest part of town. Westburrough was the old money side of town. Most of the founding members of the city lived there or their families were still there. Oil barons, Judges, City council, those types. Natoli's restaurant sat on the corner of the three areas run by east different family. I was the only one who wasn't still a family business. It was just me and my crew. They are my family though, just not the conventional type. The Natoli family came here in the early 1900's to escape the world of crime and mafia rule. When this all started there were five families and they fought constantly. Sometime in the 1950's there was disagreement that led to a shootout in Natoli's place.

Back then, it was run by the old man, Alessandro. They say he was the kindest man you'd meet until you pissed him off. It had been said that during the shootout, he was hit in the arm and completely lost his shit. He walks out from behind the counter and plugs the first three people he sees with guns. As the gun smoke clears, here's this sawed-off, very pissed off Italian guy standing on top of a table. He says, "On this day I will make this decision once and for all. Natoli's will be a common ground for those who come here. You come, you eat good, you solve your problems with your words. There will be no guns in my place of business. If I see a gun, I will shoot you dead on the spot. Are we clear?" No one argued and since that day there has never been another incident there. In fact, it's the most protected place in the state I'd say. A sanctuary if you will.

As I drove across town, I kept going over in my head the things Agent Gag (still can't remember his name) had said. I'm well aware that the Feds have been watching for a while. I'm never too concerned because I'm mostly disconnected from the dirty side of the business in the most recent years. I have methodically worked towards building and maintaining a front for all this through legitimate businesses. Granted, most of the money made on the other side was washed through those businesses, but you'd be hard pressed to ever figure it out. My business manager Pete was a genius when it came to numbers and accounting. I trusted Pete. He felt he owed me a debt he could never repay, so he pays in hard work and loyalty. He'd chew his tongue off so he couldn't speak if that's what he felt he had to do. I think everyone at this point was that way. That's what was bothering me so much about the deal with the boys. I made sure they had good jobs with great pay. Realistically, the three of them were destined to be lifetime losers had I not set them up the way I had.

Gag had said "Oh but I know so much about you now. Your name came up multiple times this morning." Was he bluffing me to see if I'd panic and make a mistake? What the fuck had those morons done? Fuck!

Remembering the tails behind me I angry smashed the gas as I whipped around the car in front of me and around the one in the other lane to blow through the intersection as the light turned red. Follow me now, you fucking twats.

12

For the next two miles I drove like a man possessed. Nothing eases my tension and anger like angry driving, and this car never disappointed in its ability to lay down rubber and move like a rocket.

As I pulled into Natoli's I was a lot more composed than I had been on the way here. I showed up early so I could have a quick conversation with Francesco and pay my respects to Alessandro. Francesco ran the place now that his father had finally stepped back due to his age. The man didn't understand the concept of retirement. I can remember years of the two arguing over him stepping down. When the economy turned down, Francesco came to me for help. Not as much for a loan as it was about me talking to the old man about retirement. The Natoli's knew my grandparents. They were close friends of the family and had worked closely together to start Natoli's in 1910. My grandfather built this building with Alessandro's father. They often all went out dancing together, and all met their untimely deaths on the same night in 1967. Some punk kid had robbed a gas station nearby and, in his escape, ran the intersection and hit their car. No one survived the accident. Francesco was about 10 years older than me, but he understood the way of things. We understood each other, and there was a respect that never had to be spoken between us.

The money He had borrowed to save the restaurant, he paid every penny back. I took every payment he gave me, and I slid it back to his wife Chiara. I had run into her at the market one day and cornered her into telling me how things were really going with the business. She managed all the bills and paid all the vendors, so she knew better than anyone what the truth was. While my loan had kept the doors open, they were still struggling to survive beyond the restaurant's expenses. I made her promise she'd never speak a word of our conversation, and I advised her how to manage the money to create a turnaround. Basically, every payment I got from Francesco; I gave back to Chiara. I had convinced Francesco to increase menu prices and because he didn't oversee the finances. He had no idea for years that the influx of cash and profit wasn't just because of the price increases. He finally caught on but never challenged me.

He simply came to me one day, hugged me, and said, "Our family is

13

your family."

As I walked through the door I was met with an ornery smirk. It always made me smile to see that wily old man sitting there hustling people over a game of Scopa. An old Italian card game that I never quite got the hang of. He loved it though and he loved to take people money playing it.

Alessandro: (in Italian) *"Ah, il mio figlio in più preferito. Come ti tratta il mondo in questi giorni?"* (*Ah, my favorite extra child. How does the world treat you these days?*)

Kyl: *"È un cane mangia cane per quanto riguarda il mondo. Saggio signore."* (*It's a dog eat dog as far as the world is concerned. Wise sir.*)

My Italian isn't great, but I keep up with it for the old man. He loves it.

Alessandro: *"It's been a while young man. I fear that you come with a troubled mind today. What brings you down my son?"*

Kyl: *"A violation of the rules. I'm meeting Kessler here."*

He wrinkled up his face immediately. Alessandro hates Phillip Kessler with a passion. The Kessler's had started the shootout in the 50's and it was Phillip's great uncle who met his demise first at the other end of Alessandro's gun that day. There's always been animosity between their families.

Alessandro: *"I hope he brings his gun so I can rid this world of him. Smug fuck he is. Just say the word and I'll plug him for ya kiddo."*

He was smiling as he said that, but he meant it with every fiber of his being. I genuinely believed if he didn't have to worry about the rest of the family, he'd do it without much reason needed.

Kyl: *"I appreciate it, but I'll handle things today. You just keep that hustle strong on that ridiculous card game."*

Alessandro: *"Ah, so you don't want to lose your money to an old man huh? That's okay, plenty of people play."*

He winked as I patted him on the shoulder and walked towards the kitchen.
Francesco came out as I reached the doors. He had his own eyes and ears in the streets. The Italian community made it a point to always know what was going on. That's part of why I wanted to see him. I was quite concerned that this was happening right under my nose, and I had no idea, and no one had brought it to my attention.

Francesco: *"Hey there's my favorite brother from another mother. How are you holding up?"*

Kyl: *"I'm in a foul mood. I need to understand how this went down and my people didn't know, and your people didn't know or didn't tell me."*

Francesco was a horrible liar, so I'd know if he was bullshitting me. He didn't waiver though, he simply motioned me back to the office.

Francesco: *"I know what you're thinking, none of my people knew shit. We were just as surprised to hear it this morning as I'd imagine you were. But I can tell you this, your boy Spilz is in on it. Marco rattled a few chains this morning and apparently Spilz is the middleman. It gets worse, Spilz is working with the Latin Crowns. That's where the heroin is going."*

I just closed my eyes and took it all in. I was angry at myself for becoming so distanced from it all that I didn't even know what my own people were doing. What the fuck was happening? Had I not treated these fucking people well enough that suddenly I was in question of everyone's loyalty? Moreover, how in the fuck had Luka missed this? Was he not as feared as he has always been suddenly? Had we become too soft? Worst of all the fucking Latin Crowns....They had numbers and that's the only reason they even existed as far as I'm concerned. The cartel had disapproved of any business with them, the largest Mexican gang in the city, Coyote Loco, was constantly at war with them. I left the Coyotes alone as long as they followed the rules. About 5 years prior the cartel received 15 of their own in individual boxes. I think they got the point and agreed to stop trying to push their way into our area. The Coyotes found their place among things pretty quickly. The Latin Crowns, however, are fucking scum. They're known to rape and several of their members are fucking pedophiles. The only reason they're not dead is their value to Kessler's chop shop business.

The look on my face must've said a thousand words. Francesco was fidgeting nervously.

Kyl: *"I want your eyes and ears in every corner, nook, cranny, and gutter."*
(Pulling $10k out of my pocket)

Kyl: *"You keep five and use the other five to pay your people."*

Francesco started to say something but stopped. I knew he intended to tell me I didn't have to give him money, but by this point he knew not to argue. It wasn't the time for it. He nodded and said he'd show me to my table. There was darkness growing inside of me that had been suppressed for quite some time. It's a fury that once unleashed could burn the city down in a matter of hours. They didn't want the old me to come back to the streets, but it sure felt like they were pushing me to it. It would be best for everyone that didn't happen.

Francesco: *"The Veal Saltimbocca?"*

Kyl: *"Yes please. And Francesco...A sturdy steak knife with my dish as well."*

He swallowed hard and nodded. Everyone knew the Veal was so tender you could cut it with your fork.

Chapter 3

A little bit of a history lesson, boring, right?

To really understand what's about to happen, you have to know the history of how we all got here. No, I don't mean our divine creation by God. I'm referring to how there got to be three families and why I'm such the odd man out on the traditional meaning of "crime family."

In the beginning, there were five founding families in the state. The Kessler's, Cretchfeld's, Mardechi's, Stephon's, and Vonnet's. You couldn't put them all in the same room together or anywhere at the same time for that matter. The amount of animosity between these five families was enough to fill a stadium. The constant power struggle through the 20's and 30's constantly spilled over into the streets. Drive-by shootings, burning businesses, and retaliation got to be so frequent that innocent people were getting caught in the crossfire more and more. The local police were too scared to intervene and at the time, the feds were still being organized but had most of their focus on places like Chicago and New York, where the really big-time families were operating.

Late one night somewhere around 1942, one of the rival families firebombed a deli owned by the Cretchfeld family. What they didn't know was there were two newly immigrated families staying upstairs. The fire had spread so quickly, no one was able to get out. The next morning as they carried out the nine charred bodies of babies and small children, Leo Cretchfeld, head of the family wept in the streets joined by Marcello Stephon. The two agreed that something had to change and dedicated the next several weeks to working together to create a set of peace talks between all the families. They designated Natoli's Restaurant a neutral place to meet every Tuesday night to work on negotiating terms and zones. It took six months to iron out the details and all came to agreeable terms. That's how Natoli's became the center of the five regions. That peace would last for nine years until that day in 1951 when the seams let out and the peace treaty would crumble. Eleven people lost their lives that day. Two innocent bystanders and nine members of the families. Three of those lives taken by Alessandro Natoli, which led to the restaurant being off limits to anyone not a high-ranking member of one of the families.

Over the next nearly forty years, the families stayed at war. Never anything bigger than small skirmishes over zones and the occasional throw down when two opposing groups ended up in the same place. The push to expand was always on the agenda. One family would move in on a block and take over. Maybe lose it, then take it back again. A viscous never-ending cycle that only got worse the more drugs that hit the streets.

So how do I fit into all this? My mother was a Vonnet. The family tried to arrange a marriage between her and one of the up-and-coming Mardechi's, who were big in their own rights on the industrial side of business. The Vonnet's were businessmen first. Their forte was real estate and development. You don't build in this in the town unless you go through them. Over the course of time, they had secured around fifty two percent of all the open real estate, both residential and commercial. It also made it easier for them to operate out of almost every part of town because they owned it.

My mother however, had other ideas, and she fell in love with a man she'd met during a summer trip to a concert after her sophomore year, Lennox Ingerham. He'd come to town with friends for a music festival. He and my mother hit it off and started on their dreams of owning a farm. Then came me. They weren't bad parents, just had zero compassion, and didn't ever impress upon me that value. Loving in their own way, I guess, but cold none the less. We'll leave it at that. When I was around twelve, Lennox became ill with some sort of kidney disease and passed away very quickly and unexpectedly. My mother followed within a year. They told me she died from depression. I later discovered what they meant was she ate a fistful of Vicodin and chased it with a fifth of vodka.

They had been really good with their money, the problem though, I was only fourteen and still a minor. My mother had kept me fairly distanced from the family outside of holidays. She had always said she didn't want me falling into their way of life. Something she

18

probably should have considered before she fucking off'd herself. Because that's exactly where I ended up. Right in the middle of their way of life. My uncle had become my guardian and his bitch wife made sure I knew I had to earn my keep. What should have been my inheritance was auctioned off, and the money spent. Mostly by my aunt, I suspect. My Uncle Mac was a good guy, to me at least. He had a temper and a violent streak when things didn't go his way. I learned some unbelievably valuable skills about making people talk, body disposal, and construction in the years that followed.

I kept my head down and for the most part did as I was told. Because I was so oddly cold and disconnected, they figured out pretty quickly that I was perfect for delivering messages in nonconventional ways. Most people weren't going to expect to be stabbed by some kid. I can't say I enjoyed it, but I didn't hate it either.
Everything had started to go surprisingly good for me until my uncle got sick. That left his bitch wife in charge and his oldest son Damian to step up in his place. I had mostly avoided him because he was a piece of shit to me. Picked on me constantly and under my bitch aunt's watch, I wasn't allowed to do anything back to him. Damian had his own plans for the business and family. He'd already begun to heavily push drugs and because he had a degree in chemistry, he was extremely proficient in teaching others how to cook meth. Which became the main trafficked drug alongside others like LSD and mushrooms. When you own so much real estate, your options to move around with labs and store houses are much easier.

I wasn't ever really impressed with the drug trade or manufacturing. I had a knack for being accurate and precise in completing tasks and ensuring others followed suit. Damian saw that and put me in charge of collections from all the dealers. Until one regularly troublesome dealer decided to push me around because I was just some kid, and I didn't tell him what to do. Guy poured a beer on me and pushed me down a half a flight of stairs. I vaguely remember the feeling that overcame me as I heard him and his boys laughing at me. I was very perceptive, so I had noticed the wooden Louisville slugger propped up behind the door. I remember my turning body back towards the door and my pace quickening. It happened so fast no one was able to grasp what was occurring until it was too late. I had charged back

19

through the door, grabbing the bat, and in one fluid motion swung and smashed into his open still laughing mouth. Someone let out a scream, a woman, bits and pieces of teeth and blood were flying in all directions. As I drew the bat back to swing, his jaw shattered and hanging slack, he wobbled and fell to the ground. The bat, already in motion, slammed into his knee making the most awful cracking sound you'd heard. I'm not sure if it was the bat, his knee, or both. He was screaming in anguish. The pain and shock must've been terrible. I was going to hit him again when the woman who had screamed was shoving a bag of money in my direction, sobbing, and saying something. My ears were ringing, I started to ease back out of my rage to see the room full of terrified people. I took the bag from her and dropped the bat. I didn't know what to say so I said the first thing that came to mind. "I won't be so nice next time."

As I walked out of the building, I felt almost high. But it was a different high, not like a drug high. Way better. Ya, I'm definitely twisted I told myself. That night when I got back, I hadn't considered I'd be in any trouble at all. As soon as I walked through the door, my bitch Aunt was on me. She slapped me, hard, right on the cheek, then again. She was in my face; her stale cigarette and vodka breath stung my nose. My head wasn't registering what she was yelling at me. Another slap.

Damian: *"Ma stop, go sit the fuck down."*

He was coming towards me. He paused to tell her she didn't slap his people.
I almost felt good for a second that he had defended me. I was too quick on that thought as my head rocked sideways from him smacking the shit out of me.

Damian: *"What the fuck were you thinking? Do you think you can just go around beating my dealers with bats? I'm going to have to take care of that guy now you fucking idiot. You got thirty seconds to explain yourself before I really fuck you up."*

My fucking ears were ringing from getting hit. I was still dazed.

Kyl: *"I went to collect, and he told me to get fucked. I said I needed to collect, and he poured beer on me and pushed me down the stairs. What did you want me to do? Come back without the fucking money?"*

He just stared at me for a second and looked around the room at his guys. No one seemed to offer anything up for the situation. I don't think he knew exactly what to do, so he smacked me again. I was about to lose my temper with him. Hit me again bitch.

Damian: *"You don't make decisions, I do. I run this shit. You come to me."*

Kyl: *"So you want people thinking they can just walk all over us out there. What's to keep them from shitting on you thinking you're weak?!"*

He raised his hand again but this time I stepped back and balled up my fists. His eyes got big with surprise

Kyl: *"I swear to God if you hit me one more time, they'll have to wheel you in there next to Mac. You fucking listen to me, while you're up in here eating good, getting fat, and counting the money brought in. Those of us like me are out in these streets. Its up to us to keep the dealers in line and make sure people know not to fuck with this family or your money. There's movement out there and one wrong step, you're on your ass losing it all. I'm not some street corner punk Damian, I'm blood and I take protecting this family seriously."*

I wasn't stupid. I had been watching the game evolve. Damian was book smart but dumb to the dope game on the street level. The tension in the room was at a boiling point and about to roll over when Lewis, my uncle's long-time advisor stepped in.

Lewis: *"He's right Damian, he's done this family a service keeping us strong out there. It was only a matter of time before someone felt like they could test that. I bet no one tests it again for quite a while after this. Let him be."*

He nodded at me as he turned to go back to his chair.

Damian glared at me.

Damian: *"Don't ever flex at me again kid. Be here tomorrow at noon. Get out of my house."*

I didn't say a word and just walked out. This mother fucker, some day he's going to push me the wrong way.

I was the only family member not allowed to live in the family compound. When my uncle fell ill, Damian said he was taking my room for an around the clock nurse. That of course, was bullshit.

I went home, I needed to change my shirt. I had gotten blood on it either from the dick faced dealer or it was mine, not sure. I couldn't sit down; I was to wound up. I put my pistol in my waistband and decided to go for a walk. That was the night I met Luka. That was the night that set the stage for the coming days.

Over the course of the next several months everything we knew about life would change so dramatically it would alter the course of everyone's lives forever and rewrite the rules. But, first, let's get down to some facts.
The Kessler's ran drugs (mostly heroin), chop shops, and prostitution. The Kessler family was known for their trucking company and two dozen laundromats.
As I said previously, the Vonnet's were real estate and now meth, LSD, and mushrooms.

The Mardechi family controlled most of the industrial side of the city. Aircraft, manufacturing, and production of several types of industrial and household items and whatnot. Their dark side included bank robbery, stolen property, and guns.

When it came to bakeries and food, the Cretchfeld's had their hand in it all. They forcefully acquired every business they owned and specialized in money laundering and a multitude of politically motivated crimes. Bribery, extortion, you name it.

At their side, you'll find Marcello Stephon Jr and family. The Stephon family was big into Prostitution and political extortion. They have aspired to be in politics for decades. The problem was always that everyone knew they were dirty. So, they teamed up with the Cretchfeld's. They let Prostitution slide off to the Kessler's for a percentage of course. Everything runs through the Cretchfeld's on the promise they'll continue to support the family's campaign for power in political positions.

So there's your five. How do we get down to three? Buckle up buttercup. It's about to get real fucking wild.

$\mathcal{C}$hapter 4
Looking back, I should've gotten the tacos

My uncle Mac passed away in his sleep about a month after Damian and I had our face off. The funeral was massive, which was not surprising. I don't think I've ever seen so many people come to pay their respects to one man. It was also the only time you'd see all five families in one place so well behaved. The death of the head of a family just hit differently, it was one time you could count on everyone seemingly forgetting all the years of animosity and fighting.

Within the following week, all five of the heads of family gathered to officially acknowledge Damian as the new face of the Vonnet family. It was no secret that everyone hated Damian. He was not his father in any sense of the word, and everyone had made it clear they wouldn't put up with his cockiness. Lewis had requested that I accompany him, and even though Damian objected, I was still there. Whether he liked it or not, I was the captain of the street trades and businesses. Thanks to Lewis of course, he was second in command. He was the only one who treated me as good as my uncle had.

Lewis: *"Today is an important day, Kyl. Not for why we'll be there, but for you. You need to take in every detail of every second. Watch who flocks together, watch for side talking, look at the reactions, and read their faces. There's going to be a story written today."*

Kyl: *"A story?"*

Lewis: *"Yes. These men hate Damian, and he's not going to do himself any favors when he opens his mouth. They respected Mac. They feared Mac. They don't fear Damian. They're going to be looking for any way they can to start pushing the Vonnet family back, and it's going to be violent. Learn what you can today and be ready, son."*

I just simply nodded. Out of the corner of my eye, I could see Damian glaring at us. He hated that Lewis watched over me so well. He had grown up around Lewis and had always seen him like an uncle. Lewis had told him multiple times as he had gotten older to watch how he treated people. He tried to advise him on the decisions he was making. When he saw, that Damian wasn't going to listen to him, he pulled back. Lewis is not one to waste words on those who refused to listen. I always had the feeling that without Lewis to watch, Damian might try to knock me off. I had in fact learned plenty that day and I was going to make my own plans to be ready.

The next year things got twice as violent. We were making money hand over fist on the drug trade. Damian had ordered the seizures of multiple properties that had been gifted to the other families during Mac's time. He pushed rents and leases up with the threat of harm if they tried to leave. Luka had learned English very well and had become my right-hand man. Everywhere I was, he was close. Damian hated that he had no control over Luka. He hated even more that every time he tried to speak to Luka, he suddenly didn't speak English. Lewis had been the same to Mac before Mac took over so he understood and kept Damian at bay mostly.

I was very well known for being extremely violent when necessary and most didn't want to find out what would happen to them if they crossed me. That intensified as Luka became my number one. He had his own way about him. Tough as nails and there weren't many who could stand and throw hands with him. He became so feared that no one dared even say a cross word to me. Even the other members of the family wouldn't fuck with me. Things would happen to people. More than once after I'd had a disagreement with someone, they'd end up in the hospital following some unfortunate accident. One of Damian's top three generals disappeared after he and I had an altercation. Of course, I got blamed for it, but luckily, I had been on a date that night and had a solid alibi from being at Natoli's. My childhood sweetheart had come back to town. Gianvonna Mardechi. Yep, it was 100% complicated and even more so now. Had I known she would end up the catalyst to the world burning down, I might have stayed home that night. No, that's a lie. I loved that girl. Had since I was like 4 years old, I'm fairly sure.

Gia was the niece of Eli Mardechi, who of course was the head of the family. Gia's dad, Dale, had taken the wrap for a bank robbery back in the day and been sentenced to 10 years in prison. Unfortunately for him, he ended up in the same penitentiary as Eli's former bank robbery partner. Eli had left him behind when things went sideways, and he took the wrap for the whole thing. He tried to turn states witness for amnesty and it backfired on him. It did, however, get him fifteen years instead of twenty. Dale stepped up and said it had been him and not his brother. The Judge sentenced him to a reduced sentence of ten years as an accomplice and for owning up to his mistake. He was dead two days after he got there. Gia and her mother were well taken care of. If I had been anyone else in the world, I'd have been dead for trying to date her. Fortunately for me, Eli had always liked me. He and Dale had not only been close to my dad, but their wives had grown up with my mother. They had offered to take me in when my dad passed away but back peddled when they found out Mac had guardianship of me.

Because of all the issues with Damian and the current state of things, it was not acceptable for her and me to be seeing each other. Not that we gave a shit what anyone thought and the only one who knew was Luka. Who was clear, he thought relationships were a waste of time. He had always maintained he was only interested in catch and release pussy. That's what he called it, I couldn't help but laugh every time I heard it. I was by no means innocent either. I had quite a reputation in the street and in the sheets. If you could get a Master's of fucking, I'd have had two. I loved to fuck, and I had learned enough about my body and how to control it to be a stamina guy. I had sent more than my fair share of women home walking funny for the next few days. You'd be surprised how many women will not object to being choked and even whipped during sex.

Gia was no exception to that. She loved it rough. The rougher the better and she had no problem telling me over and over that she belonged to me in every way. I'm fairly certain the night I threw her legs over my shoulders and held her against the wall by her throat while I licked her pussy and then dropped her onto my dick while still pinned to the wall had sealed the deal between us forever.

26

I never let my relationship come between me and my work for the family. Some might say I had that backwards, but she got it. It was never even a debate. I could always count on Luka if I wanted to step out to see Gia. Damian couldn't say much for that reason, but he still did. He hated to see me with her. He had wanted her years ago, but she'd rejected him. It drove him nuts, no one rejected Damian Vonnet.

He thought everyone owed him something and it led to a lot of half-cocked stupid decisions.

Prime example, his next set of decisions would make would seal the fate of two families and change the way everything had been in this town for decades.

I'll never forgot the day, it was fall, October. My birthday was just two weeks away. Luka was leaning against my Supra talking to some cute little gal. Gia and I were near the water, curled up arm in arm on a blanket. She kissed my lips and said, "I need to tell you something."

Kyl: *"What is it doll? You love me!?"*

Gia: *"Of course I do! It's more than that though.... I... umm..."*

I was almost worried to the point it made me sit up straight. Gia never had a problem saying what was on her mind.

Kyl: *"Gia, what it is babe? Tell me."*

Gia: *"I'm pregnant, Kyl."*

If you could have seen what just transpired in my head... I was so shocked I flew to my feet.

Kyl: *"Are you fucking for real?!"*

Gia: *"Yes, I'm for real!"*

She had tears in her eyes, and she looked panicked. Shit, I'm a dick.

That wasn't the right reaction, was it? I don't fucking know, I was shocked but, I was...excited. Happy. This was a happy feeling. I rushed back to her side and wiped her tears.

Gia: *"Are you upset with me?"*

Kyl: *"Oh Gia, no baby girl, I'm not upset. Are you?!"*

Gia: *"Not at all, Kyl. I want us to be a family. I want a life with you. I fucking love you."*

I'm certain I had no idea what was happening inside of me at this point, but I started to cry, and I just grabbed her and squeezed so tight.
Meanwhile, I had completely forgotten about Luka being nearby. He had seen the weird reaction and interaction. He rushed over and was so absolutely stunned to see the tears in my eyes that he instinctively reached for his pistol.

Luka: *"What the fuck is happening? Is everything okay? Kyl?"*

Kyl: *"We're going to have a baby, Luka! You're going to be an uncle!"*

He was completely caught off guard, that he almost looked terrified for a moment. Then what I had said sunk in.

Luka: *"I'm going to be an uncle? You want me to be a part of your family?"*

His reaction caught me off guard, and before I could even respond, Gia did.

Gia: *"Of course stupid! Who else is going to teach our kid to be tough?!"*

I had never seen Luka's lip quiver like it did just then. He grabbed us both and just held us and laughed the happiest laugh I think I had ever heard from him. It was probably the happiest moment I had ever felt and yet I had no idea that everything I never knew I wanted or needed until that moment, would disappear that day.

The chain of events that came next, I'll never understand. I didn't even try.

My phone rang, it was Damian. I answered.

Damian: "*Kyl, they killed Lewis. He's gone Kyl.*"

My heart fell into my stomach, and I went into autopilot.

Kyl: "*What are you telling me Damian? Who killed Lewis?*"

Damian: "*Eli Mardechi. I sent Lewis to tell him to vacate the Plaza and he just killed him, Kyl.*"

I couldn't wrap my head around what he was saying. I hadn't remembered ever hearing Damian cry, but it sounded forced. Fake. Something felt off.

Damian: "*We're going to war Kyl, get ready bro. We're going to war. Get Luka and get over here asap.*"

I said I was on my way and hung up. The look on my face must've been terrible. It had both Gia and Luka looking at me with anticipation.

Kyl: "*Lewis is dead.*"

Almost in unison...

Luka/Gia: "*What happened!?*"

Kyl: "*Luka, go get in the car.*"

Luka looked puzzled, but he didn't argue. He hugged Gia and walked off.

Gia: *"What's going on Kyl?"*

Kyl: *" Damian just told me he had sent Lewis to tell Eli to vacate the Plaza and Eli killed him..."*

Gia: *"There's no fucking way Eli would ever kill Lewis Kyl! You know that!"*

Kyl: *"I know, something is off. Something is wrong. Listen to me, DO NOT go home. You go to my house, and you lock the doors, and you don't open the door for anyone. Do you understand me?"*

Gia: *"I understand, please be careful Kyl. I love you."*

She embraced me, then she held my face and looked into my eyes.

Gia: *"You come back to me, you understand me? You come back to me."*

Kyl: *"I promise, I love you, Gia. Go, now."*

I had the most uneasy feeling I had ever felt. As I got into the car, I looked at Luka, and I could tell he felt it too. What the fuck was about to happen...

As I pulled out of the park, I turned left towards Damian's and made it probably half a block before I grabbed the e brake and spun the car around, dropped a gear, and laid waste to my tires as I headed the other direction towards Eli.

Luka: *"What's your thought here?"*

Kyl: *"Something is off. It's all wrong. Gia said it, too. Eli would never kill Lewis. Not in cold blood, and Lewis would never provoke such a reaction. We're going to see Eli first. You agree?"*

Luka: *" We're on the same page."*

30

I was one hundred and twenty-five deep on the speedometer when I noticed all the cars at Plaza. The Plaza was a multi unit shopping center Mac had lost in a poker game to Eli. I downshifted and hit the brakes hard sliding sideways into the parking lot. As I parked and got out, I was met by a dozen armed men led by Charlo Mardechi, Eli's son.

Charlo: *"Let's see those hands boys before I add two more of you fucks to the list of the dead."*

I could tell he'd been crying. Charlo didn't have a mean bone in his body, so I knew he was hurting right now. I pulled my pistol slowly from my waistline and laid it on top of the car. I gave Luka the hold your place look.

Kyl: *"Charlo, let's talk man. I know something is fucked up bro. I just don't know what yet. Talk to me."*

He looked at me, and he knew I didn't know. He lowered his gun and nearly collapsed. I caught him just as he started to drop.

Charlo: *"He's gone, Kyl. My dad is dead."*

I was so confused now...

Kyl: *"What? What are you talking about? I thought Lewis was dead?"*

Charlo: *"They're both in there, Kyl. They're both dead, bro. I don't understand what the fuck is going on."*

Kyl: *"Okay, we're going to figure this out. Something isn't right. Luka, get a perimeter set and find out who saw what. We know someone saw. You four, you help him."*

Charlo motioned to them to do it. He was a mess. I had to see for myself.

Kyl: *"Are they inside? I need to see"*

Charlo: *"Ya, I'm coming with you."*

Kyl: *"You sure, Charlo? There's no shame in waiting out here."*

Charlo: *"No, I'm coming."*

What I would see as I entered the building would tell me everything I needed to know. It broke my heart and invoked that dark anger I fought so hard to keep down. They had been ambushed. Lewis was propped up against a pillar with Eli next to him. Lewis had held his hand as they both died. I felt sick. I felt rage. I already knew who had done this. Fucking Damian. I'll kill him. He's already dead. He just doesn't know it yet.

Luka came running towards me and stopped dead in his tracks. The sight before him rattled him as badly as it had me.

Luka: *"There was one camera they forgot. It was Bash and Hudson."*

Bash was Damian's first general, which hadn't shocked me as much as Hudson being there. Hudson was the street captain for the Cretchfeld's. Shit just got deep. How the fuck was I going to sort this one out? I knew I had to deal with Damian first. As far as I was concerned, I was done with the Vonnet family. I had my own family to start now. My own family... Oh my god. Gia.

Kyl: *"Luka, we have to move now! Charlo, I have to go. It's Gia."*

He went completely pale. It clicked for him the same way it just had for me. Damian knew how close I was with Lewis, and he knew his death would unleash the wrath of both me and Luka. Unfortunately, Damian knew I would go directly to Eli. When Luka and I didn't show up immediately, he'd had the time to do the unthinkable. He'd been watching us. My heart dropped, I couldn't breathe, I couldn't fucking see straight. Luka saw it. He grabbed me and we rushed to the door. I knew I couldn't drive and so did Luka.

Kyl: *"My house, quickly."*

The stone-faced look Luka always had was replaced by a deep worry. A look I had never seen...I'll never forget it.

As we pulled up, my world collapsed. The front door was kicked in. I slipped as I got out of the car. I felt as if I could throw up, I already knew. I fucking felt it. Death is something that is thick in the air. You feel it, it just feels different. The air is heavier. I reached for my gun as I ran towards the door. I slipped again as I ran inside. There was blood everywhere. She had given them one hell of a fight. I scrambled across the entryway towards the living room. Everything was fucked up. Holes in the wall, everything broken, all the furniture out of place or flipped. She was in the corner of the room, covered in blood, savagely beaten, and stabbed. In her dying moments, she had drawn a heart and U on the wall in her own blood. I pulled her into my arms. I had just lost my love, my family, and my life. I don't remember ever sobbing like this, but whatever broken should feel like, this was it. I could hear myself screaming when I finally realized Luka was holding me. He had tears streaming down his face. It made me angry. Luka doesn't have tears. He doesn't deserve to be hurt. I was so confused. I wanted up. He helped me to my feet. I looked at Gia, kissed her forehead, and covered her with a blanket.

Kyl: *"They all die, Luka. The Vonnet's. The Cretchfeld's. They all die tonight."*

Luka: *"I'm with you, Kyl. They all die."*

I made several calls to all those I knew would stand with me. When Charlo learned about Gia and our baby, he didn't even hesitate. He said he was bringing fifty men. Luka and I armed ourselves to the teeth. Vests and all. Everyone would remember this night as the bloodiest night in the history of the state. There would be no speaking.

I parked in my usual spot, gun in hand, I walked into the Vonnet family home, shot Bash in the face first, and laid waste to every member there. I took extreme pleasure in blowing the lower half of my bitch aunts face off and watching her bleed out. Luka moved like a fucking demon through the house, room by room, until everyone was dead. I had shot Damian in both legs. I stood over him as he begged for his life.

I knelt down, face to face with him...I was disgusted. It sickened me to breathe the same air.

Damian: *"I didn't have a choice Kyl, the Cretchfeld's were going to turn the family over. It was just politics. I'm sorry, we can work this out together and get back at them. Kyl, please bro. "*

He was lying of course. This was a power move to activate the two most violent members of this family and set us on a path of destruction towards the Mardechi family. He wanted them out of the way so he could assume control of all those businesses and areas. He had killed my mentor, my Gia, and our child over his own greed.

I moved in so close my nose was against his. I stared straight into his eyes.

Kyl: *"She was fucking pregnant Damian."*

His eyes went wide with fear and disbelief.

Damian: *"Kyl, oh my god Kyl...I didn't know. I'm fucking sorry okay. I so fucking sorry..."*

He hadn't noticed that it was my pistol pressing into his groin. I looked him in the eyes and pulled the trigger and blew his dick and balls off. He screamed in agonizing pain. I grabbed him by the face as he screamed and held his terrified gaze. He was trying to pass out on me. No, you don't bitch. I slapped the fuck out of him.

Kyl: *"Luka, the night I met you. You cut that kid's eyes out. Why?"*

I hadn't forgotten the oddity of him cutting that kid's eyes out and putting them in his pocket.

Luka: "*So that he would have to spend eternity in hell blind but was stuck seeing the man who took his eyes forever. I look at them in a jar every day.*"

Fucking sick Luka. I loved it. I wanted the same. I sat my gun down and reached into my pocket for my knife. Damian was barely conscious, but he came to when I sunk that knife into the first eye socket and carved out his eye, and then the next. I looked into them as they sat in my hand.

Kyl: "*Rot in hell you fucking piece of shit. Fuck you.*"

I stood up and put a single bullet between his empty eye sockets. We had just massacred the whole Vonnet family in one fatal blow. Now, it was the Cretchfeld's turn.

As we walked outside, we were met by Charlo and his crew. I still had Damian's eyes in my hand. One of his guys gagged and said, "*Jesus Christ, are those eyes Kyl?*"

I looked down and stuck them in my pocket and smiled. A cold fear swept over Charlo and his crew; it was as plain as day. No one brought it up again.

Kyl: "*We hit the Cretchfeld's now. The whole family dies. All of them.*"

Some second-hand goon voiced his apprehension towards the idea, and it was the last thing he ever said. Luka walked directly up to him and shot him dead. Point blank.

Luka: "*Anyone else?*"

Not a fucking word. I'm certain no one was even breathing. Charlo looked at me with wide eyes. Shaking.

Kyl: "*We'll meet outside the family grounds. I'm hungry, going to grab a bite on the way. See you there.*"

I couldn't have looked like any more of a pure psychopath than in that moment. I don't fucking know why but I was legitimately hungry. I wanted food.

The Cretchfeld's had about thirty family members and around forty crew in their compound. As I walked to the gate out back casually munching on my tater tots, it opened suddenly. Standing there was Darren Cretchfeld. Darren was a bitch; he was the soft middle son and was never cut out for this life. But he was extraordinary intelligent, so his dad forced him to run numbers and finances.

Darren: *"Please don't kill me. I know what they did, and I knew you'd figure it out. If you'll let me and my wife, go, I'll change my name and disappear forever. Please. The door code on the east side is four three four five."*

I believed Darren; he hated being a Cretchfeld. He used to cry as a kid about being forced into the family business and they treated him awfully over the years. How fitting he was now the gatekeeper to their demise.
I laughed aloud at the thought.

Kyl: *"If I find out you're still a Cretchfeld somewhere out there. I'll come and kill you myself. Go."*

He didn't hesitate. They were gone.
As we moved across the compound, Luka stealthily executed the perimeter guards one by one. I punched in the door code and walked in. Hudson was sitting there looking at a magazine and didn't even look up.

Hudson: *"I thought I told you fucks not to be running in and...."*

He never got to finish the sentence as I sunk my blade into his neck. I looked into his eyes without a word and then let his body crumble to the floor. I motioned for Luka to round up all the family.
It had become slightly chilly outside, and I thought a fire would be rather cozy. It was a gas fireplace; I loved these things. Something

calming and comforting about it.

It took less than ten minutes to gather everyone in the house. I sat down next to Leonard Cretchfeld Jr and pulled the table closer to me so I could unpack my food. Every time Leo Jr tried to speak, I would Shush him.

I looked up at Charlo.

Kyl: *"Charlo, you should go. You aren't going to want to see this. I promise you; it burns into your brain. Leave me Devin, Louis, and Pratt. They work for me now, go home."*

I scanned the three of them, they all nodded in approval.

Those guys were old school cats. Legitimate savages. They knew what was about to happen and were well versed in it. Between them and Luka it wasn't going to be a pretty sight.

Charlo: *"Kyl, my family is indebted to you. I'll meet with you when you're ready."*

I just nodded and waved them off. Devin tied Leo to the chair and managed to duct taped his eyes open. How skillful I'd thought to myself. He was going to watch every single member of his family die a horrible death. I remembered the eyes in my pocket and pulled them out to set them on the table. Several of the guys looked me quizzically.

Kyl: *"I thought Damian might want to see this too."*

One by one each member of the Cretchfeld family was killed in the most horribly slow and painful way as Leo Jr was forced to watch. As the last member was killed. I reached over and slammed my knife through Leo's throat as I took the last bite of my food. I was sort of disappointed. Looking back, I should've gotten the tacos.

Chapter 5

To catch a Kessler

After all the violence so many years ago, I took over most of the Cretchfeld area. The businesses were split between the Mardechi, Kessler, and Stephon Families.

Marcus Stephon announced that they would keep all the businesses but would be forgoing their zone and leaving the organized crime life behind to pursue politics. So, most of their zone went to me.
I had built quite the empire, on both the sides it all. The infighting didn't really exist between the three power families. The Mardechi's just wanted a premium pick at real estate deals and fair pricing from my construction company. Luka had suggested we negotiate for the gun market, which Charlo readily agreed to. The guns were his dad's deal and he never felt as confident in, so it was easy to let go. Charlo and I were both adamantly opposed to any street gangs moving into either of our areas. They'd try but would realize quickly they had no place here. With new construction booming, it meant there were plenty of places to make people disappear.

Kessler on the other hand, was a lazy piece of shit. He had one reject son, Russ, one who aspired to lead and follow in his father's footsteps, Mitch, and a daughter, Leah.
She was a viscous woman and ran their prostitution ring with an iron fist.

Pretty much all the issues we had over the course of time were a result of Russ. He had tried more than once to step on my cocaine trade by pushing some cartel backed gang into my zones to deal. It never went well for them and eventually they stopped trying. He doubled the heroin volume in the streets. He was too stupid to understand, higher volume means lower prices. He was either smoked out high or ripped out of his mind on coke. He thought he was some badass gangster on the street. Walked around a lot dressed like Al Capone half the time. He wasn't right in the head and Phillip

Kessler wasn't good at keeping him reeled in. I had begun to understand by this point, it was intentional. Mitch was feeding the city's growing pill epidemic and gaining ground with it. They had tried to push the cartel into smuggling guns in. That stopped after they got all the neatly packed boxes of their own guys delivered back to them. The cartel announced they would not be working in areas belonging to me or the Mardechi Family. All of it was starting to make sense now though. I was focused on the clean side of the business; Luka and his guys were constantly dealing with bullshit issues with the smaller street gangs. It was all so Phil could work under the cover of it to move the Latin Crowns in place to make a run at taking over my areas.

My brain was flashing back to all the stupid graffiti around town I'd been seeing.

They were communicating their intent, setting up their own zones. I chuckled to myself, not bad Phil. That's going to cost you though. I hadn't gone soft, just mistakenly complacent.

Francesco appeared with my Veal Saltimbocca. Hands down the best dish in the city. As he sat my plate down, he placed a steak knife there next to me slowly and cautiously.

Francesco: *"I've asked the girls not to sit anyone back here, so you'll have your privacy. Can I get you anything else?"*

Kyl: *"A single of your oldest Scotch, on the rocks, and whatever Kessler's usual is."*

Francesco: *"Absolutely, I get right on it."*

Kyl: *"And Francesco... find out who the troll is. I need a name within the hour."*

He looked down at his feet, then turned and walked away. I didn't need to explain myself. He knew as well as I did.

When you have a troll in your community, they implant negativity and create animosity based on lack of any attention to those people in the area. "Look at Kyl and all his people living it up. Just expecting us to feed them information to keep them safe. What are they doing for us? We need to eat too!"

It's meant to replace loyalty with a sense of entitlement. Creates an environment where if you're not asked you don't tell and if I'm not paid, I don't say much. Which is why all these things were happening and I wasn't aware. I had become complacent. Reliant on their loyalty to keep me informed. I had made a very vital mistake and a dangerous one.

Just as I began to enjoy my Veal, Kessler walked in. Normally, I'd stand and give a man a proper and respectful greeting. When I felt it was deserved of course. Kessler stood there expecting it.

Kyl: *"Sit down Phil."*

I could see the smug displeasure on his fat face.

Phil: *"Your uncle never left a man hanging like that you know."*

Kyl: *"I never leave a man hanging either, Phil."*

It took him a second to catch that but when he did, his face turned beet red.

Phil: *"You keep insulting me and we're not going to end up on very good terms here."*

Kyl: *"That's okay, we're already not on good terms are we Phil?"*

He mulled this over for a few seconds as he sipped on his drink. I could tell he was torn between saying something stupid and saying what he thought I'd want to hear.

Phil: *"Look, I didn't know the little shit was doing business with your guys behind your back. I was just as surprised as you were, I'd imagine. I haven't had the chance to speak to him yet. He's no doubt sleeping off a bender somewhere still. I'll take care of it."*

Kyl: *"You've had the Veal Saltimbocca? Right Phil? Best in the state. You should try a piece."*

I cut a piece off and slid it towards the edge of the plate.

Phil: *"I'm not much on Veal really. Kyl, I didn't come here to have some culinary experience with...."*

Kyl: *"Try the fucking Veal Kessler. Now."*

I could see the confusion in his eyes, he couldn't figure out why the fuck I was so adamant about the damn Veal.

He reached across the table towards the chunk of Veal I had cut away for him. As his hand reached the plate, this was my moment to catch a Kessler where I wanted him.

I moved before he could even flinch, snatched the steak knife, and stabbed it through his hand pinning it to the table. Before he could let out a scream I shoved the napkin in his mouth, then grabbed him by the back of the head forcing his eye almost onto my fork. I could feel it just scrapping the lens of his eye.

Kyl: *"Shhhh...we don't want to scare the other customers Phil. Stop fucking moving around before I accidentally on purpose stab you in your fucking eye. You listen to me you fat greasy fuck. I may not have been paying attention, but it doesn't take me long to catch up. You've been intentionally causing distractions to keep Luka busy knowing I was more business minded these days. I'm very aware of the presence of your pussy street gang. All that's one thing but your retard son's actions have caused me a lot of extremely uncomfortable issues that I'm now going to have to deal with. Men who should have no voices spoke very loudly this morning and the Feds are now involved on top of it all. (I pushed his eye into the fork just a little more) ON MY FUCKING BLOCK RIGHT DOWN FROM MY HOUSE, PHIL. FEDS IN MY FUCKING YARD AND IN MY FACE FIRST THING THIS MORNING, PHIL. Do you know how badly that upsets me? This is a deep violation of the rules. I want the Latin Crowns out of my zone and in exchange for the four of mine I now has to deal with, I want Russ brought to me."*

Kessler's blood was running off the table onto the floor, I could hear the little splattering of it. He was whimpering through the cloth napkin still loudly enough, that I'm positive it could be heard through the restaurant. I let go of him and he immediately clutched his eye. I pulled the steak knife out twisting as I did to make sure it hurt even more. He let out a yelp and quickly wrapped it.

Kyl: *"I could call your actions a declaration of war. I'll give one opportunity to redeem yourself Kessler. One. You have heard my demands. Now get the fuck out of my sight."*

He didn't say another word but scurried out as quickly as his fat ass could possibly go.

I sat there looking at the pool of blood on the table and floor. I owed the Natoli's an apology for my behavior and the mess. I started to lean down to mop up the blood with my napkin when I heard the shuffling feet of Alessandro.

Alessandro: *"Leave it, leave it. We'll get it."*

He pulled up a chair and sat at the table with me. Francesco stood behind him.

Kyl: *"My deepest apolo…"*

But he cut me off.

Alessandro: *"Do not apologize for this. That fat fuck is lucky any of us let him walk out of here. I'm glad you fucked him up. He deserves it. But it us who owes you an apology."*

I was extremely puzzled by this. Why the fuck would Alessandro or Francesco owe me an apology?

Francesco handed me a piece of folded paper

Francesco: *"Before you open that, I want...we want you to know that we support whatever decision you have to make regarding what's on there."*

Puzzled, I looked down and opened the paper. What the fuck? I couldn't believe what I had just read. I looked up quickly, searching for something from either of them. They both were looking down in complete shame. The name on the paper was Matteo.

Kyl: *"Francesco, please tell me this is not your son?"*

Tears welled up in his eyes and began to run down his cheeks. Alessandro pursed his lips and wrung the napkin in his hand.

Kyl: *"Explain this to me."*

Francesco: *"My son is the mole. We've been hiding his heroin addiction for some time now. It's why he's never here."*

He paused for a minute to wipe his eyes and take a deep breath.

Francesco: *"He's been on Kessler's payroll for a few months now. Causing unrest and building up how you'd forgotten about the people. That's why no one saw you anymore. You saw yourself as too good. Kessler cared about the people. That's why he'd come down and been giving out free smack and money.... Kyl, I'm so embarrassed. With all my heart I'm sorry. I will accept whatever his fate is."*

Alessandro: *"Our family has disgraced the relationship that has been a lifetime between us. However, we must repay you, the Natoli's will make it right."*

Kyl: *"Stop it. Both of you, this family, has not disgraced me. My heart hurts that Matteo has chosen this, but this isn't your fault. This isn't even Matteo's fault. Heroin is a devil, and it grabs hold and won't let go. I will not take his life."*

As the words came out of my mouth, I heard Francesco's wife let out a cry outside of the room and Francesco grabbed my hand and began to weep. I hugged him for a minute and let him cry.

Kyl: *"Look at me. He will pay a price for his betrayal, but we will decide together how to handle it. But he will have his life, I give you, my word."*

Alessandro: *"Kessler has to go…."*

I just nodded at the old man, I agreed but it wasn't going to be that easy. I turned and walked out the door. Today was going to be a long one and many to follow, I was sure.

Chapter 6

A long overdue visit and dead men don't speak kind of day.

As I went to pull out Natoli's, I sat there staring off into the distance. I really couldn't remember the last time shit had gotten this complicated. Even though I had a fairly good idea what needed to happen next, I still needed time to think. I wasn't due to meet with Luka for several hours still. I kind of wanted to call him but I really needed him to focus on the tasks I'd have given him. I looked at my phone, I hit Charlo's name and hit call. It rang a few times…

Charlo: *"Hey hey my friend, it's been a while."*

Kyl: *"Yes it has, too long. How are you?"*

Charlo: *"Oh you know, trying to keep up with all these fucking kids my wife says we need. What's new?"*

Kyl: *"I bet! You're on your way to a soccer team soon! But hey, so…I'm going to come visit her."*

The line was quiet. I hadn't been back to her grave since the day we laid her to rest. It's been six years.

Charlo: *"Oh…It's been a long time. Are you okay?"*

I took a deep breath and let it out.

Kyl: *"There's a lot and I need to clear my head. Don't ask me why now. Because I don't have an answer. You and I need to speak too, though."*

Charlo: *"I'll have the guys let you in the gate. I'll give you a few and then come down. I need to pay respects to the old man anyway. Been a while too."*

Kyl: "See *you there.*"

As I hung up it really hit me that it had been six years. Why so long, you may ask? Seeing her and the baby's headstone had been almost too much for me that day. I spent a significant amount of time buried in bottle after bottle of whiskey. My violence was hard to contain. I spent my nights hunting down anyone that had been loyal to Damian and the Cretchfeld's. A lot of people lost their lives who likely had no idea what they were dying for. Worse, Luka had taken it upon himself to execute all those people for me. I was too drunk most of the time to even shoot anyone point blank. He suffered with me, but he chose to be my hand of vengeance when all he really wanted was to bury himself in a bottle too. I robbed him of that. It was Really Luka who kept everything together until I came out of my fog. All credit to Devin, Louis, and Pratt too, they stayed at my side loyally for the next three years. They were older than me back then and I had promised to give them a better life for their loyalty. On the three-year anniversary of that night, I gave them each enough money to retire and be normal family men. They argued but eventually complied with my request out of respect. They deserved it.

As I turned down the road to the Mardechi Family cemetery, I suddenly felt heavy. I think ashamed I hadn't been back all this time. I dreamt many a night of coming out here and lying next to their graves and ending my life. I have never been one who could take my own life. I'm self-destructive but suicide, no. I just suffered until it stopped hurting so much.

I never got into another relationship. I did have what you'd call a mutually understood agreement. Diamond, this beautiful little native woman. We both had enough of our own trauma that we felt comfortable just being what each other needed when we needed it. It wasn't complicated and she was one of my absolute best friends. I trusted her very much. She'd had a rough go at life too. An abusive marriage that nearly took her life. She has an amazing soul, and she deserved a chance at a good life. So, I had given her a home to call her own and taught her how to oversee my Property Management division. She was good at it, so good that people stopped being late on rent. I had thought it was because she was so sweet. I later found out she'd put more than a few heads through walls and even charged them for the repair afterwards. I never told her I knew that I just made sure to fuck her in every way she needed and loved. She was a good girl, the type that would grab my hand and put it around her neck. A rare breed of woman for sure, I more than appreciated her.

I had distracted myself. I was procrastinating. I put the car back into drive and headed towards the gates. Two of Charlo's long time Generals were waiting at the gate. I parked and got out.

They both smiled as I approached.

Kyl: *"Tim. Frank. Good to see you both."*

Tim: *"Good to see you sir, it's been a while."*

I embraced them both.

Frank didn't really speak. It wasn't that he couldn't, he'd been shot in the mouth during the night of our "cleansing of the families" and lost part of his tongue. He was self-conscious of how he sounded. He was a giant man though, when you're that big, you don't really need to speak.

Tim: *"We'll be right here if you need us. Just holler"*

I nodded and walked through the gates. I closed my eyes, took a deep breath, and started towards their graves. My heart was beating so hard I could feel it in my ears. I was already near tears as I drew closer. Before I knew it, I was standing there. Tears streamed down my face. We'd never even gotten to talk about names. The headstone simply said,

"An angel too soon" Baby Ingerham. Gia's was adorned with the simple drawn heart and U. I crumbled to my knees and sobbed.

Kyl: *"I'm sorry it's been so long my loves. I had to stay away; I couldn't handle this then. I hope you can forgive me."*

As if she had heard me, or God had wanted me to know I was forgiven…a rabbit cautiously hopped from behind the headstone. I completely lost it. I buried my face in the grass atop her grave. Why did a rabbit set me off so badly? Gia's nickname was Bunny, and she had the rabbit "Ms. Bunny" from Bambi tattooed on her left thigh.

I sat back on my heels and wiped my face.

Kyl: *"I'm not sure I'm going to make it out of this one Gia. Things are at a level I'm not certain I know how to manage. I wish you were here, and I'd have walked away from all this years ago. I don't know what to do Bunny."*

The wind picked up and a weird chill hit me. I swear I heard her voice in my head. She had said, one simple phrase. *"Burn it all down."* It had been plain as day and as quickly as the breeze had come it was calm again. Burn it all down, okay. I would do exactly that.

I wiped my eyes and stood up as I heard footsteps approaching. It was Charlo, he'd put on some weight and had seemed to age a lot. I was a little shocked. We embraced like old friends.

Charlo: *"How is it you never age? Did you sell your soul or something for the fountain of youth? Jesus Kyl, you look great brother."*

Kyl: *"Funny, I feel like I'm getting old! You look great!"*

Charlo: *"Stop. I know I'm fat and haven't aged well bro. You don't need to stroke my ego. That damn woman and kids have worn my ass out!"*

We both laughed and I caught his gaze shift to the headstones behind me and his face immediately shifted to discomfort.

Charlo: *"I understand why you haven't come back Kyl. If I'm being honest, I haven't come much either. Dad was hard enough, but they didn't deserve this. I questioned my faith over this one. I spent week after week, in confession expressing my failing faith because of this. No one thinks badly of you for not coming. Just so you know."*

It made me feel better to hear that. Not that it fixed how I felt but at least someone else understood.

I cleared my throat; I didn't want to talk about it anymore...

Kyl: *"We need to talk Charlo. There's a war on the horizon."*

Charlo was pretty disconnected from things these days. Most of their business was legit and the goon's kept things in line under the rule of his Generals.

Charlo: *"Shit...what the fuck have I been missing?"*

I laid it all out and explained what had just happened with Kessler and the Natoli's. It was a lot to take in, I was still processing it too.

Charlo: *"I don't even know what to say Kyl. We haven't had much to deal with after taking out the Cretchfeld's. Your zone is so deep between us and Kessler, I think he's forgotten we're over here."*

Kyl: *"Charlo, I didn't come here to drag you into a war. I came out of respect to let you know so you can protect yourself and yours if things get bad. The game changes when the Feds are involved. I don't know yet just how deep that goes. But I'm at the end of a double-edged sword. I have to deal with both."*

Charlo: *"No you don't! For fucks sake Kyl! Cash out and let him have the shit. You've done enough, ride off into the sunset."*

Kyl: *"You realize if I were to step down and secede that it would be a matter of time before he came after you right? I have to end this. It's on me to stop this where it started which is with me. I created this whole thing and then got complacent and ignorant of what was happening around me. This is my fault."*

Charlo picked up a rock and chucked it as far as he could.

Charlo*: "Fuck man. I can't leave you to fend for yourself."*

Kyl: *"Charlo, I'm not here to guilt you into anything. You're my friend, I wanted you to be on alert. What you're going to do is get your defenses up. Put everyone on alert. You need to activate zone patrols. Eyes open and ready. That's all. I don't want you involved. Luka and I have it. I assure you."*

I could tell Charlo didn't have the stomach for this anymore. Shit, he didn't have it all those years ago. I had spared him from it and sent him away.

Kyl: *"Listen, I need a favor from you. I'm not sure how this is going to go. The reality is, I might not make it out of this one. Promise, every year on her birthday, you'll put flowers on her grave from me, please."*

Charlo looked like a kid who lost his puppy right now.

Charlo: *"I should be at your side in this…"*

Kyl: *"Shut the fuck up Charlo. We're not having this conversation. You have a wife and kids. They need you. You have it good. PROTECT THAT UNDERSTOOD?"*

He flinched at my tone, but he nodded in acknowledgement. Charlo was a good man, a great friend, and that's why I had to make sure he was separated from this.

Kyl: *"You have enough to go completely legitimate. Nothing wrong with keeping a crew to protect the family. Get out of the rest Charlo. This life isn't for you. Never was."*

Charlo: *"I give you, my word. On both. You have my word."*

I laid my hand on his shoulder and turned to leave. Ready or not, it was time for the bad shit to start. It couldn't be put off any longer.

I couldn't wait until seven to talk to Luka. I had to start making moves before Kessler could get his feet under him. He's a hot head but he's not completely stupid.

Now, you're probably thinking to yourself; "Is it really a good idea to start a turf war with the Feds so close at hand?" The simple answer, yes. Smoke and mirrors There was going to be so much going on they'd have trouble keeping track of what was really happening

Realistically I should've moved to take Kessler out years ago. The honest truth is it was easier to keep him around at the time until I had fully established all the new area I had taken over. It's a lot to keep up with. Imagine you have fifty cats, and you must keep track of them all in an NFL sized football stadium. I don't know if that's a great analogy or not, but it seems like a lot of work to me. Keeping everything in order, the pop-up street gangs, and the bullshit with managing local law enforcement and other officials. Luckily, I had spent an exceptionally large and significant amount of money supporting the Stephon's in all their newly established political positions. Most city officials were far more inclined to accept the money they were offered rather than risk a run in with Luka.

Speaking of Luka, I needed to get to him. I sent him a Zero four seven. That was the country club. I was likely over paranoid and using the pager system was a bit more of a hassle at times. I wasn't ready to give up on it yet.

I always shot a few holes a couple times a week so it wouldn't be unusual or out of character to do so now.

I had swung by one of the shops and switched cars. Nothing I had was really just plain when it came to cars. I had a sizable collection, but most were sports cars and stood out like a sore thumb. Especially the red Viper I had been driving all morning. I kept cars in a few separate places. Mostly because I liked to be sporadic and just swap around between them. I had my silver E55 AMG here which would be far less noticeable than the Viper. Comfort, class, and still fast enough to get away from just about anything. I hadn't noticed my tails since losing them and I'd prefer to keep it that way.

I had decided to just stick to the driving range today. As much as I hated to admit it, I sucked at golf. I could never find any consistency in my game. But I had fun. I just knew not to bet on myself.

Luka joined me not long after I got there. He was a lot better than me, and he never went easy on me. I liked that about him.

Kyl: *"I pinned Kessler to the table with a steak knife."*

That caught Luka off guard, and he almost lost his driver. I laughed as he looked at me with that "inquiring minds want to know" look.

Luka: *"So the meeting went as planned? Was that what you had in mind going there? Because I didn't get that vibe."*

It had been so long since I had done anything violent that I think it genuinely perplexed Luka.

I took a second to reflect on his question, mostly for effect, I think.

Kyl: *"Here's the thing…a lot transpired in a short amount of time. You and I, we've been looking in the wrong direction. While I got complacent, you have been operating with a narrowed focus."*

He immediately looked ashamed. I can't even think of a time when I ever had to point out a flaw when it came to Luka.

Luka: *"Narrowed focus."*

I could see he was chewing on this, and I wanted him to. I wanted to see if he was still as sharp as I have always given him credit for being.

He bit his bottom lip and his head suddenly popped up.

Luka: *"Son of a bitch. It's all been a fucking distraction. Fuck. Narrowed focus. Kyl I'm fucking sorry man. I should've seen that before now."*

Kyl: *"We're both guilty. Things have been relatively smooth, and we've gotten into a lull and been comfortable. I think what irritated me the most is that we let Kessler have the room to move like this. It's a lot worse than you realize. "*

I proceeded to fill him in on everything I had noticed about the gangs, the mole being Francesco's son, and what I believed was Kessler's real objective. Which by the way, had come to me on my drive here. As far as I could tell, Kessler wanted to cause unrest amongst the people in my zone, create some sort of rift within my own circle, (which I had yet to completely figure out) and because of my close ties to our local government, I surmise that Kessler had known he'd have no help from the local authorities and set my people up to take a fall from probably an anonymous tip to the Feds. In turn putting federal heat on me.

Luka: *"So what's our play here. You think it's a good idea to start war in the middle of all this?"*

I smiled and put my arm around Luka's shoulders and explained my smoke and mirrors idea. Using Kessler's method to distract the Feds. The idea, which I'll figure out as we go, is to have Kessler end up their focus.

Luka smiled and shook his head.

Luka: *"So are we full scale at war?"*

Kyl: *"I set demands in place so let's see what his first move is. I'm 100% certain he doesn't comply; we need to get the word out too quickly and activate everyone we can to be on guard. I guarantee he throws the Latin Crowns into action. Have Diego and some of his boys, color up and quick hit the Lotus Club. They had a rift last week, so it won't seem off. We'll tie the Crowns up fighting with Boks Laos Killas. Give them the full go ahead when they call you."*

The BLK's were a violent Asian gang that had taken me years to wrangle in. The infighting amongst the Asian culture here had been extremely ugly. There had originally been seven different gangs and they all fought constantly. I had made multiple attempts to create negotiations between them all to no avail. I finally got sick of it and saw the only path for a change, was a change in leadership. I called a meeting of the OG's and sent a clear message. Luka and his hit squad walked in and laid waste to all seven leaders. With their leadership all dead they decided it was better to cooperate and followed my recommendation to form one gang and work for me. It worked out for both sides. Fortunately, they have been itching for conflict and this was the perfect opportunity for that.

I basically needed to set the city on fire. I didn't have it all in my head yet, but it was coming together. I was going to be doing a lot of this on the fly. I didn't mind.

As I was going over things in my head Luka's phone rang. His face contorted into a look of pure anger, and I knew this wasn't going to make me happy at all.

Luka: *"Someone just slumped Spilz outside of Jazzabelle's."*

Jazzabelle's was another of my many businesses and off limits to family related issues. It was becoming clearer the rules weren't going to be followed.

So, they had made the first move. Spilz had been working with Russ and the Crowns. No one knew what his real name was or if he had ever had one. Spilz came about because when he was a kid, he spilled everything. To the best of my knowledge, Spilz was one of probably many of Cretchfeld Jr's illegitimate children. He never could keep his dick in his pants and apparently the dude was super fertile. Typically, some woman he'd knocked up would come to him and he'd give them a small chunk of money and tell them to go away with the promise of ending up in a ditch if they ever said anything. Spilz had been unlucky enough to be born to a severe addict mother. Diamond had found him eating stale crackers in one of the properties I bought as a rental. But it was actually Luka who asked to keep him around. Spilz's mother was a Croatian immigrant, so Luka seemed to identify with him. Even though he wasn't quite right, he had always been loyal after I took him in. Guess I was never going to get the chance to understand why he double-crossed me.

Kyl: *"Get things moving and find Russ. I want him in our hands as soon as possible. You know what to do with him."*

Luka nodded and walked off. He was pissed, no one took the life of one of ours even if they were going to end up ground meat in the end anyway. Luka did a lot of work on his own, the creative work anyways. Most people didn't really know just how violent, twisted, and scary Luka was because no one lived to talk about it. We had a "Don't ask, don't tell" agreement between us. A lot of times I just didn't need to know, and I trusted his judgment. Shit was about to get really interesting, that's for sure.

After I left the Country club, I knew it wouldn't be long before things erupted into chaos. I had a penthouse downtown in a building called the Epic Tower that I'd purchased several years ago. Most of the buildings were commercial use offices. Only the top five floors had apartments. I'd use it periodically for guests from out of town or if I wanted to have any type of get-together. It was quite spacious at thirty-seven hundred square feet, and it worked out better because I hated having too many people in my house. I'm a bit of an OCD clean freak so it bothers me to have people in my personal space. I also liked that it was on the twenty third floor and the front was secured entry. You'd have to get past the door man, the lobby guards, and the elevator didn't go directly to my penthouse. You had to get off on the floor below, which of course was heavily guarded, then use a set of stairs to get to my door. Why not live here full-time?

I like my yard. I have rose bushes and nice flower beds. Go ahead, laugh. I love the simplicity and peace of working to keep them pruned and everything growing perfectly. It's rewarding.

As I opened the doors to my balcony patio, I took a deep breath and closed my eyes for a minute to reflect on the day so far. Amongst everything it had been, it had also been a long overdue visit and dead men don't speak kind of day. As I really started to delve into that thought, I was interrupted by the echo of automatic gunfire in the direction of the Lotus Club. It had begun.

Chapter 7

Bazooka. Ya know, like the bubblegum.

Luka was a no bullshit type of guy when it came to business and orders. People knew he'd cut your finger off if he felt like to were taking too long to answer his question. It was quite common to see people start talking as soon as they saw him headed their direction. I would guess that was to get enough out as quickly as possible in order to keep all their fingers. I don't think anyone really knew the Luka I knew. He didn't really like people and beyond his personal crew, I don't think he ever spoke to anyone else. It had taken years for his guys to not flinch every time Luka moved. They had learned what to expect from him and they respected him to the highest level. He was kind in his own way, he'd help an old woman cross the street and then go back and threaten to cut the dicks off every man standing on the other side of the street who wasn't man enough to step up in the moment.

Luka was also extremely proficient when it came to getting information on in the streets quickly. He made two stops before he had the whereabouts of Russ Kessler. The man wasn't smart enough to not to get fucked up and end up in one of the trap houses in my zone. In his mind, he was staying off his old man's radar and wouldn't have to answer for his constant benders. He never thought about the fact he'd been violating the rules and was hiding where he was violating them. Stupid ass.

Luka wasn't subtle when he was pissed off. He walked into the trap house to find Russ passed out next to some dope whore on a mattress in the back room. She didn't have to be told to leave; she went right out the window with no clothes on.

(Luka's point of view)

Luka: *"What a fucktard. Someone go and get her and get clothes on her."*

It sounded like they had all tripped over each other trying to get out the door first.

I stood there over the passed-out Kessler. It wouldn't be anything to jab something through his ear into his brain and just be done with it. Things are not always that cut and dry though. I needed to get information out of him and with someone like Russ, you had to make it spectacular if you were going to take them out. I had already been putting it all together in my head. I had told Diego what I needed after he made the Lotus hit. Diego was my best Captain; I was extremely honored when Kyl had told me I could put together my own crew. I owed my life to Kyl, and it still shocked me when he'd once again do something to reward me.

Don't get me wrong, I appreciate it always, but it was like fuck, I'm still trying to pay you back for saving my life. Can I catch up before you do anything else? I didn't have family here; Kyl was my family. Watching him lose Gia nearly broke me seeing him be so broken. I'd never even seen him cry until that day. He found out he was going to have a family and lost that family all on the same day. He always tells me how violent I am, to be honest, I learned what love, loss, and vengeance were all about from him that day. I think Death himself would've slunk into the shadows to avoid Kyl during all that and the year after. I'm violent because I owe him and it's my duty to make sure he never feels that way again. I'm violent so he doesn't have to be. Because I owe him my life.

I needed to take a piss. I laughed aloud as I pulled out my dick and started to piss on Russ' head. It took him a minute to come to but when he realized he was being pissed on, he initially lost his shit and rolled away, jumped to his feet, and started to come at me as he was wiping his eyes. As soon as he realized it was me, he stopped dead in his tracks. He just froze and started to tremble.

Luka: *"Get a hold of yourself. If I wanted you dead, you wouldn't be standing here like a soggy bitch."*

Russ: *"I didn't know it was you Luka. I-I-ummm...shit. What's going to happen now?"*

Luka: *"Boss wants to have a chat with you. He knows you were pushing dope to his boys. You know they go popped this morning?"*

Russ: *"Man I've been out. I don't even know what day it is if I'm being real. So, they got popped? I mean can't Kyl just make it go away?"*

Luka: *"DEA and ATF. A little bit outside of our normal playground. Know anything about that? "*

Russ: *"Come on man, you know I can't just be telling you anything."*

Luka: *"Russ, they killed Spilz an hour ago. The Latin Crowns attacked the BLK's. Kyl knows what you've been doing. We've never had any real beef with you. I think you're just doing what your old man ordered you to do. Crazy that he'd put his own son in such a precarious position. It's almost like he was willing to sacrifice you. Shitty man. That can't feel good."*

I could see the burned-out gears in his dope hazed brain grinding. It hadn't occurred to him that his pops would toss him to the wolves so easily.

Russ: *"Fuck...Luka, I don't want to die man."*

Tears were welling up in his eyes and he had started to shake.

Luka: *"I told you, if Kyl had wanted you dead, I'd have already cut your head off to send back to your dad. He wants to talk and give you the opportunity to help. You know, help us, we help you."*

Russ: *"How can you help me? Clearly my old man isn't real concerned with my safety so I'm kind of fucked here. I help you; he probably kills me, I don't help you, you kill me."*

I chuckled; he wasn't wrong. I was kind of surprised to hear him put all that together. He wasn't amused.

Luka: *"Don't start crying, I hate that shit. Look, you are definitely in a bad spot. The thing is though, it was your pop who put you here. We don't have anything to gain from killing you. Think about it. If he didn't care if you died what good are you dead to us? Kyl thinks we could use your help. I mean, you must know this isn't going to end well for the Kessler clan. I mean, I know it looks like we were caught off guard with all this. Pushing dope to his boys was a good one, that one did get us. We've been watching everything else though. We let it happen. Hell, Kyl almost killed your old man today and let me him go just to fuck with him. Look at your phone, I bet he's told you."*

Luckily, Kyl is as smart as he is. I'm blown away by his ability to figure out everything he did so quickly and meticulously set in action what he has so far. The shit he did to Kessler was fucking genius. He knew Kessler wouldn't know where Russ was, and he knew doing what he did would invoke a reaction from the old man to freak out on Russ.

As Russ looked at his phone, I'm fairly sure his spirit left his body.

Russ: *"Fuck, the old man has lost it. He said he's going to beat me with a two-by-four. My brother is talking mad shit too. Fuck fuck FUCK…. Alright man, what do I have to do?"*

Stupid ass, he fell right into it.

Luka: *"Just tell me everything you know about what the plan is and give me the weak spot in your dad's house."*

Russ: *"You swear you're not going to just shoot me after I give you what you want?"*

Luka: *"Russ, who knows heroin and whores better than you? We need someone to run all that after we take the old man and your brother down. That's you bud. All you. Even get your own crew."*

God he was dumb. He stood there with a stupid smile on his face daydreaming about it for a minute.

Russ: *"I get my own crew? Fuck ya, okay. Deal."*

Yes, he's really that stupid. He just completely sold out his whole family so he could have his own crew and be in charge.

I let him get high before we left. As I drove across town he just kept talking, I knew the complete ins and outs of the security, where they kept their money, all their store houses, and even that old man Kessler's dick hadn't worked for several years, and his brother liked to be pegged. Weird as fuck. I pulled into the old industrial park on the outer edge of town. We used this location as a shooting range to test most of the weapons we purchased. We also stored some things out here in the old underground chambers. Mostly explosives and rocket launchers. Because everyone needs a rocket launcher.

Diego was already there and had everything set up for me. I wanted to be sure the camera was set up and had a good angle.

Luka: *"How we looking?"*

Diego: *"Everything is in place. Camera is good and everything else is hanging there like you wanted it."*

I patted him on the shoulder and walked back towards Russ. I just needed to get him in the right spot. See, Russ was a tweaker, to avoid grinding his teeth he always chewed gum. There was a bunker-like wall and a table set in front of it. The distance looked good. I tossed a pack of gum on the table.

Luka: *"I have to piss. Russ you ever been hit by a Bazooka?"*

Russ: *"Huh?"*

As I stepped behind the wall I continued talking.

Luka: *Bazooka. Ya know, like the bubblegum. There's a pack on the table for you. Help yourself."*

He smiled and started working on the wrapper. I lined him up in the sights, looked over to make sure the camera was recording, and Diego gave me a thumbs up. Russel Kessler was about to chew his last piece of gum and had no idea what was about to happen to him. As I pulled the trigger the whoosh startled Russ who had just enough time to look up as the rocket propelled grenade impacted into his chest making a spectacular explosion of human shrapnel and blood spray.

Holy fuck, I wasn't even quite prepared for that, and Diego gagged at the sight of the mess.

Luka: *"You got all that?"*

He just nodded and handed me the memory card.

Luka: *"Get the cleaners here to take care of this then get back to town and get the guys ready for the next phase.*

I kind of wanted to watch this so I could see it again before I had it delivered.

Chapter 8

When you have so many ears, it can be hard to hear.

One of the bonuses to having a deep in with local law enforcement and the political powers, was the advantage of knowing what was coming your way and the inside line to information to which you'd normally not be privy. It had always been kind of a blessing. However, today was unlike anything I'd experienced up to this point. People didn't double cross me, and my close friends certainly didn't speak on me. Or so I thought. I'd learn a powerful lesson in the coming hours that would change me forever.

I woke up before my alarm went off. An annoying habit I'd had for most of my life. A side effect of growing up on a farm and having to get up before the sun every morning. Oddly enough, I had slept decently. I'm sure the three glasses of whiskey had played a part in that also. I made my coffee and stepped out onto the balcony. As I looked out over the city, it hit me that I'd never really noticed the view from up here. Life hadn't really slowed down since the Cleansing. I guess I just hadn't really thought about it. It was tranquil and I could honestly say, I wanted life to slow down.

That wasn't going to happen today though. I saw Luka's car pull up at valet. You couldn't miss his cars either, his passion for fast and flashy was just as bad as mine. He'd always loved my Supra and had imported an S15 Silva. Right hand drive and all. It was beautiful. I'm sure whatever he was coming to tell me was going to ruin my morning in some form or fashion. So, I decided I'd fuck with him. I called down to the lobby and told them to be sure and ID him at every check point on the way up.

It made me laugh thinking about how frustrated he'd be.

About fifteen minutes later, there was finally a knock at the door. I took my time getting there and as I opened the door, there stood a very unamused Luka. I played it off.

Kyl: *"Well good morning, Luka, why the sour face?"*

Luka: *"Fuck you, and I mean that in the nicest way possible. Really bro? Making me show my ID all the way up here?"*

I turned and headed to the kitchen, so he didn't see me smile.

Kyl: *"Man they made you show ID? That's crazy. You must've woken up looking like a bitch today."*

The was too much for him, Luka busted out into laughter. He tried so hard to me this dry immovable emotionless rock. I know how to break him though.

Luka: *"You're such an amazing asshole. How did not ever end up a fucking comedian?"*

Kyl: *"Well, the truth is, that was my dream. But then I had to take care of your bitch ass, so I chose organized crime instead."*

He'd almost spit his coffee out on that one. We had a good laugh over it all. I think we both knew today was going to be fucked up. More often than not, when shit wasn't great, we'd always take a moment to laugh about something. You had to, or you'd end up a full-time psycho. We were content with being part time.

Luka: *"So, business then?"*

Kyl: *"Ya, might as well get started. It's going to be another long day I'd assume. Any minute I should have the boy's interview tapes. What do you have for me?"*

He tossed me a memory card and forewarned me it was raw as fuck and had a different level of shock factor. I popped it into the memory card port and plugged it into my computer. As I watched the video, I thought about all the years I had watched Russ Kessler be a complete loser. Watching him now, jabbering away giving up his own family, reminded me that I had come to be in the same position with my own lifelong friends. I wasn't sure I'd ever completely know the truth of what they'd said.

I didn't ever have to tell Luka what to do or how to do it really when it came to making an example out of someone. All I had said was *"make his end become a nightmare for those in his family."* Per the usual, Luka did not disappoint. It only took me a couple seconds to put together what was happening. The bubblegum thing was as brilliant as the climactic build up to an RPG hitting Russ as he exploded into pieces from basically the waist up. Well fucking done my friend; this had more shock value than anything we'd ever done. This was even more shocking than cutting up cartel members and shipping them to their boss in individual boxes. This was a Mona Lisa all its own. I knew how weak a stomach Mitch Kessler had. He was definitely going to puke. Wish I could be in the room when they watched this.

Just as I had finished watching it for the third time, there was a knock at the door. Luka answered and let my courier David in. He had a thick Manila envelope for me. I traded him for the memory card and his instructions then sent him on his way. The Kessler's were about to receive their first dose of real retribution for the death of Spilz.

In the background I noticed the echoes of gunfire. Damn, the BLK's and Latin Crowns were on it early this morning. Good for them, violence is the answer to this question.

As I tore open the envelope I paused, Luka had noticed it. I think he knew this was not going to be easy for me. I hoped we were wrong.

But it kept ringing in my head one of the things Russ had said to Luka. *"They wanted a piece of the action and they felt let out because Kyl never let them into the business. They were super salty about it."* It made me angry. I didn't let any of my close personal friends into the dirt side. I made sure everyone got to party and have the benefits of the life without being in the life. I gave them legit, exceptionally good paying jobs. To be honest, they weren't even that good at it. I just had enough good people in place to make sure things got done right. I closed my eyes as I started the video of the interviews. Maybe I thought if I didn't see them, it wouldn't hurt as bad, or I could disassociate them from what was being said. That was not going to happen. Fortunately, I also never told them much in the way of specifics, but they knew enough to do damage. What they did was definitely damaging. More to me personally than to anything the Feds could really use. Circumstantial evidence, hearsay, but they had given up some store houses, trap houses, and drop spots. Put my name on all of them. For what you might ask? A free pass. A get out of jail free card for talking. No charges have been filed against them yet.

I sat down, I was dazed, and heartbroken. When you have so many ears, it can be hard to hear. As in I wish I hadn't heard any of this. What hurt the most was listening to them laugh and sound so proud of each other for telling. They even talked about how they'd "split up the pie" once I was out of the way.

Luka put his hand on my shoulder, he knew I was hurt. I could see the anger festering in his eyes. The cold truth of it was, they'd signed their death warrants, and I was left to make sure they were served those warrants.

Luka: *"How do you want to handle it? You just want me to take care of it?"*

Kyl: *"No.... This is way more personal. But we have to be smart. Give me a minute"*

As I walked out onto the balcony, what I really wanted was to tie them all to a chair and make them watch as I threw them off over one by one. Of course that was not feasible, but it sounded good to me. No, I had to make this look like it was coming from someone else. They had mentioned the Latin Crowns a couple times in their interrogations. I could use that.

I was hurt and I was angry, but this hit me on a different level. This pulled at my soul. This is exactly the reason I had made such a defined separation between this side of business and my close personal friends. Even though I had done this out of love and friendship, they felt slighted and insulted by it. They really are fucking idiots.

When you live the life, I have lived, you learn to value love, family, friendship, and loyalty in a different way. You also learn the absolute and definitive cost necessary for betrayal. Friend or family. This was one of the hardest decisions I'd have to face in a long time. As I closed my eyes to look within myself as the doubt bubbled up, I was immediately reminded of how I got here. My own flesh and blood had betrayed me. They're all dead now and my next move had become crystal clear.

Kyl: *"Get audio clips out on the streets. I want it known they gave up the Crowns. Let it slip they'll be at Pawnee Heights Edition this afternoon."*

Luka just nodded and turned to leave.

Kyl: *"Luka, I want you away from this one. Understand?"*

Luka: *"Ya, I understand Kyl. I really do."*

I couldn't ask for a better man at my side during all this. Realistically, all these years too. As bad as he wanted to personally kill each one of them, he understood this was one of those things I needed him on the outside of. He didn't even question it. He just knew.

Chapter 9

Not everything that glitters is gold. Sometimes it really is just a shiny turd.

I made another cup of coffee and sat down to think. If you've been paying attention, this shit has gotten extremely complex and complicated. So many irons in the fire at once I really needed to put some sort of priority list together in my head. I was deep into the thought process getting a good ass scratching in when the phone in my apartment rang. The only people who had that number were the staff downstairs, Luka, and the mayor.

As I reached for the phone, I was thinking to myself what else could go wrong and almost laughed. What I heard next certainly wasn't funny.

Lobby Staff: *"I'm sorry to bother you sir, there's an Agent Hague here that says he needs to speak with you immediately."*

Kyl: *"Make his bitch ass wait twenty minutes and then send him up."*

I could hear the clerk stifle a laugh and acknowledge my request.

Dammit. Not who I wanted to deal with first thing this morning. This federal cum stain was starting to make a really bad habit of fucking up my mornings. It was really starting to piss me off.

I took my time deciding to get dressed and really all that equated to was a pair of sweats and house shoes. I wasn't ready to be dressed for the day, so fuck him. Dammit, what was his name? Shit. He wasn't going to be happy with me again. I laughed aloud at the thought of calling him Agent Gag yet again.

There was a knock at the door, damn. Had it been twenty minutes already? I stared at the door waiting for the next knock. No reason to not being an asshole at this point but I made my way to the door and answered it.

Standing there was a slightly flustered Agent Gag.

Agent Hogue: *"It's about fucking time; I waited down there forever and it takes forever to get up here. Interesting setup for an average businessman."*

Kyl: *"Well good morning to you as well Agent Gag. (Couldn't help myself) Would you like to come in? Of course you would, come on in."*

He was already fuming at this point.

Agent Hague: *"Its Ha...."*

I cut him off before he could finish.

Kyl: *"You should know by this point I don't actually give a fuck. You're in my home so let's be a little more personal. Drop the Agent Douche shit. First name basis."*

He just stared at me. I think he was genuinely perplexed that I had the balls to speak to him that way. Honestly, I couldn't give two fucks and a shit about his government title.

Agent Hague: *"Marcus. Marcus Hague."*

Kyl: *"See, that's way better than Agent Gag or whatever the fuck your name is. Marcus, nice to meet you. Coffee? It's imported."*

Agent Hague: *"Imported coffee? Does that really matter?"*

Kyl: *"Oh boy, I figured you federal boys might have better taste. Guess not. Check it out, you have your standard South American coffee beans that are used for most of your domestic coffee brands.*

Then there are those from around the world. This coffee is Kopi Luwak. I won't go into the particulars of it, but it's one of the most expensive coffees in the world. I buy it fresh roasted bean and fresh grind it right before brewing."

Agent Gag: *"Alright, I'm sold. I'll have a cup."*

I forgot for a minute that this sack of shit was here to ruin my morning. Fuck it, I'd culture him a little before things got verbally ugly. Because I had no doubt it was going to.

I finished brewing us both a cup and headed to the balcony as I handed him his cup.

As we sat down, he finally tried a sip and his head popped up immediately in apparent shock.

Agent Hague: *"Holy shit, how is this coffee? How is anything else able to be called coffee after this?"*

Kyl: *"Honesty, because most people will never get the opportunity to try it."*

As he sipped his coffee, I could tell he was reflecting on what he would say next. The business was about to come out.

Agent Hague: *"You live quite a comfortable and.... expensive lifestyle Kyl. This coffee is great, amazing actually. But I came here to reiterate what I originally told you. I am well aware of what you're doing and I'm closer to taking you down. You're no more than a steppingstone for me to excel in my career. I will have enough to take you down within the week. Unless you decide you'd like to collaborate with me. I have some pull and could likely convince the right people to decrease your sentence and get you some place comfortable to do your time."*

He actually believed the shit coming out of his mouth. I had genuinely tried to keep my composure. It didn't work at. Not even close.

I burst into laughter and even spit some of my coffee out trying not to laugh. Gag's face turned bright red.

Kyl: "*You're a natural comedian. I think you chose the wrong line of work. Let's get something clear here. You don't have shit on me. The circumstantial bullshit some troubled reject friends of mine likely told you is neither meaningful nor grounds for any substantial action. Which is why you're here trying to flex your tiny government dick. You know you don't have shit. You're a fucking loser and drew this case because you're probably good at sucking dick. If you genuinely had something of substance I'd be under arrest. You know that and I know that. The only thing you can prove is that I live an extremely expensive and comfortable lifestyle. I'm a successful businessman. You're a fucking loser douche wanna-be agent that's reaching in the wrong place for a promotion. You're fucking with the wrong guy, and I can say that with assured confidence. You don't have shit on me and you're wasting my fucking time. Fucking gnat. That's all you are.*"

This drove to his core and rattled him so badly he made a vital mistake. The next few moments would dictate how much longer he would live.

He was so enraged by my articulated beat down that he forgot his place and came at me.

Agent Hague: "*Fuck you, you'll be lucky to make it to prison you piece of shit. I'll kill you myself.*"

He didn't realize his error until it was too late. I'm no slouch when it comes to martial arts, and I've trained with some of the best in the world. His biggest mistake was coming across the table at me, his swing and miss punch had caused him to end up off balance. I pushed the table aside as I grabbed his arm, using his off balanced momentum to my advantage, and pulled him towards me. I twisted his arm towards the balcony rail. As we met nearly face to face, I switched the direction of the momentum, grabbed him by the throat, and pushed him over the railing. I had locked one of his legs between mine, so I was able to let go of his arm and grab his gun. Now I had him nearly upside over the railing with his own gun shoved hard into his right eye socket.

Kyl: *"You scream or move, and I'll shoot you in the eye with your own gun and drop you off this fucking balcony. Do you understand me bitch?"*

He was so purely terrified he couldn't even muster any type of response and to add insult to injury, he was currently pissing himself. Which, if you're upside down, you can probably guess where the was running to. Not sure I'd ever had a grown man's piss on my hand for any reason. Ever. I was so locked in and furious he'd come at me in my home, I didn't even care.

Kyl: *"You listen to me you halfwit, fucking reject piece of shit...You don't ever threaten me. You think you know shit. You don't. You come into my home and take my kindness and hospitality for weakness. You have the nerve to disrespect me and even worse, try to strike me. I should fucking drop you just for that alone. I'm done with you and your bullshit already. You don't approach me again, do you understand? I have nothing to say to you and if you have anything to say to me, I don't fucking care. You'll contact my lawyers, and they can reach out to me and when I feel like I might answer. Got it? I'm going to extend one last courtesy to you and pull you back up. You're going to take you piss covered bitch ass out of my house and get the fuck out of my building. Don't make the mistake of coming back."*

I slid his gun back into the holster and pulled him back over the rail tossing him to the floor. He didn't even look back as he scrambled for the door and out.

Fuck. Talk about ruining a guy's morning. I stared down at my broken coffee cup, that was my favorite cup. Not how I wanted to start off today. My lawyers had already been fast at work, but I took the time to call them and relay the events of the morning, better safe than sorry.

I pushed my way through a quick morning workout, showered, ate, and headed out to take on whatever other dumb shit was going to happen today. For starters, I had the go see the three stooges and pretend I didn't know shit. There's a significant difference between playing off hurt feelings and acting like you hadn't been completely betrayed. It was making sick to my stomach even thinking about it. As I reached the lobby, I asked a valet to bring me my Maserati. Another day for a less noticeable car, based on how the day had started, it felt necessary. No one in the lobby had even mentioned the piss-soaked DEA agent running out of the building. My employees were all well paid and taken care of, so they knew to just keep their mouths shut. It was pretty well known amongst them all that the wrong type of fuck up would result in a visit from Luka and no one wanted that.

As I drove across town, I noticed a very familiar Lincoln Town Car pull out and start following me. I opened the console and reached in for my gun as I saw the headlights flash, then flash again. That was universal code for *"Let's talk."*

I turned off into the parking lot of a small mom and pop restaurant. I tucked my gun into my lower back and got out. It was Raymundo Salis, better known on the streets and El Tiburon, or The Shark. He was a ranking member of the Latin Crowns. This should be interesting…

He stepped out showing me his hands to say he was coming in peace. I nodded and he motioned for his guards to stay in the car.

Raymundo: *"Good morning ese, I apologize for the intrusion, but I needed to speak to you urgently."*

Kyl: *"No apology needed, I'm aware of the state of things. What's up?"*

Raymundo: *"I'm certain you know about the beef between us and the BLK's, we had to act after they attacked us. I'm not sure who hit the Lotus but as you know it's started a war. I want to assure you we will keep it to their spots only and won't disrespect any other places in your zones. What I came to speak on is different though, are you aware of the word on the streets about your boys?"*

I looked off into the distance and let the question hang for a minute before I turned my head back and locked into eye contact with him.

Kyl: *"While we're here let's cover a few things. Number one, I'm not certain if you received the message yet, but Kessler was put on notice to get all of you Latin fucks out of my zone. That needs to happen before the end of the day. Number two, if I hear of one of you coming into my zone to hit anyone not first approved by me, you will sign a death warrant for your whole gang. I will unleash Luka and the Reapers on everyone including your families."*

The Reapers are an elite group of prior special forces and highly trained killers from around the world I keep on hand for the worst of situations.

Raymundo for all his tough gangster appearance had begun to tremble. He and I had not had much interaction, but he had heard that I was ruthless and not to be taken lightly. To further impress upon him the severity of failing to heed my warning I took a step towards him. Before he could warn him off the rear passenger door opened and one of his guards started out. He had a pistol in his hand but was met by my revolver in his face. I didn't even look at him and continued to address Raymundo.

Kyl: *"As for the three idiot friends of mine…. We all understand the rules and I won't make excuses or exempt them from this. They spoke heavily on your crew, and they violated the laws in my world and yours. Handle your business. Are we clear?"*

He just simply nodded and looked sideways at the gun in my hand. I turned my attention back to the stupid fuck on the end of my gun.

I lowered the revolver away from his face, I fired a single round into his leg. Raymundo rushed to put his hand over his mouth to keep him from screaming and looked back at me in pure fear and shock. I leaned down and spoke to him.

Kyl: *"Don't ever try to get out of the car on me when men are speaking business, next time I'll kill you."*

I looked up at Raymundo and his eyes said all I needed to see. I got back in my car and sped off. What is wrong with these stupid ass people? I really had made far too much of a separation from everything. Who else thinks I'm soft? The Latin Crowns had just found out for certain now I wasn't. I had also sealed the fate of three of my best friends. My chest was suddenly heavy. With a deep sigh I smashed the gas pedal to the floor as I entered the highway. It was time to get this part over with.

As I pulled outside of the house where Mikey, Shane, and Jeremiah lived my stomach felt sick and I almost felt a touch of anxiety. This isn't your average everyday type of situation. I had no issues looking my own blood family in the eyes as I took their lives. They had taken from me in a way no one ever has again, and I've been so many years removed from all that, I had forgotten what it felt like to be betrayed by someone I loved. People who had become my family to me. I heard the front door open, so I quickly shook it off and stepped out of the car. It was Jeremiah, he and I were closest of the three. He had a look of combined fear and worry in his eyes. I shook my head as I approached him, we hit a bro dap and I put my arm around his shoulder as we headed in.

Jeremiah: *"How much trouble are we in? With you?"*

As I walked in, I didn't answer him right away. Mikey and Shane were standing there with a deer in the headlights look. I did our standard fist bump and sat down. They all stood there looking lost and honestly terrified.

Kyl: *"Sit."*

Shane: *"Bro, we fucked up bad."*

Kyl: *"You think"!? For fucks sake guys, what were you thinking?"*

Jeremiah: *"We weren't Kyl. Man, I'm sorry,"*

Mikey: *"Come on guys bullshit."*

Mikey was always the most outspoken and if I had to guess, was probably the instigator in all this who encouraged the whole thing. He had always had a jealous streak about my success and their lack of involvement.

Mikey: *"Look Kyl, you kept us on the outside of all the action. You're out here with Luka and all these other guys raking in the money, the bitches, the fast cars, and clout. We're fucking construction superintendents. It's like a slap in the face."*

Before he could speak another word, I exploded from my seat and floored him with a backhand across the face.

Kyl: *"You want to speak on a slap in the face? You unappreciative shit bag. How about the fact you're the highest paid superintendents in the whole fucking state? How about the fact all three of you constantly fuck up and never loss your jobs? You three suck at almost everything you do and no matter how much coaching I give you or how many chances, you still can't get it right. It's never even crossed my mind to fire you. No, I pay people to go around behind you and fix your fuck ups. I give all three of you brand new trucks every year and multiple times a year I either take you on a trip or pay for you to go on one. How dare you downplay the life I've given you! You'd be nothing without me you. Want more proof? You three retards couldn't even push dope to a gang doing all the street work without getting caught. I protected you for YEARS from your own failures and stupidity. All you had to do was be loyal and be the friends we've always been! FUCK YOU!"*

I was fuming. All three of them were scared shitless and Jeremiah looked like he was about to cry. Dammit, this is not what I wanted but I couldn't undo it now. Part of me wanted to have them beaten nearly to death and shipped off somewhere to live out their days. The problem is, I could no longer trust them. I was in a pure rage and on the verge of losing my composure completely. I don't get this angry. I spun around and planted a kick right into Shane's solar plexus knocking him back. I moved so quickly Jeremiah barely had time to cover his face and I landed a hard hook to the body on him.

He immediately dropped. As I looked around the room, not one of them could even look at me. I was surprised that out of all of them, Mikey was the one who chose to speak at that moment.

Mikey: *"You're right. I'm a piece of shit Kyl. I've always been jealous of you and wanted what you had. I just wanted a taste of the power you have. This is my fault; it was my idea. I take responsibility for it all. I'll pack my things and go. Just don't punish these guys that bad. I deserve to carry this."*

You'd think I'd have really softened to hear that. Not in the slightest. You know what that told me? It told me that he had not only still stood behind what he had done, but by playing martyr in all this, he could separate himself from the group. Why? Because he fully intended to continue working with the Feds against me and in his mind, I was sunk, and he'd be able to take up with the Kessler family and the Latin Crowns for the power and clout he wanted. I almost shot his snide ass in the face right there. Instead, I laughed.

Now they were all looking at me.

Kyl: *"Look, I'm fucking angry with all three of you and Mikey, I appreciate you taking responsibility. But, at the end of the day, this was all three of you. I'm going to deal with Kessler and the Crowns. Ya'll broke my trust and that is going to have to be earned back. I can't believe you idiots really thought working with Kessler was a good idea. You should know that not everything that glitters is gold, sometimes it really is just a shiny turd. I want your fucking word this bullshit is done. I'll get the attorneys on this asap."*

They all looked a little sick at that comment. They were realizing I didn't know they hadn't been charged or so they thought anyways.

Shane: *"We weren't charged Kyl, we sold out Kessler to the Feds. We figured it was the least we could do for fucking up like this so close to the house."*

Man, do you know what it does to a man's soul when one of your best friends looks you in the eyes and tells the worst lie and you know the truth already. The emotions I was experiencing inside was like a complete war zone. I rubbed my hands together and took a deep breath. It was time to push this to the end.

Kyl: *"While I understand what you were trying to do, you have created a whole new issue here. Fuck guys, anything else you want to shit on me with. No? Okay, look, we're going to get through this. Right now, I need you three back to work. I have to move another crew into Pawnee Heights. Gerald's crew got pulled over and not one of those fuckers was legal. I need y'all to go through the houses they were building and figure out what's next on each one so the new crews that show up this afternoon can get right into it. Go."*

All three of them looked at each other then back at me. I just put my hand up to indicate I didn't want to hear it.

Kyl: *"Get your asses moving."*

I walked out without another word. This would be the last time I saw them.

Jeremiah*: "Well, he didn't kill us. That a bonus."*

Mikey*: "As long as Kessler keeps his word, we have nothing to worry about. Those Feds are going to do all the work for us, and we'll be off the hook and in the positions of power we all wanted."*

Shane: *"I hope so man. That shit was fucking scary."*

Mikey: *"Everything went as we had planned. Ya he lost it on us, but I told you he had gone soft. We're good from here on out boys. Load up and let's go do this bullshit job one more day. I'm still trying to get a hold of Kessler. Probably still passed out."*

When I had sat down, I slid the burner phone I had called myself from down into the couch. As I drove away, I heard it all. Every word. Greed is a wicked thing. It will turn the oldest of friends against one another. I had just witnessed the proof firsthand. A tear rolled down my cheek, I had been holding them back the whole time. I don't care who you are. Betrayal from those you love hurts in a way that isn't easily ignored or written off.

The Pawnee Heights Edition sat on the outer edge of town. It was going to the most exclusive gated community with a full golf course, Club house, large fitness center, and indoor/outdoor aquatics center. It sat in the middle of a sunken area of land that was originally created to be an overflow flood plain. After the Army Corp of Engineers rerouted the river and moved the dam, this was left behind and thought to be useless. But after several geological tests and surveys, I found if to be actually very solid and perfect for building on. On the east end of the valley was an overlook that would be connected to the nature center and trails yet to be built. But I had liked to come up here and look out over the area to imagine it in all its finished glory. Today, I came to oversee the deaths of my friends. I had lied about Gerald's crew; I gave them the day off paid. I just told them they had been working so hard, they deserved a day off. They really had been busting ass, in a little over three weeks they had five houses already in the process of being erected. I didn't rush them; quality was what expected. These homes would start in the one and half million-dollar range and go up to three million dollars as they got further back.

My greatest accomplishment yet is in real estate development. There would be no cookie cutter designs here and no house would have less than a three-acre lot. I was a little upset at myself that I would be tainting my prized development with their blood. If I was being honest though, I don't think there were many developments or new construction that didn't have bodies under them or in them rather. Years ago, I had capitalized on a process my uncle Mac had created. He'd originally taken up the practice of drilling a deep hole on a spot he'd intended to pour concrete on. In the early days, he'd drop the body down the hole with a special mix of chemicals to help decompose the body, then back filled the hole and pour a foundation over the top. Pretty solid idea if you ask me. I like science though, so I wanted to take it a step further. Mac thought it was a fool proof system, and I don't necessarily disagree. Not many people are to think to tear down a house, rip up a cement foundation, and dig down eight to ten feet in a specific spot to be able to find a body. With all the advancements in forensics, I thought the process needed some modifications. This is pretty fucked up, but when you need to be sure someone really disappears. You have to be creative. We figured out that grinding up the body wasn't all that difficult with the right woodchipper, further the process by adding the that to the rock crusher and kiln process, add your sand, aggregate, mix it all up and you have concrete. Pour your foundation and voila! No more body. I'd made sure the boys were used in the concrete to be poured for the bathrooms somewhere out here. Shitty right?

As I looked out over everything, I saw Mikey's truck pull into the edition. Not far behind was a couple of unassuming white vans that were reminiscent of any other white van you'd see in a construction site. If anything, I could certainly say the Crowns were definitely prompt. Mikey and the boys had wandered into a house unaware of the fate to befall them shortly. The white vans pulled up and honked, this drew all three out of the house. As they stepped out into the open, all the van doors flew open and about nine Latin Crowns jumped out, opening fire immediately. They never even had the chance to run. I watched as they stood over each one and pumped at least fifteen more rounds into each one of them. It was done.

Thanks to the arrogance of the Crowns, they always left a calling card. Usually in the form of one of their color rags to claim the hit. It was common knowledge I had no ties to the Crowns.

The Feds had documented knowledge that the boys had been working with the Latin Crowns and that they were directly tied to Kessler family. They got busted with dope being pushed by the gang that took them out. It would be impossible for Agent Gag to prove any type of connection for this to me and now his witnesses were dead. The bodies were starting to stack up already and we were just getting started.

Chapter 10

Being a Columbian drug lord doesn't give you a pass

There's an old saying my Uncle Mac used to say a lot. *"Not even a good plan can prevent a stupid person from doing the wrong thing in the wrong place at the wrong time. You just have to try not to be there for it."*

When I was younger, I seemed to have a knack for ending up in the wrong place at the wrong time. But, looking back I had to consider what came out of those situations. For example, I found Luka in a bad situation. Diamond had been running down a county road in the dark when I found her. Lots of times I'd go "What the fuck, why does this always happen to me!" But again, in retrospect, I ended up with some of the best people in life that way though.

Another such unforgettable situation that had been burned into my brain, happened years ago when Luka and I had gone to Miami to check some product for the now head of the family, Damian. Some of our prior business partners opted not to deal with the family after Mac passed. A lot of people didn't like Damian and he was so paranoid, he wouldn't travel or meet anyone. Since I dealt with the drug trade, he agreed to send me as I knew product and negotiations better than anyone.

We'd tested a little more of the product than we should have. I'm thinking Luka and I were about eighteen at the time. Not old enough to get into the bars and clubs but the guys we'd come to meet took care of all that. Columbians definitely know how to party, and we went right along with it. With all the cocaine in our systems the liquor just went down like water, and I felt completely sober. Wired as fuck but certainly not drunk. Miami is a different world, especially to a couple of young up and coming hustlers. We had the money to throw around and the company clout to get us VIP everywhere we went. More gorgeous woman than any man would know what to do with. We had met a couple of fun loving ready to party girls who were on a different level that night. This was the first time I'd ever had my dick sucked in public. I'd heard there's no sex in the champagne room, but no one ever said shit about getting head. That chick looked me in the eyes the whole time she was throat fucking herself and swallowed my cum with a smile on her face.

I was a little embarrassed at the end of the whole thing. I had plenty of attention and experiences back at home but none like this, so I didn't know how to react. I told her that was amazing and asked her what I owed her. She blushed a little and said, *"I'm not a working girl, I did that because I thought you were hot and maybe we could finish things up at the hotel later."* I felt like a dumbass, but I definitely wanted to continue things later, so I agreed to meet her. I had asked her to at least let me buy her a drink to which she agreed. Luka had been on the other side of the room with her friend and apparently had much the same interaction I did. We both felt like kings in that moment.

As we all headed to the bar, my Columbian partner, Oscar, stopped us and asked if we were having a fun time.

Oscar: *"Ahhh my friends! Are you having good time?"*

Kyl: *"Fuck ya Oscar, this is awesome man. Ya'll know how to party hard."*

Oscar: *"Good, good my friend. Just remember, tomorrow we meet the boss. Don't get too fucked up that you can't stand up straight."*

He winked, walked off, and I suddenly remembered why we were here. I was feeling surprisingly good, and I really wanted to fuck this girl. I made my way to the bar where the girls and Luka were. The vibe was so good and easy to roll with. I didn't want to ruin it, so I stayed casual as I spoke.

Kyl: *"Luka, we can't forget why we're here. We have business tomorrow."*

Luka nodded in acknowledgement, the girls got the point I was getting to, and we agreed to leave. They had a suite nearby and invited us to come over, Rachel and Jessica were their names. They were in town from Arizona for Rachel's sister's wedding in a couple of days.

Once we got back to their place Luka wasted no time taking Jessica off to her room. Rachel was a lot more of an intellectual than I'd first realized. She was sexy, beautiful, and highly intelligent.

Rachel: *"So tell me, what kind of business brings you two to Miami?"*

I laughed in my head at the idea of telling her the truth.

Kyl: *"We're in sales and investment. We survey products for future investment."*

Her eyes twinkled and she laughed.

Rachel: *"That is the most elaborate explanation I've ever heard for a drug dealer. A couple guys hanging out with Columbians in high-end clubs in Miami, says a lot about your type of investment."*

Kyl: *"Oh you're a smart girl huh, think you know it all."*

She moved in closer to me as her hands moved across my body, her lips met mine.

Rachel: *"I don't give a fuck what you do, tonight we're just here to fuck and have fun. Show me what you're made of."*

Kyl: *"Oh you're going to challenge me?"*

I smiled and grabbed her by the throat pushing back against the wall. I kissed her deeply and passionately. She fumbled to get my clothes off as I worked to get hers off. It flashed through my head how well she'd sucked my dick earlier and I thought I'd pay her back for that. I reached down with both arms and pushed her legs apart. She wasn't expecting what I did next. I squatted down, throwing her legs over my shoulders, lifting her into the air, against the wall, and began to lick her pussy. Sucking her clit in and out, swirling my tongue around it as she sunk her nails into my upper back. She let out a scream as she gushed and came. Her body shaking and convulsing every time my tongue flickered on her clit. She looked down at me, breathing heavily.

Rachel: *"Please fuck me!"*

Without another word I slid her legs off my shoulders and onto my arms dropping her down so that her wet pussy fell onto my dick. She was so fucking wet yet still tight. She gasped as I drew her down onto my rock-hard cock. As I penetrated her, she whimpered and asked me to take her to the room. As I made my way there, I gripped her ass and continued to slide her up and down on my dick. For the next hour I took her from every possible position, and she came over and over until there were not dry spots left on the bed. We laid there out of breath but absolutely satisfied.

Rachel: *"I've never experienced anything like that. Holy shit. You think we could keep in touch and do this again?"*

Kyl: *"I won't say no. We'll see how it plays out for sure. You know I gotta go now though."*

Rachel: *"I figured Mr. Sales and investment. I'm glad we met, and I want you to know that's the best I've ever been fucked."*

Kyl: *"I can say that's the best my dick has ever been sucked and your pussy is premium."*

She kissed me as I got dressed and made sure I had her number. I walked out of the room, and it was like Luka was on the same wavelength. He was dressed ready to move already. He smiled and headed towards the door.

Luka: *"Damn bro, did you kill her?"*

Kyl: *"What are you talking about?"*

Luka: *"Mother fucker we fucked and spend the next 45 minutes listening to her scream and call you Daddy. I don't know how you do it. I got like 20 minutes in me, and I'm done."*

Kyl: *"You've always been quick to blow up though."*

We both erupted in laughter as we made our way out of the hotel. We weren't far from where we were staying so we just decided to walk. It had been a crazy night, a good one though. But that was about to change.

As we made out way towards our hotel, we reflected on how far we'd come. Luka had always expressed to me that he appreciated me for saving his life. I think the coke and alcohol must've gotten to him.

Luka: *"Man, I just want to say something. I wouldn't be here if it weren't for you. I'm literally alive because of you and it's more than that. I have a life I'd have never known of you hadn't told me to come with you. Kyl, there's never going to be a moment ever that I don't owe you my life and have your back. I mean that."*

It was touching and I felt what he was saying. The best decision I'd ever made was not letting him just walk away. I hugged him and slugged him in the shoulder.

Kyl: *"I appreciate you too shithead"*

I was so ready for bed. I felt like nothing could've kept me from my bed at that moment. How wrong I was. As I headed to my room, I heard a muffled scream. A few doors down from my room, the door cracked open, and a kid peaked out. I'm talking like an eleven- or twelve-year-old, he was bleeding and looked like he'd had his ass beat. I looked back at Luka, and he noticed what I'd seen. I didn't hesitate at all; I opened the door and grabbed the boy. I pushed him to Luka and rushed into the room. I was not ready for what I was about to see. The young woman on the bed was severely beaten and bleeding badly. She was being raped; her pussy was leaking blood like she was on a heavy period. There was blood all over the room. I grabbed the piece of shit raping her and spun him around. Of course this was happening....

It was Oscar's brother, our Columbian counterparts. He smiled at me and asked if I wanted some too. I didn't even think as I socked him in the face and continued to beat the fuck out of him until he was knocked out. I wrapped her in a blanket and sent her out of the room to Luka.

Kyl: *"Give her one of our rooms."*

I went back into the room as he was regaining consciousness. He asked me if I knew who he was, to which I replied, "A dead man." I don't care who you are when you commit these types of atrocities. A woman and a child. Fuck this guy. I grabbed his face and told him *"Being a Columbian drug lord doesn't give you a pass to rape a woman and hurt a child you fucking piece of shit."* I reached down and ripped his belt from his waist and wrapped it around his neck. I choked him so hard one of his eyes was protruding from the socket.

Fortunately, this hotel had no cameras in it, I made sure as I walked to Luka's rooms, I hadn't realized I was covered in blood. When I walked in the boy winced and Luka looked at me shocked.

Luka: *"Damn bro, are you okay?"*

Kyl: *"Its not my blood. I'm fine."*

I looked at the boy shaking and scared in the corner. As I approached him, he started to cry and covered himself up in a ball.

Kyl: *"Hey kid, it's okay now. You and your mom are safe. He's never going to hurt you again, I promise."*

He lunged forward into my arms and sobbed. All this shit wasn't really my realm, but I still knew right from wrong and even in my line of work, you didn't beat kids or rape women. Fuck that piece of shit. Tomorrow was going to be interesting for sure.

I helped the woman clean herself up as best as possible and Luka had gotten their stuff from the room they were in. Her car had broken down and the Columbian piece of shit had put her up in the room expecting to be repaid in sex. When she refused, he had taken what he wanted. The poor kid had tried to help his mom and not only gotten his ass beat but had to watch what was being done to his mother. A scene I'm sure he'd never forget. Shit boiled my blood. I gave her all the money I'd pulled off the dead Columbian and Luka and I both added to it. We sent her on her way with about five thousand dollars. Plenty to get far away and hopefully start over.

I don't think we got to sleep until close to four in the morning. We weren't supposed to meet up for business until eleven but it sure didn't feel like we had gotten any sleep. We had cleaned up the room well and gotten rid of anything covered in blood. I had no desire to be here when house keeping found what had transpired in that room with the dead guy in it.

As we turned in our room keys and checked out, the prior night was on my mind. Talk about two complete ends of the spectrum. It had been so good and yet ended so much differently. I couldn't even call it a bad ending because two lives had been saved. Not sure how things would go on the business front yet or if it would even come up. I certainly wasn't going to offer up any information myself.

Miami was rich in exotic cars, and you could rent just about anything you could dream of driving. Of course we were going to take advantage of that. I've been a car fanatic since I was little, my dream was to one day own a fleet of all my favorite cars. I rented a Ferrari F355 spider in its classic Ferrari red. You rent a car like this in a beach town, and it had to have to be a convertible. Luka and I felt like we were straight out of the movie Scarface even if we were the real-life version of that lifestyle. We just didn't have Tony Montana level money. I doubted we'd ever see that kind of power.

As I drove across town, I tried to put everything out of my mind and just take this all in. This was a way different world than the Midwest where we lived. I could get used to this I thought.

Kyl: *"I think it best we don't mention anything about what happened."*

Luka: *"I'd agree with that. What happens if it comes up?"*

Kyl: *"Deny any knowledge of it."*

We were both quiet until we got there. It was a high-end beachside restaurant, and it seemed a little empty. My guess was it was likely either owned by the Columbians or they had paid for the privacy. Either way, I was glad it was a restaurant. I was hungry because we'd skipped breakfast.

Oscar stood as we approached and shook both our hands. He didn't look like a man who knew his brother was dead.

Oscar: *"Hello my friends, I hope you didn't party too hard! You look a little tired. Would you like a little bump to perk you up?"*

Kyl: *"That's not a bad idea but I think we'd like to eat and talk some business on a clear head, first."*

Oscar: *"This is a good plan. I like you, always business first. I apologize for the absence of my brother. He did not return to the hotel last night and I cannot get a hold of him. Hopefully, he's not gotten himself in any trouble. My brother...has, some bad habits we'll say."*

I looked out at the beach because I wasn't sure how well I had hidden the disdain I felt had crossed my face just then. So, he knew his brother was a rapist piece of shit. I suddenly wasn't as hungry, and I wanted to tell this guy to go fuck himself and walk out. All feelings aside, I was here for business. I just wanted to get it over with and move on at this point.

As we sat there talking, one of Oscar's men hurried to his side and spoke in his ear. Oscar's face went solemn. Shit, they'd found him. Luka looked at me and his eye said be ready as I noticed his hand come to rest near the knife on the table.

Oscar: *"It would seem my brother has been found. It would appear his bad habit has caught up with him and cost his life. I must leave to deal with this. We are settled?"*

Kyl: *"My condolences and yes, we are settled."*

As I stood to leave, I shook Oscar's hand and again offered my condolences. He looked at my hand in his and it suddenly hit me they were bruised and cut. Shit.

Oscar: *"Between you and I, he was a burden and caused me lots of issues and unnecessary money. He was a rapist, but my mother could never know of this, so I could do nothing but protect him. I am free of that now."*

He held my gaze for a moment longer and then turned and walked away. I'm not sure I had been breathing because I had to take a deep breath as soon as he was gone.

Luka: *"Do you think he knows?"*

Kyl: *"I think if he ever figures out, we were staying in the same hotel it might be an issue. Nothing we can do now. Let's go, we need to get home and start making arrangements for new shipments."*

I didn't regret saving that woman and her kid, but I had to learn to start using more discretion when inserting myself into situations. This could've gone very badly and to be honest, was something that would be a loose end lingering over my head.

Chapter 11

Old dogs don't need new tricks

The last couple of days had been thick with a lot of police presence and conversations with detectives. I had left their bullet riddled bodies for the rodents overnight and to be found the next morning. Being that they hadn't just disappeared, and it was clear it had been a legitimate hit by the Latin Crowns, it took the heat off me. Detectives had verified the word on the street about the Crowns getting wind of the boys snitching on them which even more reinforced things.

Agent Hague had kept his distance since our last meeting, but it hadn't deterred Agent Lewis from the ATF from coming around asking questions. Hague had accused the Police department of having a leak within their ranks after information had gotten out. The police chief quietly told him to go fuck himself and it was likely due to the boys' own bragging that caused the leak. The only real question I had to answer and explain had been my sudden decision to give all the crews the day off leaving the boys to be out there alone. It was an unavoidable side effect of the plan I'd had. But the simple answer was, I'd been distracted and with my three leads out of pocket during their day long interrogation, I felt I needed to get a better insight into where things were and what was next.

So, I'd given the guys a paid day off to rest up. It made sense easily and apparently Agent Lewis had thought so too. He wasn't an unlikable guy at all. Nothing like Hague. Something about the way he looked at me was bothering me though. There was something oddly familiar about it. I just couldn't put my finger on it though.

The orders I'd given in reference to the delivery of the memory card were a bit more intricate and maniacal than I'd led on in the beginning. I'd had the video edited to ensure that Luka's voice was not on it and then transferred to another memory card. Luka had ordered a clean up crew which consisted of picking up all the pieces, scrubbing the area, cutting up the rest of the body not blown apart, and placing it all in a bag and then a nice wax lined box. You had to wait a few days too, so the body would start to decompose. The bag and box did an excellent job of sealing in the smell. Today, that box along with the video will be delivered to Phil Kessler and family. I'd also needed a few days to move people and things around to prepare for what was about to come. Phil and his other son, Mitch, were about to get a nasty surprise and a clear declaration of the war they had started.

Luka was concerned about keeping me safe and well guarded. He'd expressed the common sentiment from all my top commanders.

So, I'd be staying at my Epic Tower penthouse apartment for a while. I didn't really mind and to be honest, my neighbors didn't deserve to be drawn into all this. Not that I was just going to hide through all this, that's not my style. I'd definitely be reducing my movements, but I can't be caged up. No telling how long this would take to play out. Phil Kessler was not to be taken lightly, especially at this point. I was kind of impressed at the tenacity he'd shown to get us to this point. I didn't think he had it in him. He had the resources to give me a hard time, but not to beat me. I still had the Mardechi's at my back if things got beyond my ability to contain and control. I wasn't worried.

I owed our fine Mayor Marcus Stephon, and the Police Chief, William Stephon, a visit to converse on the impending chaos that was about to erupt in their city. We'd passed some messages back and forth between us to keep up with current events. But things were about to go completely sideways, and I always gave them both the respect of an in person visit for the more important things. I was proud of the strides they had made in "leaving" the crime family life.

Realistically, they were just as dirty as they had always been, but they had city offices and political positions to stand behind.

As I walked into City Hall, I was waved through the metal detectors. It was common knowledge I had a long-standing relationship with the Stephon family.

I was one of their main donors and had done more charity events and fundraisers than I could count. My last donation to the police department had brought the department into the top three of the most up-to-date and most well-equipped departments in the country. As far as they were concerned, I was a Saint in the community. Even if they did know the truth about me, they turned a blind eye to it.

I was privileged enough to use the private elevator that the mayor himself used. As I stepped off the elevator, Chief Stephon greeted me with a warm smile and a hug. He held onto me as he leaned back to look at me.

William: *"Hard to believe you grew so much from the knuckle headed kid you were to now. It's been a while, Kyl."*

His smile faded for a second and he grabbed my hand.

William: *"My condolences on the boys. I hated to hear how things ended up. I know they were family to you."*

He knew the truth even if he didn't know the details. I had knowledge of more than several of his officers that met untimely deaths for their mistakes or betrayals too. William was the Stephon Family enforcer when he was younger. That man had a body count higher than likely half the murders in the state prisons combined.

Kyl: *"Thanks Will, definitely a hard one to get off the mind."*

The truth is, I hadn't even really tried to deal with it in my head. I was cold to it all. Not that it didn't hurt, it's just that after Gia, I'm not sure I ever really felt emotional pain the same. It sucked and I was usually just more disappointed and angrier.

I had spaced off for a minute and almost forgot where I was.

William: *"What a fucking thing ya know. I have to wait like the common folk to see my own older brother!"*

We both laughed. We'd all come a long way.

Marcus opened his office door and waved us in. He had an impressive office, the man had impeccable taste. He hugged Will and pointed him towards the dry bar in the corner of the office. He embraced me like I was his own family. It had been a while…No, scratch that. We hadn't had to have a talk like this. This would be different for sure. They had ears in the streets too. They knew it was brewing.

Marcus: *"You look good Kyl; I swear you never age. Still look like you're not a day over eighteen! How are you? I know the shit with the boys has to hurt."*

Everyone was always poking at me for having a baby face. I was only twenty-five but considering what I'd been through to get here, it felt like I'd lived a lifetime already.

Marcus: *"It seems like the six almost seven years ago has been forever since…since that night. You know, I owe where this family is today, to you."*

Kyl: "*Come on Marcus, you were already pushing towards this on your own.*"

Marcus: "*Yes, but to be honest. We weren't making the moves we needed to make. My father's ties and loyalty to the Cretchfeld's would've held us back forever. My father was blind to their toxic hold over our family. You changed the course of life for our family. Accept it or don't but we know the truth.*"

96

William: *"He's right Kyl, and because of that, we're here today. Tell us how we can help."*

It was a blessing to have such admiration and support, but it always felt like a burden to me. I'm not sure why. I just struggled seeing the value others saw in me. I'm just a guy trying to make it and not end up dead doing it.

Kyl: *"There is a war coming. Kessler is behind everything that's transpired. They killed Spilz, Russ Kessler is dead, the BLKs and the Crowns are going to war, I hung our federal friend from the DEA off my balcony, I told the Mardechi's to stay clear but be on guard, and I'm about to reactivate the Four Horsemen."*

(I'll explain the last part soon)

No matter how well you think you're informed, there's always going to be more than you were ready to hear. That's exactly what was happening to Will and Marcus right now.

William: *"So do I need to worry about Russ? What about the Fed? Is he going to be a problem?"*

Kyl: *"Russ is basically ground beef in a box that's going to be delivered today. The fed, I don't know. The guy has a hard on for me, I haven't figured out the ATF guy yet. Something is off with him."*

Marcus: *"So what I need from you, is a chain of events to come, what we can do to help, and I need to figure out how to minimize the effect on the community and the media coverage. More importantly, I need a timeline. How long is this going to last. I'm telling you now, it needs to be over as quickly as possible. Next year is an election year Kyl. I need Kessler out of the picture if you catch my drift. Like Cretchfeld gone."*

Damn, I hadn't honestly thought about taking it that far. He was looking to take my situation and completely exercise one of the cities demons. The heroin and pill trade had hit our town hard, so I was starting to see where he was headed with this. Fucking politicians. I couldn't keep from smiling.

Kyl: "*You're a mother fucker Marcus. Always an agenda with you politicians.*"

They both smirked but clearly were waiting for me to delve into what my plan was.

Kyl: "*This changes things a bit, but I can work with it. The BLKs are far better armed than the Crowns. I will push them into an all-out elimination war. They'll be the tip of the spear. What I need from you there is the department to be the double-edged sword. We know they're all going to be armed all the time. Have your gang units and any other uniforms you can count on, start dropping them. No one will flinch at some piece of shit gang members getting dropped during the uptick in violence. Your department will look like it's on top of the issue and eliminating the problem. I'll handle the Kessler's. Just be aware of the impact all these bodies are going to have.*"

William: "*My gang unit has been chomping at the bit to do some real work and most of my beat cops will be on board to drop Crowns after the incident earlier this year when they killed Det. Lakin. You know my Detectives; we'll cover the spread on the bodies.*"

Marcus: "*We'll PR this as a gang war and link it to the Kessler family. No one will think anything of it when we feed the media a predesigned story about some type of double cross between the Crowns and Kessler's. Two burdens on the city taking each other out is a win win. We'll attribute the final blow and end to our great Special Ops Gang unit and the outstanding and brave actions of our police department.*"

Kyl: "*Sounds like a win for all of us.*"

We all chuckled and agreed to the plan. It was definitely a win for me. I wouldn't have to focus so many people and resources on making this happen. I just needed to focus on Kessler now.

So, let's talk about the Four Horsemen. If you remember back to the days when we had taken out the Vonnet and Cretchfeld Families, Devin, Louis, and Pratt had been instrumental in the elimination of the Cretchfeld's and any remaining loyalists to either family. Who's the fourth? Luka of course. Those four became known as the Four Horsemen of the Apocalypse. For the first year after the cleansing, they moved through this city, making example of anyone who spoke ill of me or even hinted to any loyalty to either of the former families. Anyone who even said I'd gone too far ended up dead. That was their way of managing it. I didn't hold order over how they handled things. I gave them free rein to do as they saw fit. It was time for them to come out of retirement for one last cleansing.

Luka was waiting in the parking garage for me, and I think I noticed at least six other guards. I wanted to call it excessive, but the truth was, Luka knew what he was doing. He'd devoted his life to protecting me and I didn't ever question his judgment. I filled him in as we walked to the car.

Luka: *"Kessler's delivery was made. He knows."*

Well, here we go. No turning back now. It was on my mind how we were going to take out the entire Kessler family. A lot has changed in the world since the last cleansing. Not that I'd gotten too soft to do it. I'd figured Phil would be upset about Russ but inevitably find the silver lining and eventually agree to negotiate to the terms I'd wanted. All that was off the table now. The mayor had spoken about his desire and intentions. Like it or not, I still had to play ball to a certain point. As much as they attributed their success to me, I had to attribute my success and position to them as well. We didn't exist in the capacity without each other. That's the truth of it all.

As I drove across town towards my penthouse, my phone vibrated. It was Phil Kessler. Shit, that was a lot sooner than I'd expected. "Meet me at Natoli's. Back lot, just you and I. Headed there now."

Not going go lie, this caught me off guard. I had several tails including Luka. I needed to pull over and let him know.

As I pulled over, I looked down and realized I didn't have my pistol in this car. There was a shotgun in the trunk. But it was Natoli's. No gun rule and oddly enough, Phil could've picked anywhere else other than our neutral meeting spots. I wasn't sure what he had up his sleeve.

I informed Luka of the current situation and even though he didn't like it, he agreed to hold up across the street and wait. I guess we were all about to find out what was about to happen next.

As I pulled into Natoli's, I rounded the building towards the back parking lot. I saw Phil's Cadillac and pulled in a few spots from it. He wasn't in the car. I sat for a second and collected my thoughts. As I was getting out of the car, Phil came out of the back door. He stopped in his tracks and the look on his face puzzled me. It wasn't the anger I'd expected. It was a cross between confusion and fear. Now I was getting anxious.

Phil: *"That's far enough Kyl, we can talk from here."*

I noticed he'd pulled a 9mm from his jacket. I didn't have one in the car. Stupid. So much for the rules. Shit.

Phil: *"You need to know I didn't want this, Kyl. None of it."*

Kyl: *"Bullshit Phil. A man doesn't set in motion the things you did without ill intentions. You broke the rules, and you crossed lines that can't be uncrossed."*

Phil: *"That's the thing Kyl, I didn't know what was going on. You have to believe me. This was Mitch, Leah, and Russ. I've been on the heavy side of retirement and not been paying attention. Kyl, you know I'd never involve your people like that."*

Kyl: *"I have a tough time believe any of that. Your fat ass was in my zone passing out money and heroin. Stop fucking lying to me. You're not making your case any better standing there with that pistol either. You forget the rules here too?"*

Phil: *"You stabbed me in the fucking hand and nearly took my eye out you fucking shit. My mind isn't so sharp any more Kyl. The kids have been doing their own thing and I'm not as clear on everything as I used to be. You sent my son to me in a fucking box Kyl. All fucking cut up and not even all there because you fucking blew him up with a rocket you son of bitch. I didn't ask for this, and a war wasn't what I wanted. You can't have my other kids Kyl. They're shitheads but they've got new insight into things I don't have. They're teaching an old dog new tricks Kyl. So, fuck you."*

My eyes darted in both directions. I was in the wide open and had no cover. Fuck, Kessler was shaking and sweating. I saw his hand tighten on that 9mm and suddenly the world shifted and turned on its head.

As Phil looked like he was about to raise his gun, the unexpected occurred. It happened so fast I couldn't even process it. I hadn't noticed the door behind Kessler had slowly crept open. I hadn't seen anyone lurking there. In one single movement, Alessandro Natoli stepped the rest of the way out of the door spoke one simple statement, *"I made clear if I ever saw a gun on these grounds I shoot a man on site. Fuck you Kessler."* Then Alessandro shot him point blank in the head. *"Old dogs don't need new tricks, you smug fuck."*

I watched as Kessler's body slumped to the ground with a profound thud. I was in such shock I couldn't fucking speak. The fragile old man I thought could barely get around had moved with directed purpose and shot Phil Kessler dead on the spot.

Luka's car and two others came sliding into the parking lot. All were shocked at what they were seeing, and no one spoke a word.

Kyl: "*Alessandro…*"

He raised his hand and spoke before I could say anything else.

Alessandro: "*Kyl, he's had it coming for decades and I have wanted to be the one to do. The son of a bitch finally broke the rules so I could justify it. You spared my grandson, I owed you. Now get out of here. We'll take care of this.*"

Kyl: "*Stick around for a while old man, I owe you a couple games of Scopa*"

He smiled ear to ear….

Alessandro: "*Now that's what I wanted to hear; I'll certainly take your money kiddo. Now go.*"

He gave me his signature wink and I turned to leave.

Kyl: "*Luka, get some guys over here and on the Natoli homes. They don't move without our people close behind until this is over.*"

Luka: "*Yes boss.*"

Kyl: "*Let the BLKs know they have a full go. We take out the Crowns first. Meet me at the Penthouse. I'm calling a meeting of the Horsemen.*"

Luka stood up a little straighter and his eyes glazed over as if I'd said some sort of incantation. He knew what was about to happen and he loved the idea already.

Chapter 12

The Four Horsemen, and an unexpected ally

I couldn't leave the Natoli's to fend for themselves on taking care of Kessler. My clean up crew was very efficient. Oddly enough, sometimes the best thing you can do is provide the police with the murder weapon. My crew would strip down the gun and thoroughly wipe it clean and put Phil's prints on all the various parts as they put it back together. His prints would be the only ones on the gun and each round in the mag. They'd scrub the scene to appear nothing had ever happened there. Phil would end up in the river appearing to have committed suicide. The number of questions and lack of evidence would leave the possibility of suicide the most viable option for anyone investigating.

Knowing that was taken care of would alleviate some unnecessary stress I didn't need to deal with right now. Shit would be hitting the fan soon, there was zero doubt about that. I just had to get out ahead of it. Bringing Devin, Louis, and Pratt out of retirement was the right move here. I hadn't always stayed connected with them all, so they wouldn't know exactly where things were as of current. I had forced them into retirement. They were grateful for the financial security and the blessing of family time. But the reality is they were killers. Three of the most savage and devastating men I've ever know. Aside from Luka and his Reapers. The combination of the Four Horsemen and Luka's Reapers was going to be the deadliest force on the streets. We were at war; I'd be a fool not to take advantage and just have everyone even questionable taken out at this point. Marcus had his own list, that's part of how this all worked. You scratch my back, I'll scratch yours. These men were impartial to who was who or what they did. They operated on orders alone.

I'd sent out a page to all those I needed to meet me. It was just a matter of waiting now.

As I pulled into the parking garage, the garage guard informed me that I had company in the lobby. Gee, I wonder who it could be now. I was sick of surprise visits. I put the car in park and let the valet take over as I headed to the lobby. I had a feeling that I wasn't going to be excited about whoever was there waiting.

As I walked into the lobby, my temperament went from calm to anxious and angry. I took a deep breath and walked towards Agent Hague who was standing not far from Agent Lewis. I walked directly to him and stopped face to face and nose to nose. He flinched as I stepped closer.

Kyl: *"What the fuck are you doing here Gag. You didn't get enough last time?"*

He reached up like he was going to grab my shirt and stopped just short of doing it.

Agent Hague: *"You know I could arrest your fucking ass right now for assault on a federal agent? Maybe I should."*

Kyl: *"Do it pussy. You have no evidence anything ever happened to you. Except you showed up at my personal residence alone. Maybe I tell it like you showed up unannounced and started coming onto me. Acting all queer and offered to suck me off."*

I'm not sure I'd ever seen someone turn so red so fast. If steam could've come out of his ear right then, it would've. I'd struck a nerve.

Agent Hague: *"Fuck you bitch. I'm not some queer. I'll you take out right here and now."*

Kyl: *"There you go again. Now you're offering to take me out. Not my type bud. I like tits, ass, and pussy. Ya know, on a woman. I'm going to need you stop making all these homosexual advances towards me please."*

That was all it took to trip his trigger. He came at me and as he moved, he pulled his gun. But, before he could draw down on me, Agent Lewis had grabbed his arm.

Agent Lewis: *"Enough Hague. Put it away, now. Let's go."*

Kyl: *"I'd have thought you learned your lesson after the last time you tried to get tough with me Agent Gag. You tell your partner you pissed in your own face hanging off the balcony after you tried to attack me in my own home?"*

The look on his face and the look on Agent Lewis' face caused me to burst into a fit of laughter.

Agent Hague: *"Get your fucking hands off me. Don't forget your place, I'm lead investigator here bitch. (Turning his focus back to me) I swear to you Kyl, I'll kill you myself if I don't end up the one taking your ass to prison. This isn't over."*

I could've let it go but that's no fun. I could barely stop laughing.

Kyl: *"Nobody is scared of your bitch ass Agent Gag. Make sure you keep an extra pair of pants with you when you're fucking with me. Oh, and don't ever threaten me you fucking piss stain."*

By this point Agent Lewis was pushing him away towards the door. As he pushed him out of the door, he turned back and looked at me.

Agent Lewis: *"You've got to stop antagonizing him before something bad really does happen Kyl."*

I watched him walk out, something about him still nagged at me.

As I stood there staring at the door, Luka walked up behind me.

Luka: *"What the fuck was that all about?"*

Kyl: *"That douchebag DEA agent and his ATF pal. Agent Gag told me he'd kill me himself if he didn't get to put me in prison."*

I chuckled at hearing myself say that, but Luka wasn't amused. I saw his eyes narrow, and that killer instinct start to come out.

Kyl: *"Hey, it's alright. Don't do that. You hear me. We drop a Fed, and we create a whole new issue. Things are in a good place. You hear me?"*

He looked at me for a minute and then his rational side came back.

Luka: *"I understand, I don't like this dude creeping around. You say the word and I'll make him appear six states away Kyl."*

Kyl: *"I know you will. I appreciate you Luka. We're okay though. The other guy though, something is bugging me about him. I can't put my finger on it. It's his eyes, I'm telling you, I've seen those eyes before."*

Luka: *"That's weird bro. Want me to look into him?"*

Kyl: *"Not right now. We'll come back to it. More important things to do currently."*

Just as I said that, Devin, Louis, and Pratt came walking in. I actually hadn't seen any of them for at least eight or nine months now. Far too long.

Kyl: *"Well I'll be damned, y'all still looking good for some middle aged, retired gangsters. I figured y'all would be fat by now."*

Devin: *"Shit, have you met my wife? She never lets up on me. Gym gym gym and always eating healthy. She's got us all on the same damn routine and diets. I'm certainly not arguing with her!"*

Louis: *"Not a man alive wants to argue with that woman. Why do you think we all just show up and do what she says?"*

Pratt: *"No doubt, my wife is almost as bad. I'm not arguing either."*

They all chuckled and one by one hugged Luka and I and paid their respects to us.

Kyl: *"Let's head up so we can chat."*

The mood changed to more serious immediately. I wanted to get into a more private setting before anything else was said.

As we worked our way up to my penthouse we joked and laughed like the old days. I had genuinely missed these guys and a part of me felt guilty for bringing them back into this. They'd done so much already.

Once we got behind closed doors, I took the time to catch them up on everything that had transpired over the course of the last week. It was a lot and almost unbelievable to think there had been so much in such a short time. I answered all the questions and explained my vision for how this would all work out. I didn't mean it would all go as I had planned because as it had been so far, shit had a way of working out in the most unexpected ways. No one could believe Alessandro had smoked Phil Kessler. I was still chewing on that one myself.

As we were going over everything, my phone rang. It was Dho, the second in command over the BLKs.

Kyl: *"What's up Dho?"*

Dho: *"I'm sorry to call you like this, are we good to talk?"*

Kyl: *"Ya, go ahead. Talk to me."*

Dho: *"Xhan is in ICU. They followed him to the fucking school and popped him in broad daylight as he was headed in for some award ceremony for his kid. They killed both of his guards and I'm not sure he's going to make it Kyl."*

Fuck, seriously? That's where we were? I was about to make one of the most brash decisions I'd made yet.

Kyl: *"Dho, you're in charge now. This is all out war. You have my permission to bring in the other Asian gangs from wherever you need to. You hit them in their homes. At their jobs. You hit them all. Take the leash off and let all hell break loose. There is to be no Latin Crown left breathing. Do you understand me?"*

Dho: *"Yes sir, I will end this at whatever cost."*

I hung up before anything else could be said. I was angry. Even though they were a street level thug gang, I had always held them to a standard. A level of integrity. I felt foolish at that moment. Like gangs had integrity anymore. Stupid.

I was joined on the balcony by all four men. They stood there quietly as an affirmation they had my back but were waiting for me to fill them in.

Kyl: *"The Crowns hit Xhan at his kids' school and killed both his guards. Broad daylight. I just told Dho to assume command and unleash hell."*

Pratt: *"My brother in-law is close to the Oliver St. 316's. They hate the Crowns."*

Kyl: *"Do it. Make the call."*

Luka: *"You're planning a complete takedown then?"*

Kyl: *"Here's what it is fellas. Every Crown, every Kessler, every affiliated associate of the Kessler family ceases to exist. I brought you three back in because I want every Captain, every Lieutenant, every General in the Kessler's ranks taken out. I want you to hit their Royal Guard."*

The Kessler family had employed nearly two dozen former Serbian special forces as their closest guard. They had become known as the "Royal Guard." Taking them out would be difficult but not impossible and would send a message to the remaining Kessler's that their days were numbered. I was reverting to some of the old ways in this, I wanted to kill Mitch Kessler myself and I had yet to decide how Leah Kessler would meet her demise.

Luka: *"We'll handle it all. Let's get down to the details of how we're doing this. We got this boss; we won't let you down."*

My Four Horsemen were back together and about to plan the full-on Apocalypse of the Kessler family leaders and guard. I had full trust and faith that it would be taken care of. I just wanted them all to make it back home. It's hard to pray for safety when you're sending men out to take the lives of your enemies. I'm not sure where God and I stood on this, but I was fairly certain he'd not be very happy with the decisions I was making.

As I sat back and watched the four most dangerous men, I'd ever known work together go plan the most violent attack this city had seen in years, I reflected on everything it had taken to get here. All the lives lost, all the violence, and all the damage we had all sustained. It made me angry the Kessler's had pushed it to this. When we all agreed on these zones and the peace between us, it had been good. Everyone was profiting, everyone was pulling in money hand over fist. Greed is a mother fucker. It had already cost them two of the top members of their family and yet they still wanted to continue. Fucking idiots.

I was lost in thought when the apartment phone rang. I answered, there was a woman in the lobby waiting to see me. She hadn't given a name but said it was urgent. I really didn't want to go all the way back to the lobby, so I had them bring her to me.

I let Luka know what was going on so he could inform the others. They had cleared the woman in the lobby, she had no weapons. I was intrigued by this point. Who could this be and what would she want?

The doorbell rang. I tucked my pistol into the small of my back and answered the door. Standing there was a beautiful green eyed brunette. Small framed. Very fit. Very well built. Ya know, because all that's super important. I rolled my eyes at myself. I did feel like I'd seen her before.

Kyl: *"Who the fuck are you and what do you want?"*

Woman: *"My name is Deedra and I want to help you, but I need your help too."*

Kyl: *"Deedra"*

Why did that sound familiar?

Kyl: *"How are you going to help me, Deedra?"*

Deedra: *"I'm Leah Kessler's first general."*

My hand slipped behind me as I gripped my pistol. It would probably be in my best interest to just shoot her right here. I knew I'd recognized her. The ruthless general over the prostitution ring the Kessler family ran.

She saw me tense and, in an attempt, to ease my anxiety she lowered herself to her knees.

Deedra: *"Look, I know this doesn't look good and you have every right to be apprehensive. I'm coming here in good faith to give you information you'll need and devote myself to your family."*

Kyl: *"And I'm supposed to just believe you and take you in. You think I'm fucking stupid? Why the fuck would you want to help me?*

110

Why the FUCK would I ever trust you bitch?"

She was visibly shaking, and I could see genuine fear in her eyes. I still needed to be sure. Most people will tell you the truth when they're hanging by their feet over two hundred and fifty feet above the ground.

I pulled my pistol and grabbed her by the hair. I dragged her to the balcony as she stumbled and tried to keep her footing.

Kyl: *"By the feet."*

I didn't even have to explain myself. Luka and Devin grabbed her and hoisted her over the railing before she could even object or fight back. She was screaming as she hung there by her feet.

Kyl: *"Stop fucking screaming!"*

She put both her hands over her mouth. There was nothing but pure fear in her eyes.

Kyl: *"Why the fuck are you here?"*

She was so scared she couldn't even answer. I reached over the railing and put the pistol near her temple and pulled the trigger. Her eyes went wide with even more fear and disbelief. Her hands flew away from her mouth immediately and she began to speak. There were tears in her eyes.

Deedra: *"I'm not stupid. I know the Kessler's can't win this and I don't want to fucking die for some stupid ass bitch I don't even really like. I came here because I can help you in exchange for protection. Please, I'm telling the fucking truth. I'll do whatever you want or say. I don't want to die. I'm begging you, Kyl. Let me prove it to you please!"*

I stared at her hanging there. I didn't have a bad gut feeling. For a moment I thought I might believe her.

Kyl: *"Pull her up. Go wipe your face and then sit on the couch. Don't move or say a fucking word until I tell you to. Go, now."*

As they set her on her feet she collapsed and struggled to get her legs under herself to move. She'd been honest, I felt that. She was 100% aware that I had no problem dropping her. I'd think about hearing her out.

I really just wanted all the noise to stop for just a little while. So many gears turning, so many variables, and way too many people trying to talk to me. I was by no means overwhelmed, I just needed to slow things down a bit. Although, I wasn't foreseeing that happening just yet and I had to figure out what to do with Deedra. Part of me wanted to send her back to Leah Kessler in a box with a nice letter about how she'd come to double-cross them. That was really just doing them a favor though. You have to be a pure psychopath to be held by your feet off a balcony and not be compelled to tell the truth. I had even pushed the bar by firing two inches from her face. Shit, really, you'd have to be something beyond to show up here in the first place thinking you're going to pull one over on us.

I looked at myself in the mirror as if to search my own soul. I was going to take a chance on her, I could always kill her later if I changed my mind.

I walked back into the living room. All four men were standing guard around her. Luka had his head down, cocked to the side, looking at her up. It was an ominous stare. I could tell he was uncomfortable about her being here.

Kyl: *"Do y'all have everything lined out as far as your starting place and plan?"*

Luka: *"Yes boss, everything is set to go. What are we doing with the broad? Can we toss her off the roof?"*

Everyone in the room chuckled except the girl. She was not amused. There was genuine fear in her eyes.

Kyl: *"Alright, I need you to make contact with Chief Stephon. He has list you're going to have to work into play on the fly. You have to pay to play, boys, make it happen. Let's get moving."*

Luka: *"What about the woman?"*

Kyl: *"I can handle it, but you can send Taska up and have someone replace his spot in the lobby. Feel better now?"*

Luka: *"I'd feel better if we just got rid of her, but you know best."*

Kyl: *"You're worse than having a pesky side chick."*

He laughed and threw a couple soft punches at me. I knew he was just doing his job and meant well.

Devin, Louis, and Pratt all came by and gave me respect and the customary bro embrace as they headed out. I didn't need to say anything else; they knew I expected them all to stay safe and keep coming back.

Luka hovered at the door, I winked and motioned for him to get going. He nodded and closed the door.

I sat down across from Deedra and just looked at her. She had collected herself and though I could still see the remnants of tears and the fear in her eyes, she stared back at me.

Kyl: *"I'll be honest, I'm in a bit of a conundrum here. Part of me screams I should just kill you and be done with it. The other part is I'm intrigued as to what you think you could offer me to make it worth saving your life and offering you protection. So, I suggest you take a moment and collect yourself so that you say exactly what you need to say in this moment."*

She looked at me for a few seconds and then shifted her gaze to the floor. I could tell she was going over everything in her head. It had become clear to her that her life was merely a matter of her being able to prove a worth and value to me.

Deedra: *"Look, I've spent a couple of years working for the Kessler's now. It wasn't exactly much choice place to end up and it was either I was going to be one of their whores or I was going to keep the whores in line. I was raped multiple times before and after I was able to make that choice. I didn't have anywhere else to go they made it clear no matter where I turned, they'd be there. If you live in the in the Kessler version of life, Kyl Ingerham was and has been on borrowed time. They preach it like a Bible verse that you're not as tough as you think or untouchable. It took me a little time to really look around and see the truth for myself. I'm not a fool, I'm very perceptive and I have seen the ins and outs of their operation and their capabilities. They could never win. They rely so heavily on the Latin Crowns and their supposed backing from the Sanola Cartel. What I can offer is the complete and total every day start to finish in every aspect of their operations. The strong points in their defense. The weak points in their defense. What they have planned, how they plan to execute, and how they intend to take you down. In their minds of course."*

Kyl: *"Tell me, what made you come to me. Don't give me the bullshit protection speech again. Let's talk about what it really is."*

Deedra: *"The Kessler's are the epitome of human shit. The way they treat people, the way they lie, and manipulate is disgusting. They make everyone they come in contact with, a victim of something. I've been a victim for far too long. I hate them. I hate Mitch and Leah. I want to see them die. I want to help them die."*

There was an eerie sense of pure honesty in that statement. I like it and that would be the perfect way to let her prove herself. To earn the right to show me loyalty.

Kyl: *"So you're willing to show your loyalty by any means necessary then."*

Deedra: *"As long as you promise and devote the protection it takes to ensure my safety. Whatever it takes."*

Whatever it takes huh......

Kyl: *"I want Leah Kessler's head."*

That caught her off guard. I think she thought I was joking at first because she giggled a little until she realized it wasn't a joke.

Deedra: *"You want me to cut her head off and bring it to you? Seriously?"*

Kyl: *"I want her head removed from her body and I want it left on the mantle in the Commodore."*

She swallowed hard and looked a little sick to her stomach.

Kyl: *"What's the matter? Does this exceed your skill set of carving up and scarring the whores or torturing an abusive nonpaying John? I'm well aware of everything you have done and what you're capable of. You'll have to either get really creative or push past your current abilities. It's not optional. You either do it and I'll give you the protection you seek, or I will drag you to the roof now and throw you the fuck over the ledge."*

Deedra: *"I'll do it. I'll figure it out. As long as you guarantee me safety. I'll do whatever it takes, and I'll show you unquestionable loyalty. I'll need a few days to get it done."*

Kyl: *"Forty-eight hours Deedra. After that, I send the Reapers after you, and you don't want that."*

Deedra: *"I understand. I give you my word I'll make it happen."*

We spent the next several hours conversing on her knowledge of all things Kessler. She had a lot more information than I'd actually expected her to know and if it was as accurate as she portrayed it to be, the Kessler operation was about to take some devastating hits very soon.

I put her up in one of the spare rooms and sat outside for a while. Taska had come up and would spend the night on watch, so I wasn't worried about her slipping out in the middle of the night.

The city was not at rest on this particular night. I could hear gunshots from all over the city. Cars rushing around, the wail of sirens from police, firetrucks, and ambulances. It was an all-out war between the gangs on top of having the police involved. I'd guess every traffic stop was turning into a shoot out. The Crowns had bitten off more than they could chew.

I finished my drink and got ready for bed. As I was about to crawl into bed, there was a knock at the door. It was Taska.

Taska: *"Sir, sorry to bother you. But Ms. Deedra has requested to speak to you."*

I motioned to let her in, she stood there in one of my t shirts with this almost lost puppy look on her face. Like a scared little girl, she was either a good actor or I was seeing her vulnerability.

Deedra: *"This is a lot to take in. It's been a heavy day on me and...and I don't really want to be locked in a room alone. If I could sleep in here, I'd appreciate it please. I'll sleep on the floor."*

I nodded at Taska and closed the bedroom door.

Chapter 13

The neighbors hear everything

Not everything is always as it seems. On the surface it can be perceived one way and below a completely separate way. I had learned over the years to never judge a book by its cover. People are often really good at presenting themselves one way and being total pieces of shit with a great smile. You had to pay close attention to see it.

In the midst of all the newly ordered violence between the street gangs, there was far more going on below the surface of it all. Along with the pre-determined hit list my Four Horsemen had put together, we also had to honor the list given to us by the Stephon's. That list was going to carry a lot heavier weight than ours. Fortunately, these four men were completely impartial to who someone was. A mark is a mark. You take them out and move on. No questions, no emotion, no remorse.

Luka was efficient and very intelligent, so he had cut the easier and lower risk targets out for his Reapers to handle. The Reapers were a hand selected and personally trained group Luka himself had created. Most were also Croatian and Albanian, but there were a few Germans. All were completely savage and loyal to Luka and me.

This was by no means a finished in one day type of task. I had expected this to last for several weeks to start. There's more to it than just assassinating the leaders of a rival family. It's almost more about the mental warfare of it. The methodical elimination of each one in no specific order on no specific day or time was absolutely unnerving to the other side.

The Kessler compound was not easily accessible like those of years prior. If they had learned anything it was fortification of their homes. Theirs was basically a closed off heavily guarded private neighborhood. The most important thing in this type of war was to make them feel uncomfortable and unsafe in their most guarded space. For this, Luka was an absolute ninja. Probably more accurately a wraith. He had managed to get inside of their compound neighborhood, snuck into the families top Generals home and murdered him while he was taking a shit.

A lot of what Luka did seem to be for shock factor. The truth is, he was genuinely a real psychopath. A well contained one but none the less, a psycho. He deserved every bit of credit for his creativity in the moments he let the monster out. I'm not sure anyone would really have ever said shit to him anyways.

The General he had assassinated was Kessler's number three in charge. Luka had somehow managed to silently slit his throat while on the toilet. He then cut out his eyes, put them on the counter, and drew a smiling face, nose and mouth in blood to accompany them. He then cut out his heart and tossed it into the shit filled toilet. When it came to striking fear in the hearts of enemies, no one was better than Luka at doing so.

With a complete lack of safety present even in their own homes. You could guarantee people were going to panic. People were going to start running. There was chaos in the streets with the gang war. Police involved shootings almost daily. Even with the recent appearance of the Sanola Cartel, things hadn't changed for us.

The Sanola's were from Guadalajara Mexico and not well liked in their own country. They were notorious for murdering their own people and for having started a turf war with the Tierra Caliente Cartel. The same cartel we'd already had a run in with years prior and sent their men back in boxes. I was honestly a little surprised they'd come back for another round with us. Frustrating really, now I had to find a creative new way to send these guys back to their leader.

The Kessler mob wasn't doing well, and it was about to get even worse for them. We'd only suffered twenty-three losses at the street level. So far, Mitch Kessler had lost one hundred thirty-two Latin Crowns, twenty-one street soldiers, two lieutenants, and one general. Their next loss would have an enormous impact on them.

Luka and Louis had made their way towards the most prominent person on the mayor's hit list. Much to my surprise, not everyone on that list was about political positioning. This particular person was a high court county Judge. The story was, years ago as the Stephon family was on their path to politics, Marcus had crossed paths with the man. Apparently, he had ended up with some information that could harm Marcus' climb towards mayor. The judge cornered Marcus into killing his wife in exchange for not leaking what he knew. The one condition was, Marcus had to do it himself.

On that night, Marcus sat outside the Judge's home. He didn't want to do this, but he also knew the family's past would have implications in the beginning. This was to look like a home invasion, which, during this time, was a common occurrence. Just a year earlier, a couple of thugs had done a home invasion, done horrible things, and kidnapped then executed five people. The judge had presided over their case.

As Marcus got out of the car, he nearly shit himself as the neighbor leaning on the fence said *"Don't worry about having to be too quiet, we won't be calling the police right away. We never spoke by the way."* Then he turned and walked inside. The neighbors were in on it too. Marcus would later learn that the judge had looked the other way after catching the couple raping young girls and boys. They simply owed him too. Disgusting. Marcus swore retribution for this, and that day had come.

The judge was sitting in his study reading over presumably some case he had coming up. Louis disabled the alarm system as Luka slipped into the house. He leaned against the door frame of the study quietly and stood there for several minutes before the judge noticed and let out a startled yell.

Judge: *"What the fuck are you doing here? I know who you are. Street trash."*

Luka: *"Street trash, that's cute. Don't be a shitty host. Pour us a drink, your Honor."*

The judge set a second glass out next to his and filled them both with the expensive bourbon he had been drinking.

Judge: *"This is aged forty years. Costs five thousand dollars a bottle. It's like silk on the tongue."*

He handed Luka a glass. He was right, it was extremely smooth. Impressive.

Judge: *"Who sent you and what do you want?"*

Luka: *"Do you collect anything, Judge?"*

Puzzled, the judge replied.

Judge: *"Rare books, art, expensive bourbon. I'm not going to continue this conversation if you're not going to get to the point."*

Luka: *"Just so we're clear, you don't have a choice in what happens here. Don't be disrespectful and don't make me angry. You see, I collect deaths."*

As he spoke, Luka rolled up my sleeve on his right arm.

There on that forearm, was row after row of small skulls. The judge was beginning to understand.

Luka: *"You see, most people owe a debt of some sort. Whether it's money or a life debt, they all have to be paid at some point. You've been on borrowed time for a few years. I'm sure you remember cornering an up-and-coming politician. Blackmailing him into personally killing your wife for you."*

Judge: *"That son of a bitch, he'd be in prison had I not looked the other way."*

Luka: *"Racketeering is far different than having your wife murdered, judge."*

Judge: *"You'll never get out of here before the police show up. The neighbors hear everything, and they've either already alerted the police or will soon. You're fucked."*

Luka: *"Your neighbors are already dead. See they were in on your scheme to murder your wife and as you know, they're sick fucking pedophiles that you turned a blind eye to. Oh, speaking of eyes. Here's theirs, they should watch this."*

The horrified look on the judge's face was an indication of the scream to follow. It never made it out though. Death really was an art if you had the time to work with it. Luka was an artist of death, there was no doubt about it.

I hadn't left the apartment for several days at the request of pretty much everyone around me and even Mayor Stephon. I was beginning to feel like a caged animal. I wanted to get out even though I had no real reason too. I had a private chef cooking the most amazing meals for me and pretty much anything I needed just a phone call away.

I wasn't good at doing nothing. I was working out all through the day to keep busy. I had really started to think about what was going to happen when the Kessler family was gone. That would put me in control of nearly seventy percent of the city. To think, I was just some punk kid who started out as street enforcer collecting money and keeping drug dealers in line. It's almost nonsensical to wonder if my parents would be proud of me. My uncle Mac would be proud of me. Lewis, he'd be proud of me. It's strange when you've lived your life to this point as I have and start to think about who'd be proud of you. I laughed aloud at the thought of it. I'd come to understand long ago that while some genuinely respected me, most were just honestly terrified of me. Fearful compliance is not the same as respect, although still appreciated.

This is why I keep myself so busy all the time. My brain is a ticking time bomb of tunnels, different pathways, webs, wonders, and complete fuckery. It's actually quite unnerving, it never stops. I'd considered more than once over the years that I was mentally unstable. Not like Luka, but certainly unstable. I found positive ways to keep myself stable and on a satisfactory level. The busier I was, the less of the darkness crept in. It seemed to get worse as time passed too. Or maybe I was just far too critical of myself. Either way, I was fucking bored. That's what it had come down to.

I needed to get out of here. Everyone was just going to have to accept it. One thing about me, being the leader of a crime family or not. Respect goes both ways. I called Luka to let him know I was going out. He wasn't happy about not being able to be at my side, but I let him send a couple of Reapers to be my tails. It was the least I could do for all I asked of him.

I made my way to the parking garage to decide what I'd be driving. There wasn't anything here that didn't stick out, so fuck it. I went with my bright green 911 Porsche. It was a heavily modified and probably one of my louder cars. Definitely not subtle. I waited by the exit for the Reapers to show up, I told them they'd better keep up because I need to let the horses run. I could see the anxiety on their faces. It made me smile, God I'm an asshole sometimes. I know they did not want to have to tell Luka they had lost me.

I'd be nice and not get too far ahead.

As I pulled out onto the street, I felt a little more alive, I hate being cooped up. I hadn't made it but a few blocks when my phone rang. I didn't recognize the number at first and almost didn't answer it. Then it clicked, it was Deedra. I answered quickly.

I could tell she was in a panic and sounded almost ill.

Deedra: *"Its done. I need help. I need out of here asap!"*

Shit. I'd almost forgotten I'd sent her on a suicide mission. She'd pulled it off. Holy shit.

Kyl: *"What's done Deedra?"*

Deedra: *"Don't fucking play games with me! You wanted the stupid bitches head on the mantle at the Commodore. It's done Kyl and now I need help getting away. I thought I was going to get in and get out before anyone noticed and that's not what happened. Help me! Please!"*

She was an absolute mess. I could hear the fear and panic in her voice. She was sobbing in between everything she said.

Kyl: *"Alright, listen to me Deedra. Take a deep breath. Calm yourself down. I need you to be tough right now. Are you with me?"*

I heard her take a couple deep breaths and collect herself. She was a true soldier if she had someone at her back.

Kyl: *"Where are you now?"*

Deedra: *"I'm east of Seneca on Thirty First Street, behind the Quik Stop. I had to ditch my car and run a few blocks. I can see them circling. You have to hurry Kyl. Please."*

I slammed on the brakes and slid into a parking lot. As I jumped out Both Reapers did the same. I quickly filled them in, and we were all on our way.

Kyl: *"I need about ten minutes Deedra. Keep hidden, I'm coming."*

Ten minutes was being generous. I could make it quicker, but it was going to draw attention. No choice now. As I shifted gears whipping in and out of traffic, I thought about how I was going to get in and out of there as quickly as possible. If they were looking for her it likely wasn't just a couple guys. There was likely an army after her. I was more than a little shocked she had pulled it off. I really thought she'd chicken out and end up either taking off or just trying to pretend like nothing happened and ride it out with Leah.

I checked my mirrors for my tail, they were struggling to keep up but as long as they ended up close as I was making my exit it would be fine. My phone was ringing again, it was Luka. I couldn't talk right now. He'd have to wait.

As I rounded the corner, I slowed way down in an attempt to draw as little attention as I could in a bright green Porsche. Not like I knew I'd be in this situation, but I still had to shake my head at myself. After this was all over, I was buying some lame ass plain Lincoln Town Cars to park everywhere with my others. Just for occasions like this.

I pulled into the Quik Stop and rounded the back of the building just as one of the Kessler's street soldiers rounded the other end of the building. I leaned over and flung the door open.

Kyl: *"Move your ass now!"*

As she jumped in, I was already in reverse before she could shut the door. As I cranked the wheel and spun the car around shots rang out from two different directions. I could hear the rounds slamming into my car and one hit the rear driver's side window right behind me.

124

I dumped the clutch and rolled out of there sideways, white smoking the tires. Shit another one, and another one. I was nearly boxed in by five cars. I down shifted and barely slid by as they tried to cut off my escape. As I slid back out onto Thirty First Street, I had to go left towards the stop light. A car slid to a stop in the middle of the intersection as I approached and opened fire with a barrage of automatic gun fire.

We were taking hits from straight on, my windshield was peppered with holes. I downshifted, hit the e-brake, and slid around the corner; the two Reapers who'd been my tail opened fire on the car in the intersection. It was just enough to get us a clear path out. I looked over at Deedra. She was sheet white and that's when I noticed all the blood. Shit, she'd been hit a couple times. But the look on her face seemed less self-concerned at the moment, she was staring at me. She was actually talking to me, and I wasn't sure what she was saying. She reached for me and that's when I looked down. Fuck, I was hit too. Bad. I think at least three or four times. I was sitting in a pool of my own blood. My ears were ringing. I felt funny. Damn, was I going to die like this? I should've stayed home. Luka was never going to let me live this down.

My phone rang, Deedra had answered. I couldn't drive any more. I was tired and could barely keep my eyes open. I pulled off into a parking lot and turned the car off. She was trying to put pressure on the wounds, and I knew in my head she was nearly screaming into the phone and at me, but I just couldn't put together anything she was saying. I was fading fast. For the first time in as long as I could remember, I started praying. Not for God to save me, but for forgiveness. I didn't even know if he would forgive me, but I remembered as a child being told he always forgave us of our sins. I had watched my uncle Mac say a prayer as he lay there dying. Had seen many pray to God as they were about to die. Wouldn't hurt to try, I guess. That's all I remember, and everything went black.

Chapter 14

Sometimes bad guys really aren't all that bad.

(Luka's perspective)
Everything that had been planned and all that had transpired led to
the bloodiest month anyone had seen yet. The mayor's office and the
police were spinning it as a gang and cartel war. The gang unit had
become an extension of our street army in this war. Even
coordinating attacks so the Reapers would go in first and the gang
unit would follow as a clean-up crew. People didn't end up in jail. It
was in everyone's best interest they were taken out. We needed a
"dead men don't talk" outcome here and that's what we were getting.

If you lived here, you had a fairly good idea of what was really going
on. The idea was to keep that perception from the rest of the country
and of course the Feds. There was so much happening at once, I
don't think they knew which direction to look. The Kessler's had
done us a huge favor, bringing in the Cartel. It just further
accommodated the theory that this was beyond what they had
initially thought. The only one who didn't care what else was going
on was Agent Hague. He'd not changed his mind about following
through with his promise. If there was one thing all of us had learned
that he apparently hadn't, it was that your position nor title could
protect you in all this. He was going to learn too.

With Kyl out of the picture, the chaos that followed was almost
overwhelming at times. Being the boss was not as easy as he had
made it look. There was a heavy emphasis on business and the ability
to manage all the different gears turning at once. Keeping all the
businesses running, making sure there was plenty of security at those
businesses, keeping up with the construction, and operating the war

machine. It had deepened my respect and admiration for all that he did. I'm not the businessman type and I struggled with how to make the right decisions and keep up with it.

Mitch Kessler had lost his shit when he saw Leah's head sitting on a mantle and found her badly mutilated body. He came seven cars deep and proceeded to open fire wildly on several of the businesses in our district. He didn't make it far before being met with huge resistance from our street guard and the police after that. He lost most of the men he'd taken with him, and I hear he barely made it home in one piece, unfortunately.

The other Horsemen and I had completed the mayor's list, and we were nearly halfway through our list. During the initial purge everyone was on high alert and after the rumors of Kyl's death had started to circulate, people went deep into hiding. It really was no secret that he was the decisive force behind keeping me and the Reapers reined in. Everyone learned very quickly what it meant for those reins to be dropped.

I'll admit I lost it pretty badly. I'm not the most rational person and after all these years of standing at Kyl's side, it put me in a place that honestly was scary even to me. I'm not just his enforcer. He's my best friend and the closest to a brother anyone could ever have. He's family to me. Seeing him like that, sitting there full of holes, covered in blood, not breathing, the man who had seemed like an untouchable titan all these years…. just gone. I'm not the most mentally stable person and I'm well aware of that. I'll be forever changed after that day. It's taken everything I have within myself to not go completely nuclear and kill the whole city.

I don't know if you know what it's like to have someone save your life. He stood there that day looking at me getting beat to death and made the choice to step in take the lives of several of those men to save me. Stood there as I cut out the eyes of one of my attackers and didn't say a word about it. Then offered to take me in and give me

127

the life he's given me. He was my brother, I loved him as a brother should love. I was in ruins and didn't understand exactly what to do or feel. I knew one thing for certain, I'd be at his side until the end....

(Thoughts from Deedra)

Sometimes, the hardest thing to do is wake up to the decisions you've made. There were so many of those in my life at this point, I'd lost count. If anyone in my life at the present time knew the truth, I'd be dead before I could finish a sentence. I couldn't even explain how I got to this point. I'd been here so long I had genuinely forgotten who I was. Who I used to be. I didn't know me beyond what I was today. I was all the way in with no way out.

I had done some dirty, rotten, and even atrocious things to get here. But, cutting Leah Kessler's head off was the tombstone to anything I had been previously. I had gotten too deep into things. I'd left myself without an exit except for going to Kyl for protection. I can tell you this, I could have never in one hundred years considered he'd hang me off a balcony and then demand Leah's head in exchange for safety. Kyl had been smart. The most dangerous, intellectual, and intelligent man I'd ever met. He was more than that too. His passion for the people he cared for and loved was unmatched. His passion...the man he is....no words for the intimate side of him.

I felt responsible for everything that had happened. I was sloppy and irresponsible in my actions. It was my fault things were where they were. The most feared and dangerous man in this city, didn't even hesitate to come to my rescue. He'd demanded, no, ordered what he expected from me to show my complete and total loyalty in exchange for the protection I was seeking. When I had done that, he put himself at risk to ensure he kept his word and paid the ultimate sacrifice for doing so.

After seeing him like that, seeing them cart him away. I had accepted my fate when Luka came into my room at the hospital and forced his gun into my mouth. I spoke through my heart to God to ask his mercy and forgiveness. As the tears streamed down my face, something happened I wasn't ready for. Luka was angry, he was hurting, there were tears in his eyes and I knew he was fighting to keep them from falling.

As he pulled his gun from my mouth he sat down. The tears had started to stream down his face too. He told me how they'd met, how Kyl had saved his life and afterwards taken him in. Luka didn't know anything but Kyl. They were deeply connected in a way even a traditional family couldn't understand. I felt sick to my stomach. I had been the cause of all this. He should've killed me but instead told me his story. These people, the ones we'd all been taught were just pure evil monsters, were in fact very loving, caring, and deeply passionate men.

Many a night I considered committing suicide. To live with the burden of my mistakes and what had come from them was almost too much. Kyl was a good man despite his title, position, and perceived character. I don't cry usually, but I have cried every day since this all happened. What was I to do now? How would I ever repay the care and loyalty shown and given to me?

Getting shot was a mother fucker. Getting shot multiple times was a fucker of mother fuckers. I don't even know how else to explain it. I'd been lucky and nothing vital or important had been hit.

You can breathe now, I didn't die. I could've if not for the quick actions of those around me and the paramedics. I took five rounds to the stomach, chest, and legs. I lost a lot of blood really fast and was legitimately clinically dead upon arrival. The upside to it all is I was open to the "alternative" workings of the medical world. HGH and other specific steroids were key to the express recovery I'd experienced the last month. I had a ways to go yet but I was miles ahead of the average person in my situation.

I had stepped away into solitude in order to heal and left Luka in charge. He'd done well and no matter what he thought, I was proud of him. I had to focus on my health and recovery. I was in a bad way and even if he did slightly lose it, he didn't burn the world down.

When I first came to, several days had passed. I can remember my eyes cracking open for the first time since thinking it was all over, and there she was. She was asleep when I woke, the nurse had been changing my IV bag and checking my dressings. She informed me that they'd had issues with keeping her away, so they had just let her be here. She stayed next to me the whole time, held my hand the whole time. I was looking at my hand in hers, she had such a tight grip so as not to lose hold of me it seemed.

I squeezed her hand, and she immediately woke. There were tears in her eyes instantly and she had leaped up and grasped me in a very deeply caring embrace. I could feel the flood of tears on my chest. It was weird feeling someone react this way that I barely knew. I was a little foggy still and not entirely sure what exactly had happened. It didn't take long to remember once the fog in my head cleared.

I ran my fingers through her hair and wiped her tears.

Kyl: *"What's all these tears for? I'm not dead yet"*

Deedra: *"Fuck Kyl, I really thought you were."*

She could barely speak for the sobs coming out.

Kyl: *"Hey, shhh. Slow down, breathe. I'm okay. You're okay."*

Deedra: *"I fucked up Kyl. I was sloppy and I almost got you killed. Why did you even come for me?"*

Kyl: *"There wasn't time to wait. I gave you my word, I'd protect you. I had to stand by that. Could've done without getting shot but here we are. We're both alive."*

She dropped to her knees next to my bed.

Deedra: *"I swear to you with everything I am, everything I have in me, that I'll stand at your side in complete loyalty until my last breath Kyl. If you'll allow me to that is. Please allow me to."*

I wasn't sure how I felt yet. I wasn't sure how much I trusted her. I did almost just die to save her and keep my word. She did just almost die following the orders I had given her. Damn, that's right. She had really cut Leah's fucking head off. Then sat here at my side this whole time. Shit, I couldn't ask much else from her to prove loyalty.

Every day I felt a little stronger. I could do more, push further, move faster. I stayed cooped up in the apartment day after day working out. Deedra at my side working just as hard. She understood to give me my space, but she was there in an instant to help or make sure I had what I needed. Even more odd, her and Luka had seemed to have formed some sort of bond as well. Luka was always apprehensive about anyone this close to me and even more untrusting of women. There was clearly a story there, I'd wait and see if Luka brought it up.

It was a daily occurrence that Agent Hague had tried to get onto the floor I was on in the hospital. The Stephon's had ensured that I had a private wing of the hospital, and it was heavily guarded. The Chief had assigned 24hr protection based on "perceived threat" to justify it. Luka had placed nearly two dozen guards outside of the recovery wing I was in and at least another dozen on the other side of the doors with me. The doors could only be opened from inside and it required clearance from outside those doors first. Hague had no reason to be there and had no warrant. He'd gone head-to-head with both Chief Stephon and Mayor Stephon. He'd accused them of protecting a violent criminal. To which they had responded, "The man in there has been a pivotal part of the growth and development of this city The charity work and donations alone had changed the lives of hundreds of children and families. Whatever frivolous reasons the DEA had to maliciously attack this pillar in our community was not going to be allowed."

The Federal Government had been relatively quiet publicly. They had made no efforts to publicly address anything or try to further insert themselves into anything. The FBI had been poking around but left it to the DEA and ATF being they already had agents working on an active case. Hague had made it his personal mission to take me out or take me down. I didn't perceive him as a threat and if I had, he'd have disappeared long before now. He was mostly annoying and his partner, Agent Lewis, still made me uneasy. I had yet to figure him out.

Since I'd been home, Hague had tried to enter the building multiple times a day. He threatened to arrest the guards but what he'd lacked in understanding, is that the guards on this building were licensed and certified. They were employed by my private security firm. Which requires a federal clearance. Said clearance is given through an ATF and FBI program. I bet that had chapped his ass when he figured that all out. It made me laugh. Poor little fella couldn't win for losing.

He'd been doing his homework though and had squeezed a few of Kessler's people into giving him information. He'd learned that Russ had likely met his demise at the old industrial park. He was out there poking around when he decided to call me.

My phone rang.

Kyl: *"I'm fairly certain I told you if you needed to speak to me, you were to contact my lawyers."*

Agent Hague: *"Interesting spot you have out here. This abandoned industrial park. Wonder what I could find out here? DNA? Bodies? Weapons? Drugs? I think it's time we had a talk without all your goons around. You either meet me out here in 30 minutes or I bring*

*in every agency to tear this place apart and swab every inch for
evidence."*

This son of bitch had some nerve. He also wasn't stupid. He'd said
the one thing that could actually make me be inclined to show up.

Kyl: *"See you in few Gag."*

As I hung up, I called Luka and filled him in. Deedra wanted to go
with me. I told her this one was just me and Luka. Of course, that
wasn't completely accurate either. I'd have Pratt on the scope from
across the property. He was surgical with a rifle. I'd had enough
surprises; I wasn't going into this unprepared.

Luka met me at the front of the park. Hague's car was parked outside
of the gate. Luka got into the truck with me after opening the gate. I
made my way back towards the area we used as a shooting range.
My intuition said that's likely where Hague and Lewis were. I wasn't
wrong.

I still wasn't one hundred percent, but I was moving better than I had
been. I slid my pistol into my lower back. I had no idea what this shit
bag had up his sleeve. He was looking around intently. The funny
thing was he was standing directly on top of the bunker entrance
where we stored weapons and other illegal items. I kept it covered in
close to a foot of sand and pea gravel. You had to have a tractor to
clear it away to open the bunker doors.

Agent Hague: *"We can make this easy and you can just tell me
where everything is hidden and what else I'll find when I bring in
forensics."*

Kyl: *"I'm pretty sure you can still fuck off. Gag. You don't even have
anything to pull a warrant for to even start looking around out here.
As of right now, you're trespassing. I could have you sited for it."*

Agent Hague: *"Fuck you bitch. You think I brought you here to banter and make empty threats? I'm not stupid, I know you got out of the car with a pistol. You're going to draw that pistol, Kyl. We're going to end this right here."*

As he said that he had unholstered his pistol. He intended to shoot me as I reached for mine and claim a justified shooting. I was in another spot I didn't want to be in. We were too far into the building for Pratt to get a shot. Gag was smart, he'd looked at the location and seen where the open spots were. Even with Luka here, he was already at an advantage being openly armed and both of us would have to reach. Agent Lewis had pulled his weapon as well.

Agent Hague: *"You think you're so smart. You're not smarter than me. I told you I'd get you one way or another. Checkmate Kyl."*

My pager went off, that meant Pratt had found his shot. It would be only a matter of time before this was over. Except I was completely wrong about how.

Hague raised his pistol at me.

Agent Hague: *"See you in hell mother fucker."*

A shot rang out and Hague's forehead exploded. As he collapsed to the ground, Agent Lewis was standing there, smoking gun in hand. What the fuck did I just witness? Agent Lewis had just executed Agent Hague.

He just stood there for a minute, then he lowered his gun and looked at me.

Kyl: *"What the fuck just happened?"*

His reply would forever stick in my head.

Agent Lewis: *"Sometimes bad guys really aren't all that bad."*

Kyl: *"I don't understand"*

Luka looked at me just as confused.

Agent Lewis: *"When I was a kid, my mom and I had gone on the run to escape my dad. He was an alcoholic and had beaten my mom more than once. She loaded me into the car one night after loading his food with sleeping pills and we drove away. My mom drove all night until our car broke down. This man said he'd help us; he'd put us up in a room for the night. He seemed so nice; my mom was thankful. That man then raped my mother and hit me as I tried to get him off her. A scared boy opened the door to the hotel room as a couple of older teenagers were passing by. The older boy with the blue eyes pulled me from the room and he killed the man that was hurting my mom. Then, he helped her clean herself up and gave us enough money to get away and start over. Miami Florida Kyl, I'm the boy you saved. When I saw your name come up in this investigation, I asked to be assigned to it. Hague has been mental for months about killing you. I owe you for saving my mother and me. My life has been rather good thanks to your decisions that night. I've done my research and I know, aside from criminal activity, how much good you've done as a result of your power and money. I can't guarantee this won't draw extra attention, my report will state Hague went rogue and tried go kill you in cold blood. I've been recording his rants and ramblings. I'd already reported him as compromised. End this all quickly Kyl. It's in your best interest."*

Kyl: *"Thanks Lewis, I won't forget this."*

What in the fuck. Did that really just happen? My gut hadn't been wrong. I knew those eyes were familiar. I just watched the kid I saved halfway across the country show up as a grown man and execute another federal agent. Shit, who'd ever believe this would ever happen? Luka looked just as shocked as I was.

Kyl: *"Luka, am I still on the hospital in a coma? I'm awake right? Like I'm here and that really just happened?"*

Luka: *"That really just happened Kyl, we're both here and that really just fucking happened."*

Chapter 15

Dead men dine alone

You can't ever predict what was going to happen when you live this lifestyle. You think you know. You think you're in charge and you're on top of the world, so you can see everything that's coming. That is complete and total bullshit. If you'd have tried to tell me any of what's transpired the last few months, I'd have laughed and maybe had you thrown off a building. The fact was, no matter how well I planned, no matter how many men I had in place, or how well defended I was, there was no way to account for all the crazy and unpredictable shit that could happen.

I spent the last week going over in my head everything that had happened. A kid from my past, from halfway across the country, shows up, and without hesitation, executes a fellow federal agent. Then blatantly lies to cover it up. I sat in the same room with him as he went over his report with agents from three different agencies. His calm, cool demeanor was likely a product of being desensitized to violence as a child, he reminded me of Luka. I answered about three dozen questions, they seemed satisfied, formally apologized for what had happened and went on their way. Agent Lewis, or David as he'd said to call him, had said he was going to be investigating the Kessler's. He thought he could divert attention from me. Even though I said I didn't want him putting his career at risk, that he didn't owe me anything, he insisted it was simply the right thing for him to do.

Before we parted ways, he again implored me to finish things up quickly. It wasn't bad advice but not as easily done as was spoken. Mitch Kessler wasn't about to lay down and just give up. Apparently, he was a lot more unstable than I'd ever been aware of. He hid it behind his docile demeanor and the fact he was highly intelligent. I'm told seeing his brother in a box, his father being found in the river, and then seeing Leah's head, had pushed him completely over the edge.

It was understandable, but to me, just meant he had a weakness I could exploit even further. When you start to act irrationally, you make mistakes. He'd already nearly lost his life during a tantrum. I think he saw it too. I'd still push on him, and I knew I'd be able to break him mentally again. With him though, it would be more of a chess game. Fine by me.

He brought in the Cartel, but I still had a half dozen aces up my sleeve just to deal with that. I didn't get here by being ignorant. You live prepared for war and hope for peace. One thing cartels are good at is fighting each other.

If you think I hadn't garnered respect and relationships with other cartels in all these years, then you haven't been paying attention.

Tierra Caliente Cartel had been working with us for years on the intel and drug trade game. We had done a lot of business in the gun running game. It hadn't taken them long to see that being my ally was far more beneficial than being an enemy. On top of everything, I'd collaborated the unification of the Tierra Caliente and Coyote Locos. By pushing them into their own zone outside of mine, they could operate with more freedom and with the backing of a cartel they had the power to knock out other gangs that tried to push up on them. It was time to see if they were ready to go to war.

Activating the Tierra Caliente and Coyote Locos had certain side effects that would ripple through other cities from here to the border. It meant an all-out war with the Crowns and the Sanola Cartel. A lot of people were about to lose their lives across the Southern belt and Midwest.

I had honestly had to step back and look at how we got here. It was weird to think the Kessler family had started all this and yet now somehow, I was the bad guy. I was okay with it; I'll be the bad guy. You push me, I become the boogeyman you were warned about.

I'd grown a conscience and leaned a lot further into moral values and standards over the years. It was clear I needed to put that back on the shelf for a while. I was about to show them what made me the most dangerous man even above Luka, the Four Horsemen, and the Reapers. I would flood these streets with the blood of my enemies.

There was one unexpected factor in it all and I was about to get a surprise of my own. Imagine that….

I didn't move without a shadow, even in my own apartment. Deedra was never more than five feet away from me unless I was with Luka. I didn't say anything about it because I knew what she'd been through and the level of her loyalty and devotion to me was more than admirable. She felt she owed me her life; she'd said so herself. I do like having her around. She was good company, good conversation, was willing to lay down her life for me, and I had become partial to her falling asleep next to me.

Everything we had been through, had changed her. She was a mother hen over me a lot. I was still recovering from my wounds and I'm someone who will push myself to the point of collapse just to get to the next level. Where I was nonchalant and unconcerned, she was maxed out on pushing back on me to take it slower and give myself time to heal. Funny how that only applied when it didn't involve taking it slower and going easy on her.

I was sitting on the edge of the stair stepper when my phone rang. It was Quiz, Luka's ace.

Quiz: *"Hey boss, I'm sorry to bother you but I have something you should probably know."*

Kyl: *"No problem, Quiz, whatcha got for me?"*

He cleared his throat and took a deep breath. I instantly knew I wasn't going to like what I was about to hear.

Quiz: *"So, I'm sure you're aware that the Sanola Cartel is involved in this. Word on the street is they just teamed up with Kings Disciples and there being led by someone calling himself Killa of Kyl."*

Kyl: *"Hmm. Get me more information on this Killa of Kyl. Bring in who you need to help you. I'll deal with the rest of that. Let Luka know what you told me."*

Kings Disciples. Not something I wanted to hear. The KD's were an extremely large street gang that had tried to find a place in our city. They were moving in under the watch of my cousin Damian Vonnet. When I eliminated the family, they had asked for a place here and I wasn't in a mood to accept anyone who'd been loyal to Damian. So, I expelled them. They weren't good at following rules, and they operated based on oppression of the local businesses. I didn't operate that way. They were salty about it, but I didn't care and at the time, no one was willing to stand against the man who had eliminated his own family and the Cretchfeld family.

It was time to turn up the heat and I needed to figure out who my new biggest fan was quickly. I sent Luka a text and I'd wait for him to show up.

Deedra: *"What's that worry on your face? Are you doubting your decision-making abilities?"*

Kyl: *"No...it's not that. I'm just trying to assess how far I need to push things and if I should just throw all the cards on the table."*

Deedra: *"What's the sudden urgency? You're the rock in everything you do."*

Kyl: *"It was something Agent Lewis had said. He told me to end this quickly. It's been on my mind since he first said it. I knew when this started it would be a grind, but I hadn't considered having to throw everything at this. It feels like an opportunity to fuck up."*

Deedra: *"You know what works. I think you should do what you know."*

Kyl: *"I know my dick works."*

Not even a smile, I don't think she was fond of my sense of humor. She shook her head at me.

Deedra: *"Not sure that's going to solve this whole thing or keep you alive."*

As she walked away, I just stared at her ass. She had the most amazing ass. That wasn't going to solve this either, but I sure did like looking at it.

I laid back on the mat and started to stretch out. I did some of my best thinking during a workout. I still wasn't back to one hundred percent, but I had come a long way. Deedra gets credit for a lot of my speedy recovery. She's been at my side and stayed on me about properly taking care of myself. It was annoying at times when I'd want to push myself and she'd stop me. We'd had a few exchanges of words over things, but she usually ended up getting me to stop or slow down. She had this way about her. I couldn't explain it completely, but she knew exactly what to say and do in those moments. The way she looked at me sometimes reminded me of how Gia looked at me. I considered asking her on more than one occasion how she felt towards me. Somethings are better left alone though, and to be honest, I wasn't sure I'd have been able to reciprocate that conversation if I started it. There was no doubt she and I had a deep bond and there were certain other things between us that had pulled us closer. She was deeply loyal to me. That's what was most important. I just kept going back to that.

As I was finishing up my workout, Luka came in. He stared at the healing wounds before looking up.

Kyl: *"They add character, don't they?"*

Luka blamed himself somehow for what I'd chosen to do that day.

Luka: *"Never should've happened. I hate that you have to go through this. I'm sorry."*

Kyl: *"You have to stop beating yourself up over this brother. I made the decision to go, and I knew the risks. It taught us all an important lessen and were stronger for it as a whole."*

Luka: *"Ya, I guess you're right. I just feel responsible. I see you laying there like that a lot when I close my eyes. It pisses me off."*

I put my hand on his shoulder and got right in his face.

Kyl: *"Look at me Luka, I'm fine. I'm recovering quickly and I'm right fucking here. Flesh and blood. I'm asking you as friends and family to let it go. I'm ordering you as your boss to shut that shit down and knuckle up. It's time to move on from it."*

He nodded and almost looked ashamed that he had to be told that. Luka was uniquely one of a kind.

Luka: *"You certainly acquired quite the trophy out of all this. Good grief, how is your dick not hard constantly watching her walk around here dressed like that?"*

Kyl: *"I usually just look at her ears."*

We both laughed and headed to the kitchen so I could get a protein shake and talk business. It was good to see him laugh. I thought about how much he devoted to this life, and I wondered if he was genuinely happy. He always told me there was no better place to be and no greater honor than being my friend and associate. All these people around me had so much admiration, respect, and loyalty to me. I had to protect them too.

Kyl: *"So you spoke to Quiz then?"*

Luka: *"I did. King's Disciples huh. I'm not really surprised. Who do you think the psycho is behind the lame ass name."*

Kyl: *"I honestly couldn't tell you. It's not like you leave very many open options. Could be just another Kessler stunt. Not going to just brush it off though."*

Luka: *"Oh I most certainly think we take it seriously. What's your plan of attack here? It's starting to look a little lopsided even if the Latin Crowns are getting their asses handed to them."*

I'd thought over how this needed to go but I had a special surprise for these sorry cartel fucks.

Kyl: *"Here's how this plays out. The Oliver St Three Sixteen's have already been wanting a piece of the Latin Crowns. So have them join the BLK's. I'm activating the Coyote Locos to go head-to-head with King's Disciples, and we'll utilize Chief Stephon's Gang unit to go after the Sanola Cartel. I've got another surprise for those cartel bastards too. I'll be traveling tomorrow, I'll have Deedra, Taska, and Devin."*

Luka: *"So we're outsourcing this whole war?"*

Kyl: *"I will not lose any members of this family to some street gang. We have the resources at our disposal to combat them. I need all of our people ready to go at the Kessler's when it's time. You, the rest of the Horsemen, the Reapers, will all pull back and only engage when necessary."*

I could tell he wasn't happy to be benched but I was doing this exactly the way I felt it needed to be done. They'd all get their moment.

Luka: *"Alright, I'll get the word out. We'll all pull back and wait."*

Kyl: *"You'll get plenty of action Luka, I promise."*

Luka: *"You're the boss for a reason. I don't question you even if I don't like it. You know that. You just keep your eyes on those ears."*

We both had another laugh and he headed out. I almost felt guilty not telling him everything. There was so much more at play here than I'd led on. Some of it I hadn't yet processed and in my head, I wasn't sure exactly how I was going to pull it off yet. It gave me a heavy heart to think of what I was about to put into motion.

As I sat there thinking, Deedra walked in and handed me my phone. I didn't recognize the number, but I felt compelled to answer with everything going on.

Kyl: *"Who's this?"*

Caller: *"Hello Kyl. You've been quite the busy man, haven't you?"*

I didn't recognize the voice. It was raspy and rough. Almost like someone who had throat cancer.

Kyl: *"I don't play games so why don't we get the formalities out of the way, and you just tell me who you are and what the fuck you want."*

Caller: *"The man in charge. Always thinking you run everyone and everything. See, I don't respect you and I don't fear you. I chose to call myself Killa of Kyl because I intend to slowly tear your world apart and then kill you. I will watch you bleed out and hang your mutilated body from the bell tower of St. Roman Church."*

Kyl: *"You make it sound so easy. Why don't we meet and have a face-to-face conversation? Dinners on me. What do you say tough guy?"*

Caller: *"That cockiness will be the death of you. I'll have to decline your offer, as I'm sure you know, dead men dine alone."*

The line was quiet. He'd hung up. He was certainly sure of himself. Something bothered me though, he'd said *"dead men dine alone."* Where the fuck had I heard that before? It was ringing in my head like tornado sirens. Fuck, there was an answer to who this was in that phrase….

Chapter 16

There's a pain in losing loved ones that burns like nothing else.

I was sleeping good for once when everything seemed to erupt into chaos. There's nothing worse than being awakened by the phone ringing and someone pounding on the door. I ignored the phone and grabbed my pants as I heard Taska open the door. I rushed out of my room to see Luka.

Luka: *"The Pump and Go is in flames. Boss...."*

Luka grabbed me by both arms to get my full attention.

Luka: *"Amy was working Kyl."*

Luka knew I adored Amy; she was one of the few people who had just become a good-hearted loyal person and wouldn't hurt a fly.

Kyl: *"Let me get dressed and we go. Taska, you stay with Deedra. No one comes in unless it's me or Luka."*

He nodded and Deedra poked her head out of the room. She was trying to rub the sleep out of her eyes and make sense of everything.

Kyl: *"I'll be back. Stay here."*

I ran out of the door and as we exited the elevator, I could feel myself in an almost panic. Was this an accident or had there been an attack on the store? We'd know soon enough; I could see the smoke billowing into the air as Luka raced towards it.

As we pulled up the badly charred remains of the front of the building were still smoldering. There were fire fighters and police everywhere. Chief Stephon was there, William always made it a point to be present whenever it had to do with one of my properties.

William: *"Kyl, you don't want to go in there. Please, you don't want to see her like that."*

Kyl: *"Get out of my way Will, get your people back for a minute."*

He motioned for everyone to step out. He knew not to get in my way. I took a deep breath and walked into the store. Everything was burned badly. It looked as if someone had busted out the front window and sprayed gasoline from the pump into the store before lighting it.

As I rounded the counter. There in the corner was the tiny half burned body of Amy. You could tell she'd been badly beaten, and both of her legs looked broken. She was burned so badly on one side she was unrecognizable. I knelt beside her and touched her cheek that wasn't burned.

I wanted to cry. I wanted to pull her to me and just sob. But I couldn't here. Not now. I couldn't move her, and I'd not let these people see me break down. Forcing the tears back only created anger. I said a short prayer and I stood up. William motioned for me to come to the office.

William: *"There's footage from the cameras Kyl. It's really bad, whoever did this, wanted to make a statement."*

Kyl: *"Play it."*

As the officer hit play, Amy was standing there working away and as she heard the door chime, she raised her head up with that signature smile before she saw what was standing there and the smile faded. He was a fairly big guy.

He wore all black and everything was covered. On his face, a mask that looked like a skull.

He casually walked to the counter, and you could hear Amy ask how she could help him today. He held out a twenty-dollar bill and as she reached for it, he grabbed her arm. Slamming it to the counter, you could hear the bone snap in the video. Amy fell backwards to the floor and screamed in pain.

He walked around the corner and entered the cashier's area. Without hesitation, he stomped on her leg bending it completely the wrong way. As she scrambled to get away, he drug her backwards, lifted her other leg and stomped down onto it, also breaking it. He also did the same to her other arm. Then he grabbed her by the throat and punched her in the face repeatedly before throwing her back to the floor in the exact place where I'd found her.

I was fucking shaking. My head was spinning, and I could hear my heartbeat in my ears. As the video continued, the man stopped, looked directly into the camera, and showed his middle finger and then waved before walking away. The outside camera showed he'd thrown a trash can through the window and then in fact had stood there spraying gas all over the outside of the building and inside. He drove to the edge of the entrance and lit the gas before driving off.

I could barely focus on what anyone was saying as I walked out.

William: *"Kyl, let me help you please."*

Kyl: *"I don't know what to tell you Will. Some piece of shit is calling himself Killa of Kyl and said he was going to tear my life apart before he killed me and hung my body from St. Roman's bell tower. That's all I know."*

As I walked off Luka had told him to give me time and he'd be sure to have me call. I sat in the car and waited for Luka.

Luka: *"Boss...We'll find him and make him pay. I promise you that."*

I just sat there. I had nothing to say. I was so overwhelmed and angry I could barely speak.

Kyl: *"Take me by my house."*

I needed to grab a few things from the safe.

Luka pulled out and headed north. I had barely noticed the black Cadillac hovering in the lane next to us. That is until it pulled up next to us and the back window rolled down.

My heart fucking stopped.

I reached for my gun just as Luka saw it too.

The Cadillac quickly accelerated ahead of us, and Luka gave chase.

Kyl: *"Do not lose that car Luka! Fuck!"*

No, please God, if you can hear me, if you'll listen to me, please don't let them kill her.

We were doing nearly seventy miles an hour when suddenly the car braked hard, slid sideways, and the rear door opened. My heart dropped into my stomach. I just screamed. As if almost in slow motion, whoever had been in the backseat kicked her out of the car and she hit the road in a violent tumble. Luka swerved and slammed on the brakes.

The car hadn't even stopped moving when I jumped out screaming at Luka to call 911.

The woman in the car was Diamond. As I slid to her side, she was a bloodied mess, and she was fucked up bad but still alive. She was barely conscious but recognized me. Her jaw was severely broken, and she couldn't speak. I carefully pulled her into my lap, and I began to sob. Diamond meant the world to me. We'd had years of being so close, becoming best friends, a trusted associate, and we'd been intimate in a way we both needed at times.

The world around me disappeared as she clutched onto me. I didn't hear anything. I saw nothing. I just held her and spoke softly into her ear. Her breathing was labored and shallow. I told her to be strong like she always was and hold on. We'd get her all fixed up.

Luka knelt and got my attention. The paramedics had arrived, and he was getting me back so they could help her. I looked at her as they started to take her away. *"I'll find him and kill him. I promise."*

I had barely wiped my eyes when Luka put his hand on my shoulder.

Luka: *"Boss, we have to go. There's another one."*

Kyl: *"Who?"*

Luka: *"I'm not sure. I just got a call there was a body at Cooper's shop."*

There's a pain in losing loved ones that burns like nothing else. I was livid and shaking. I was trying not to become so overwhelmed that I completely lost control. As we pulled into the parking lot, Cooper was standing outside with his brother. He was pale and looked like he'd been throwing up.

I took a deep breath and got out of the car.

Cooper's shop had been here for three generations and was the most well-known and honest shop in town. I was relieved the brothers were okay.

Cooper: *"I can't go back in there, sir. It's real bad. Real real bad."*

Kyl: *"It's okay Coop, you don't have to go back in."*

I nodded at Luka and headed in. What we were about to see was going to elevate this war to its worst point.

Inside the shop there was a body stripped down. The stomach had been sliced open and the intestines pulled out. The body was suspended in the air between the two lift pillars by those intestines. The face had been completely peeled off. I wasn't sure who I was looking at, but Luka was.

He picked up a tool laying nearby and launched it at the wall. The look in his eyes was purely murderous but there were tears on his cheeks.

Luka: *"Its fucking Quiz. The tattoo on his arm, I was there when he got it. What the fuck is happening Kyl?"*

Mother fucker. I'd sent Quiz out to find out more about this piece of shit. This was my fault. All of this was my fault. Who the fuck was this asshole and how did he know so much about me and to whom I was close?

As I walked out Luka was pacing in the parking lot. It was going to be extremely hard to keep him reeled in. I was on the verge of not being rational and I'm here to tell you, an irrational Kyl and Luka at once is not what anyone needs. Including us.

Kyl: *"Coop, take a few days off. I'll triple whatever your daily average is per day. I'll have the clean up crew take care of it all."*

As I walked towards Luka, I knew what he didn't want to hear was me telling him he was still benched. It was important I did though.

Kyl: *"Look, we can't lose it now. I know you want to go burn the city down looking for this guy. We're here because we're smarter. I have a plan and we will flush him out. I give you, my word. "*

He stepped close and just hugged me.

Luka: *"Fuck Kyl, I'm sorry. You've lost so many people close to you through all of this. Quiz was my brotha from anotha motha type of dude. I almost lost you and then this happens to the girls, now Quiz. I can't lose you bro. You're the only family I have. We have to strike back at this hard if you expect me to keep my cool."*

Kyl: *"Everything we talked about yesterday, start it. Take me back to the Penthouse and I'll take care of my end of things."*

I couldn't risk being at the hospital. It would put too many people in danger. I called to get an update on Diamond. She was in surgery still and they weren't sure yet what was going to happen. She'd slipped into a coma but was stable as they were fixing all they could fix. My heart hurt not being there. It was time to get down to business though. I had to make moves now and I had to set the war machine in motion. There was going to be no turning back now.

C*hapter 17*

You're only as good as your last mistake.

Once you cross a certain line, there's no going back. No matter how good you are, no matter whether you meant well when you did it, and regardless of what you do after. You'll always be on the other side of that line.

I had set Luka in motion to bring hell from the other gangs I'd ordered brought in. I had to get myself on the move as well. There was in impending trip to Mexico that had to be done.

I showered as I filled Deedra in on what had just taken place and what we were about to do. She looked concerned for me and yet steadfast in her resolve to be prepared for what was coming. She had stepped into the shower as I stood there letting blood run off me and water cascade over my head. Her hands ran across my body to wash away the remnants of the morning. It was probably one of the most genuine and caring things I had ever felt. I was in a weird emotional spot, and I couldn't really process my feelings at the moment.

I turned to face her, the pale lights in the shower made the perfect curves and accents of her body glimmer. She didn't speak. I searched her eyes and there was this look, I'd seen it only once before in my life. She slid her hands down to my now hard cock and grasped it as she looked back up, biting her lip, as if asking silently for approval. I wasn't going to tell her no.

I reached up and slid my hand into her hair and kissed her deeply and passionately. My emotions were all over the place. Her grip on me tightened, so I pulled her head back and she immediately went to her knees. I leaned back against the wall as she took me deep into her throat over and over. The way she moved, how her hands raked down my stomach, made me need to feel her. I reached down clutching her throat and pulled her to her feet. I looked into her eyes once more and she softly spoke one word. "Please." I spun her around pushing her against the wall and started to take her. She was tight and even in my aggressive manner, I still didn't want to hurt her, but she pushed hard back against me forcing me deep inside of her. We fucked as if it would be our last time ever.

This trip was one I had felt couldn't be done any other way than in person. As we landed at the private airport, I looked out to see a large presence of armed militants. I'd come to meet with the Tierra Caliente Cartel leader, Javier Guerrero. He was referred to as the Warrior of Mexico. I think the only thing that kept him from being the leading Cartel in Mexico was Sonola's hold on the government and the number of political positions they controlled. That was all about to change. Keep an eye on this part.

As I exited the plane Javier met me on the runway. He had a huge smile on his face and shook my hand and hugged me.

Javier: *"Welcome to Mexico my friend. I am honored to have you here! Come, let's get off this hot airstrip."*

Kyl: *"Good to see you Javier, the honor is all mine."*

He smiled even bigger and led us to our transport. Six armored vehicles accompanied by four heavily armed Humvees. Not a bad way to travel in my book. The Tierra Caliente region was comprised of several different states. The region was literally names for it being one of the hottest regions in Mexico.

As we traveled across the countryside, it was beautiful in its own way. So much open space, like being in the country back home. As we drew closer to Javier's homes, the landscape changed. A lot of dug in bunkers, guard towers, foot patrols, and even a moat as we entered his compound.

The villa itself was as big as a mansion you'd see in Beverly Hills. Heavily fortified but beautiful. I liked Javier's taste in architecture.

I was led through the house to an underground bar. One of the coolest things I'd ever seen. It was raw stone walls, it was cool, and had a natural spring trickling down in one spot. Very impressive. I felt like I was doing things all wrong, I needed as castle compound! I chuckled to myself as we reached the giant ornate table in the middle of the room.

Deedra and Devin were left at a bar upstairs along with Javier's men. This was business for our ears only, things that were about to change things as we'd previously known them.

Javier: *"So tell me Kyl, what brings you to my home? I know you're at war, I'm ready to help if that's why you're here."*

Kyl: *"This goes deeper than that Javier. Today we discuss a changing of the guard."*

He raised his eyebrow and sat up straighter. He was fully tuned in now.

Javier: *"Tell me more."*

Kyl: *"Things have to change. They can no longer stay the same and its well past time you had the power you deserve as well. The Sonola's have crossed the line against me again. There's no pass for it this time."*

Javier: *"I would love to accommodate this quest with you; however, we do not have the resources to take down the Sonola. They have too many numbers and much better weapons."*

Kyl: *"That changes today. I have garnered a deal with the Columbians and the Bolivian guerillas. The Bolivian's I paid for, and they're only interested in taking down the Sonola. For personal reasons if you remember. The Columbia's are more businessmen, I paid them but the want to work together and expand their coca processing to your region. The exchange would be sixty/forty for you. But what this means is you have twenty thousand men and plenty of high-grade weapons and vehicles to aid in your dispatching of the Sonola."*

Javier: *"You're serious about this? I thought you might be yanking my chain, as you say. Twenty thousand men? That's well more than enough plus my men. I don't pay for anything else. Why would you do this?"*

Javier looked at me suspiciously.

Kyl: *"Look.... this goes deep. I'm taking out the Kessler family, the Latin Crowns, and I have some other things in play here. We'll get into that later. Right now, I need the Sonola eliminated. Here. In Mexico. I'm funding it, fifteen million all on me. You provide the land the Columbians need, agree to partner, you both make money, and you get the power you desire."*

Javier: *"You must have a lot going on back home. This is my dream. You come here and sell me my dreams. What's the catch? I feel it sitting on your shoulders."*

As we spoke over the details of the rest of the plan, he sighed heavily and looked down at his drink. He was deep in thought.

Javier: *"You'll make it quick? Not drug out and a lengthy process. I have your word?"*

Kyl: *"Have you ever known me to bullshit or not keep my word? You have my word. It'll be done in one swift action. I just need to know you understand and agree to it. This all hinges on it, none of the rest of it works if you aren't with me on this."*

Javier: *"I understand, my heart is heavy, but this is the price of the game and the power we seek. I agree to this Kyl."*

He stood and grasped my hand; he was happy about this change but the cost of it was heavy. For both of us.

We made our way upstairs, Javier insisted we stay to eat. I was not going to turn down traditional Mexican food. Deedra looked like a ball of anxiety until she saw me walk through the door. She was immediately at my side. Devin smiled.

Devin: *"Mother hen here was a mess with you gone. Thank God you're alive, she'd have burned the whole place down!"*

Deedra: *"Shut it Dev, it's not too late to burn you."*

Devin winced and shook his head.

Devin: *"I feel like that's true. Kyl, you got to watch yourself with this one."*

Deedra glared at him but smiled at me. She was really a blessing. Every day I appreciated her more.

Kyl: *"Devin, I need two shipments of weapon pulled and delivered here immediately. As in tomorrow. No excuses. Also, I need five hundred pounds of c4 delivered to the parking garage on Garret Street. Have it locked in the basement and put twenty-four-hour security on it."*

He looked up at me immediately and the look on his face was pure shock.

Devin: *"Shit boss, that's a lot of c4. What the fuck is that for?"*

I didn't answer him and just walked off. I didn't ever have to explain myself and this was one of those times I wasn't going to. I had kept this to myself other than bringing Javier in on it. I needed to know he understood and stood with me. Sometimes, you just have to make decisions without even the closest people to you.

Deedra: *"What the fuck was that about?"*

Devin: *"I don't really know but he's chosen not to talk about it, which means it's way above our pay grade. I'd advise you to leave it alone. When he's like that, he's volatile. I trust his leadership and so should you."*

Deedra: *"How dangerous is Kyl?"*

Devin: *"You could lose your life at any moment. Kyl is the most dangerous man I've ever known. Luka is dangerous but he's just a psycho, but he wouldn't ever cross the boss. Kyl is extremely intelligent and that makes him just plain scary. The way his mind works, I don't dare even speak a cross word. Whatever he's planning, it's bad. It's going to be something so violent it'll scare everyone. I guarantee that."*

Deedra swallowed hard and shifted uncomfortably. She knew Kyl was dangerous, but she hadn't considered even the Four Horsemen being terrified of him.

As we left Javier's and our fully armed convoy made its way back to the airstrip, everyone was quiet. I'd guess that Devin had told Deedra not to inquire as to my plans. I wouldn't speak about it until it was time. It still weighed heavy in my heart and on my mind. I knew it had been a big deal for Javier to agree. Power is a strange thing; it will make you do things you'd not normally consider. Even I was struggling with this one.

As we flew home, I'd let Luka know our expected time of arrival so he could bring the necessary guard to take us home. I told him to bring Diego with him. The line was quiet, he eventually replied with *"Yes sir."*

He and Diego were close, but I'd never been completely sold on him, he rubbed me the wrong way at times. Needed him involved today though.

I'd been waiting for a call, Agent Lewis, he'd become quite useful in all things. He and I had a conversation before I left. We needed to come to an understanding about certain things. He was more receptive than I'd initially thought he might be. That line crossed, it changed men and money speaks every language. Every language.

As we landed, I was glad to be home and see Luka. I always felt safer with him around when shit was on the wire like it had been. We did our typical bro embrace and he stood back and looked at me.

Luka: *"Everything okay boss?"*

Kyl: *"You trust me right, Luka? Like all the way no questions?"*

Luka: *"Of course! Why the fuck would ask that?"*

He looked nervous, it took a lot to make Luka nervous and I was probably the only one who could do that.

Kyl: *"This is one of those moments Luka, I need your pistol."*

He'd started to pale; it had hit him what was going on. He reached back and pulled it from his waistband and shook his head as he handed it to me.

Luka: *"You're sure Kyl?"*

Kyl: *"Without a doubt"*

I stepped past him and headed towards the car. This was a private airport, wouldn't be anyone here except the tower staff, and they were on my payroll. As I walked, I briefly looked back to see Luka's face. He was sick to his stomach; I could see it in his eyes. Devin, Deedra, and Taska stood there in confusion after Luka had stopped them from going any further.

I walked to the car and shot Diego in the dick. As he screamed and collapsed, I put my foot on this throat. I looked down at him.

Kyl: *"You're only as good as your last mistake. You fucked up Diego, you betrayed this family."*

I fired again, hitting him in the left thigh.

Kyl: *"Do you know what it feels like to have a FUCKING FED tell me that my top General's number one is a fucking snake working with the Kings Disciples? You fucking piece of shit."*

Again, I fired, this time in his right thigh.

I knelt down next to him, he was sobbing. There was nothing for him to say and he knew it.

Kyl: *"What you heard in the company of this family was sacred. You broke that."*

I pulled my knife and cut both of his ears off. He was starting to fade on me, I needed him awake. I slapped the shit out of him to bring him back to consciousness.

Kyl: *"When you speak, you never speak on this family. You disgraced us. Stick out your fucking tongue."*

As he cried, he wasn't opening his mouth as I'd ordered. I took my knife and cut away his cheek from the corner of his mouth back, grabbed his tongue and cut it off. He was bleeding profusely, and I knew he'd be gone soon.

Kyl: *"You betrayed this family. You will rot in hell Diego."*

I laid his tongue over his eye and plunged my knife through the tongue into his eye so hard the hilt of the knife sunk past the eye socket.

As I wiped the blood from my hands on his clothes I stood and turned to everyone present.

Kyl: *"This is the only time I'll say this, loyalty is what keeps this family together. I catch another mother fucker betraying this family, I will personally skin you alive while you watch me, then dissect your body slowing until you're a pile of parts. I will then deliver what's left of you to your mother. I hope I'm fucking clear."*

I walked around the car and got in slamming the door shut.

Luka hung his head, he motioned for one of the Reapers to get the cleaners here.

The look of pure fear and shock on everyone's face couldn't be hidden. Deedra walked to the car and got in as Taska opened the door. Luka got in the front and Devin told Taska he'd drive. No one spoke a word. Deedra slid her hand onto mine cautiously but was careful to remain looking forward.

I spoke in a low tone as I looked out the window.

Kyl: *"He told our new friend where to find people that mattered to me. Diego's brother is a KD."*

No one said a word. They all knew it was a statement and required no response.

Chapter 18

Enough blood in the water will make a river run red

I was getting better by the day, but the trip to Mexico had taken a little more of me than I'd expected. I had Luka take Deedra out to go shopping. She'd been protected as promised, but she was getting by on the bare minimum. I wanted her to be more comfortable and feel like she had everything she needed. When she objected, Luka had told her not to be disrespectful and to take the offer. That meant getting everything she wanted and needed. It was just trying to get them both away for the day. I needed time to be alone and I had plans to work out and things I needed to put in place without other ears around. It wasn't a trust issue, I trusted everyone that was nearest to me, this was simply different. It was another level I'd not even been at.

I sat and thought about how Agent Lewis had clued me in on Diego. The guy was resourceful, and I had plans for him yet. I'd be sitting down with him soon to set some things in motion I knew he'd be able to put action too. We'll come back to that.

I made several calls and ended up getting the meeting I needed with a couple of former Army Sappers. Taska and Leon stood guard as I spoke with the two men I'd invited to meet with me. They were monstrous men, six foot seven and six foot eight. Nearly three hundred pounds but so athletic they moved like men half their size. Even from across the room I could see the nervous looks on the faces of my guests. Both sat rigid as I motioned for Taska to approach. He brought a backpack loaded with two hundred thousand dollars. I assured them he only bites if ordered. That got a smile out of them. We finished discussing the details of the plan and as we stood to shake and part ways, I gripped the first man's hand tightly, and reminded him there were no mistakes here. Flawless execution was the only acceptable result. He nodded and they left.

The gang violence had gotten so bad, it was almost constant you'd hear shots ring out across the city. I knew Marcus Stephon; the city Mayor, was catching real heat over this. He was doing an outstanding job fielding the media and even being proactive doing almost daily press conferences. Fortunately, there were no bystanders involved. With the Coyotes and Three one Sixes doing the majority of the work behind the scenes, Mayor's gang unit was looking like the savior of the city. Everything was on schedule as it needed to be.

The week had passed by quickly. I was a little anxious for the next phase of things. I had invested over Fifteen million dollars into this at this point and to be honest, there was no guarantee things would turn out how I was planning. On paper it all looked feasible and was very solidly planned. If I'd learned anything in the last year, it was that even the most well-designed plan was subject to be completely fucked up. What no one else knew, is that I'd put my own life on the line for all this. Which means, the lives of all those around me were on the line too. I just hadn't told any of them that.

I opened the doors to the balcony and looked out over the city. Money and power don't make everything okay. I had dealt with my own struggles over the years. More than once I'd questioned my existence and quality of life. Not the physical and material quality. The emotional and mental quality. Regardless of what you might think, I'm not just a stone-cold psychopath. I had different modes, that's what I called them. They were vital to survival. But, outside of those modes I was still a man. I cared, I hurt, I loved, and I suffered internally for my own sins and losses. I lost the first woman I'd every truly loved and as a result completely eradicated an opposing family and then murdered my whole family for their involvement. I felt no regret. That didn't mean it hadn't taken a toll on me. Not to mention the hundreds lives on my shoulders. That number was about to outweigh likely what most men had known. It was heavy on my mind and on my heart as I looked over the rail to the street below. Some decisions take a piece of your soul. Would this all just end if I were gone? I don't know. My analytical side was a lot more unstable and morbid at times. The rational side told me what I was about to do would hurt many in two different cultures, but free so many others from the oppression and danger that consumed their worlds. I didn't have all the answers, but I knew that my life needed to go on, at least for now.

I took a deep breath and accepted my place in things. After all, we are all a product of our previous decisions, and we have to pay our dues for those decisions.

I picked up the phone as it started to ring.

Javier: *"Hello my friend, how are things for you?"*

Kyl: *"They're good, how is the family?"*

Javier: *"The most impressive family I have ever seen. Your recommendations were far above what I had expected, and we will be more than able to change the course of our future because of this. I am honored to have been accommodated by the powerful presence of your guidance. I concede fully, we are yours to command jefe."*

Son of a bitch, that was not what I had expected. The leader of one of the largest cartels in Mexico had just pledged his allegiance to me in full. No turning back now.

Kyl: *"You honor me with your allegiance, our families will grow and prosper together. The time for change is now, you are the sword towards our enemies and for your people. Strike them down my friend."*

Javier: *"As you say, so it will be."*

As I hung up, my heart was racing. Not only had I just funded the largest cartel on cartel war, but I'd also just given the orders to start that war. Mexico was about to turn into a war zone and there would be more death than had been ever seen since the Battle of Buena Vista in 1847. I don't care who you are, that's heavy.

I had been extremely separated and reclusive from everyone, even Luka and Deedra. It had deepened their concern and worry. I'd shut Deedra down every time she tried to get me to open up. If I had to guess, it was her who had called Luka. He showed up today with a set plan to get me out of the Penthouse. He'd coordinated the Reapers and plenty of our other lower-level sergeants and street soldiers. I certainly appreciated it, I really needed to get out.

My personal get away was driving, I loved my cars and driving fast. Nothing felt freer than having the throttle wide open hauling ass. Luka had done some more work to his car and wanted to race. I was game, I fed off the competition of combined build and driver.

We sat outside the entrance to the raceway we'd grown up racing on. It had been long closed, but it was a historic place to anyone who'd grown up racing.

Luka: *"How come you never bought this place?"*

Kyl: *"Because Charlo Mardechi owns it. It belonged to his father. Eli was an avid highboy racer and had bought the track before his untimely demise. Charlo couldn't focus on everything he'd had to take on, some things went to the wayside. They shut the track down, but Charlo refuses to let it go."*

Luka: *"I get that. Sentimental value."*

He paused and looked off into the distance.

Luka: *"What's going on with you Kyl? I'm concerned about you and I'm really feeling like you've suddenly decided to push everyone out and keep us all guessing as to what's going on with you and everything else. That's not like you. You're always open and direct. Have I betrayed your trust somehow that you no longer feel like you can bring me in on what's going on?"*

Kyl: *"It's not that at all. I know if feels that way, and I'm sorry. Sometimes things come about, and I just have to shoulder them myself. I trust you brother, don't fret in that."*

Luka: *"It doesn't feel that way at all. To be real, I'm kind of feeling like you are pulling away from everyone that truly is here to protect you and follow you. It's unnerving Kyl."*

Kyl: *"You trust me, right?"*

Luka: *"Of course I do, why wouldn't I?"*

Kyl: *"Because you're sitting here fucking drilling me because I have things in play that I'm trying to protect you from. Not everything I fucking do is inclusive and sometimes I make decisions that I feel are best not spoken and if that's what I choose then that's how the fuck it is. Listen, where we are currently, is the heaviest place we may ever see. I have made some choices that could impact the world as we know it. The less you know at the present time the better for your safety. For everyone's safety. What I will tell you is this, I just funded a war between cartels in Mexico and I'm currently being seen as the Chief in charge of it. That's only a small part of it all. You feel my vibe here Luka? I'm deep in it."*

He just stared at me for a few seconds, he wasn't used to me making major decisions without him at least being involved in some sort of capacity.

Luka: *"I'm sorry I questioned you. You always include me, so it threw me off when you didn't. I trust your judgment, I'm just here to let you know you don't have to carry it alone. I always have your back. Just know that."*

Kyl: *"You're my brother for life Luka, I just need you to trust me without question right now, please."*

Luka: *"Say no more. I understand."*

As the days passed the war raged in Mexico and on our streets here. The Sonola had called all their troops home to fight. The news reported daily on the extreme violence and mounting death toll. An estimated twenty thousand dead and more dying by the hour. The sheer numbers and advantages in weapons had boosted the Tierra Caliente to the most powerful presence in all of Mexico. Even the Mexican army had chosen to keep its distance with that being supported by their president. "Let them sort out their problems and we'll spare the unnecessary deaths of any military personnel." Realistically, they were all hoping the Sonola would fall. What had begun as simple bribery of government officials turned into control by force and murder for defiance and refusal to do as they were told.

They had been ruled by fear for years now and this was their way out with absolutely nothing lost on their behalf.

What had struck me as most impressive was the speed with which they had expelled nearly the whole Sonola cartel. When you sat back and looked at it, their reign of terror and control was solely based on numbers and fear. No one had ever challenged them on their own turf. They weren't highly trained or even that well-armed for being the richest cartel in the world. Complacency is a killer. I'd experienced it myself and gotten far luckier than the Sonola. This could've easily been me and that was unnerving. I'd never be complacent again; I guarantee you that.

On day fifteen of the assault against the Sonola cartel, I received a phone call. One I'd not expected to have to take honestly. One that would change who I was forever.

Kyl: *"What's up?"*

Javier: *"Hello my friend! El jefe! I have proud news for you!"*

It was almost absurd to have the new most dangerous cartel leader in all of Mexico calling me "The Chief." It didn't stroke my ego, it felt odd honestly.

Kyl: *"Share your news with me brother, I'm excited to celebrate in your accomplishments."*

Javier: *"We have interrogated everyone necessary to ensure we have found all who must be found. We have rounded up the last of the just over three thousand men who remain of the Sonola cartel and all its leaders including Treviño Moreno Delgado. We have them all jefe. We have them lined along the river awaiting your final command."*

The river which he spoke of was the Humaya River in the state of Sinaloa, Mexico. It connected to the Tamazula River and ran directly through the city of Culiacán. Where the home-base of the Sonola cartel was and the most heavily oppressed of those suffering under its power. It had just occurred to me what he was doing, and he wanted me to order it. He was testing my durability to speak. Could I make the biggest and most violent decisions. He'd know whether to respect me or set me as weak based on my decision in this moment. Sly bastard. While caught off guard, it didn't deter what I knew needed to happen. The answer was easy.

Kyl: *"Javier, enough blood in the water, will make a river run red. Let the people of Culiacán know they are free from the rule of the Sonola and then treat them well."*

He spoke no words and the sound even over the phone was deafening. Three thousand plus men had just been executed on my command. I had just ordered the final extermination of the last of the Sonola cartel. The world had just shaken, and the news was already showing the river flowing red. The souls of nearly thirty thousand men had just found their way out on the Kyl Hades express. I was pretty sure if I hadn't sealed my fate before, there was probably a special place in hell for me now.

Chapter 19

Watch yourself, that first step
is a mother fucker.

We'd all gathered to discuss the next steps for dealing with Mitch Kessler and the self-proclaimed killer of me. Considering all the things of current, the Penthouse was still the best choice for these gatherings. Epic Tower was an impenetrable fortress. This was the first time in a while that I'd had so many people in my presence at once. It felt like the right time to show my loyal friends and family I was still in this with them. Luka, Deedra, Devin, Louis, Pratt, all the Reapers, Taska, Leon, and my other top lieutenants, and street sergeants had all shown up. Including someone no one had expected to see. As everyone chatted the door opened and suddenly the room went quiet. His sense of humor was a lot better than I'd previously known.

Agent Lewis: *"I just came for the beer and pizza, relax, I don't wear a wire on Saturdays. This is me time."*

It actually got quite a few chuckles around the room. It made me laugh, which eased the tension even more. I greeted David Lewis as I would anyone else, today he wasn't Agent, just David. He'd grown to appreciate the large sums of money he'd been receiving and my guidance on how to hide it so as not to get caught. It was no longer bribes; he was on the payroll. Essentially, a part of the family. He'd earned his keep, and I'd had him wire tapped, phone tapped, and followed to be sure. He was doing his job, being an ATF Agent pursuing an investigation. He just left out the part about working for me too. Money tends to make people leave their values behind.

Kyl: *"David has been quite instrumental in putting pressure on the Kessler family and helping to keep us up to date on things we should know. Without his help, Diego could've kept selling us out from within and we might not have known until too late. Both Luka and I are privy to other things he has done that were of great and nearly priceless value to us. I expect you to treat him as a part of this family now, he's earned his stripes."*

Luka followed up with his signature nod of approval and everyone began to greet him, converse amongst each other, and dig into the food that had been prepared. It seemed like a good opportunity to step out onto the balcony with Luka, the rest of the Horseman, and David.

David: *"Thanks for the warm welcome and introduction Kyl. You too Luka, I can see the power in your nod of acceptance."*

Luka: *"My nod just reinforces there should be no further argument. Conversation is over."*

Kyl: *"We've had more betrayal from within and just outside of the ranks than we've ever seen. Everyone is understandably apprehensive right now."*

David: *"Completely understandable, money makes people do things they normally wouldn't. Mitch is spreading it around in copious amounts to get at you."*

Kyl: *"I think I made my position clear and it's a well-known fact I'm back in old school form as are these four."*

David: *"Did you really hang Hague off the balcony? He really pissed himself?"*

Kyl: *"Pissed right in his own face. Shit ran into his nose, mouth, and eyes."*

David: *"He said you threw a pitcher of water on him. I thought it was weird he demanded to go directly to the hotel so he could shower. He was obsessed with you. Weird shit. Never shut up about it."*

Kyl: *"Well thanks to you, we're all free of his weird ass."*

Pratt: *"Did you know you were going to pop him before you got out there?"*

David: *"Honestly, I had wanted to do it before that but, I didn't know what he was planning until we got there. He basically tried to bully me into this mutual understanding that "this was the only way" shit. I had to make a choice and it just sort of happened in the moment. I don't regret it if that's what you're asking. I couldn't stand him, and I owed these two my life."*

Devin: *"Solid move in my book."*

Louis: *"Agreed, you're good with me for sure."*

David: *"Thanks guys, I'm grateful to be here and honestly, if I'd have had the opportunity to join you before now, I would've."*

Luka: *"Everything has a time and a place. Yours hasn't been chosen yet. But I'm glad you're here now. I appreciate the Diego tip. I never saw it coming."*

David: *"I know you two were close, so I'm sorry it happened the way it did. Speaking of, Kyl, I really think you need to make a move on his brother, Ramiro. I think we can make use of him to get to the nameless one."*

Kyl: *"Nameless one, I like that. You really have nothing on him?"*

David: *"Nothing. He came out of nowhere and had enough knowledge to convince the KD's to join him. Wears the mask constantly. Ramiro is heavily guarded, not going to likely catch him out without an army in tow."*

Kyl: *"Perfect, then it'll be easy for you to grab him up then."*

The look on his face was something like a deer in headlights. Luka

172

smiled; he knew exactly where I was going with this.

Kyl: *"Time to put that badge to work."*

David: *"You want me to walk in there and just arrest him?"*

Kyl: *"Absolutely. I'll get you some Gang unit guys and uniforms. Your Fed credentials will get you further than the police."*

He thought about this for a minute. I could tell he was trying to work out the details in his head.

David: *"I could pull it off. I certainly have privileged that local PD doesn't so it would only make sense I'd take the lead on it. Ya, I'll make it work. Where do you want him?"*

Kyl: *"Gang unit has a training and interrogation room on the sixteenth floor of the city building. You'll go there."*

He started to respond but stopped. I think the depth of my hold on this city had just really sunk in. He chose to simply nod.

I motioned to Luka to take everyone inside. It was time to get down to the rest of the business.

As I turned to go in, my phone rang. Another number I didn't recognize. I knew who it was.

Kyl: *"Speak nameless one."*

Nameless: *"That's cute, you know my name. It's our destiny."*

Kyl: *"It's written wrong in your head. You're already dead you just haven't realized it yet."*

Nameless: *"You're getting far too confident in yourself Kyl. Fortunately for you, I still have so many people to make you watch die before I kill you. Hey what do you think about me burying your new bitch next to the one you already lost?"*

My blood was boiling, my jaw clenched so hard I thought my teeth would shatter. I couldn't let him know he'd struck a nerve. This fucking guy, who was he? He either had done his research or he was someone close to things back then.

Kyl: *"They're all disposable, Nameless. I'm not certain you're much of a man seeing how you like to pick on women apparently. You talk so tough about how you're going to kill me but you're too much a pussy ass bitch to just face me. I think you know you're on borrowed time."*

Nameless: *"I love how cocky you are. It makes me excited to know I'll get to watch that leave your eyes and be replaced with fear. We both know without all those people around you, you're really nothing. I've been watching you. You're weak. I could walk into your little penthouse and kill you now."*

Kyl: *"I'll do you one better. I'll meet you in the lobby."*

He laughed.

Nameless: *"Have fun tonight, Kyl, you'll be burying more of your beloved family soon."*

The line went dead. I was certain I was going to do horrible things to this man when I found him. He had to be someone from my past. But who? Darren Cretchfeld had been the only person to walk away that night and I'd had him checked on for several years. He'd completely changed his name and was living a nice quiet life. He didn't have the balls for this, nor did he care, he hated his family. Whoever this was sounded way older, which made no sense at all.

I looked up at everyone else standing there who'd been listening and just shrugged my shoulders. No one else seemed to have much to add either. We'd need to move around carefully though; I did know that.

I'd already planned to have Devin, Pratt, and Louis' families moved out of the country for the time being. I'd sent them all on a nice vacation at an undisclosed location. No chances there, these men had given up their quiet lives to come back to this war. The least I could do was keep their families safe.

Inside, I addressed everyone with instructions to not travel or do anything alone. We'd double up guards on all ranking members. I just needed a little more time to coordinate what I'd been working on. Life as we knew it was about to change for so many. Made my chest heavy every time I thought about it. I'd just directly ordered the execution of three thousand men. I'd funded the war that wiped out nearly thirty thousand people. I don't care who you are, it's a weight that rests upon your soul differently. I wasn't a full-blown psychopath, more like part time. I had more normality and stability more of the time than anything else. Likely just how I justify it all to myself. I'm not sure anyone would come to the same conclusion about me as I did myself. I just knew what I'd done and what I was about to do would forever change who I was. I'd pretty much accepted that and whatever would come from it.

Deedra looked annoyed; I made my way across the room to her.

Kyl: *"What's the sour look for doll?"*

Deedra: *"I've barely seen you all evening. You left me in here to play hostess."*

I liked that Deedra wasn't like most women and tell you "Oh nothing is wrong." She was always up front and direct about how she felt. Even when it annoyed me, I appreciated it. I felt closer to her than I had anyone in a long time.

Kyl: *"You did an amazing job and I'm proud of you. Thank you for taking care of things for me while I conversed with the boys."*

I immediately saw her soften, she'd been so used to never being appreciated or just simply thanked for anything, that it was almost overwhelming it seemed when I did it.

Deedra: *"You mean that?"*

Kyl: *"Of course I do, I don't bullshit you."*

She stepped closer and leaned up to my ear.

Deedra: *"When you send everyone home, I'd like to show you my appreciation too."*

She bit her lip as she spun away from me and walked off. My dick was certainly aware of her intentions. I had to take a deep breath and adjust the jewels. I'd be fucking her until she couldn't remember her name later.

As I walked out with the last of the group, I stopped with Luka and David.

Kyl: *"I want no time wasted on this. Ramiro needs to be picked up tomorrow morning. They won't be expecting something so early. Luka, you're to coordinate with David on this one."*

Luka: *"Yes sir."*

David: *"I'll get it done."*

As they stepped onto the elevator, I was proud of Luka for accepting David so well. He'd been pretty upset about Diego and initially wanted to put the blame on others, including David. It's never a good feeling when you have to put down someone you love like a dog.

I turned back to the Penthouse door to see Deedra completely naked in the doorway touching herself. Ever since the time in the shower, we'd fucked every day. Usually, a couple times a day. She would often just start sucking my dick regardless of what I was doing. She knew she could do it just how I liked, and I couldn't say no. Which in turn would lead to me taking her and she knew that. I wasn't complaining.

I woke up early and got my workout done. I was nearly back to one hundred percent. Some of the muscles pulled or felt tight at times but I was back and stronger than before. I made my coffee and protein shake before I sat down to start on some work. I still had to keep the legitimate side of things running. I had to deal with insurance over the gas station. Being that Amy had no family, I'd just taken care of her burial and had a private service for her. It was too dangerous right now to have a full-blown funeral. My heart still hurt over it all.

Diamond was still in a coma. I had her under twenty-four-hour guard. The doctors hadn't been incredibly positive she'd wake up. She'd had a lot of head trauma. It made me sick to my stomach that this had happened to her. I'd failed to protect them both, I was struggling to accept that.

As I sat in front of my computer looking over everything, I noticed Deedra leaned against the entry into my office. The look on her face was one I hadn't seen before. I looked at her puzzled.

Kyl: *"You, okay?"*

She just stared at me for a minute.

Deedra: *"Last night..."*

Ah, yes. Last night had been something unlike anything of this world.

Deedra: *"I have never felt like that or gotten off like that. My body still isn't right, I feel like I'm still somewhere else."*

Kyl: *"It was certainly astronomical, that I can agree."*

Deedra: *"Astronomical. Ya that's a good word for it. Kyl, I'm yours. Whether it's just a thing or whatever it is. I'm loyal to you in every way, do you understand what I'm saying to you? I'll die for you and with you just to be here. You feel what I'm saying?"*

I knew exactly what she meant. Gia had said almost the same thing to me, damn. Was it possible? This feeling? What she was feeling? What I was feeling? It didn't seem like the right time to be focused on that.

Kyl: *"I feel what you're saying Deedra, I want you here with me. No question about it."*

Wasn't exactly what I wanted to say, but I wasn't sure I was ready to say more. To her though, it was more than enough. She slid into my lap and wrapped her arms around me. She whispered in my ear, *"Let's agree not to die so we can focus on this later on."* I did adore her.

My phone went off, it was Luka. They had Ramiro. Things were headed in the right direction.

(David's perspective)

Getting picked up by the Feds and Gang unit was about the worst way to start your day. You'd not think it could get any worse. But you'd be extremely wrong. Ramiro ran his mouth from the moment he was cuffed until he stepped off the elevator on the Gang unit's floor. All the way up until the moment he saw Luka sitting there. Then suddenly, his knees were weak, he was having trouble standing. He'd almost begun to whimper. It made Luka smile. Which was even more unsettling. I couldn't lie, Luka made me a little nervous too. Kyl was dangerous, extremely dangerous. But Luka, he was different. He got off on the violence. He loved it and I believed all the stories I'd heard about him. The most disturbing story I'd heard was how he'd pinned a man to the wall and cut off the hand of this man, showered in the blood, then killed the rest of his family. Kyl could switch it off, I think Luka was just completely off his rocker all the time.

Whatever it was, Ramiro recognized it immediately and had decided to cooperate. He didn't hesitate to begin bargaining with Luka. I probably could've spent all day with him and not learned as much as Luka did in 30 minutes. He walked out of the interrogation room with him. He'd somehow managed to make himself appear the businessman and less of a threat, he'd made Ramiro seem almost comfortable. It was strange seeing Luka emulate Kyl's persona. He was far more intelligent than I'd given him credit for.

David: *"That went well. Impressive. Well, what now? Are we turning him loose?"*

Luka: *"Let's all take a walk. I'd like to show you both something."*

His cool demeanor layered over his merciless ability to take a life without blinking was scary. I was genuinely terrified of him and Kyl. Even at the sacrifice of my professional integrity, I felt I'd made the right choice siding with them.

Luka: *"Ramiro, let's go grab a drink and get some fresh air. I have something I want to air out."*

As he walked past, he said *"bring up the rear and don't go through the door."*

My senses immediately told me something was off, the darkness in Luka's eyes and the smirk on his face was unnerving. What the fuck did he have planned.

Ramiro: *"This is right on time bro; I was getting thirsty. I hope we can keep things on the level with us Luka. You're going to talk to Kyl, right?"*

Luka opened the door and stepped through

Luka: *"Uh huh, I sure will. Watch yourself, that first step is a mother fucker."*

Immediately after Ramiro stepped through the door, I heard him let out a blood curdling scream that seemed to continue to get further away. Instinctively I rushed to see, only to be met by Luka to stop me. He was right in my face. I was scared, my heart racing.

David: *"What the fuck just happened?!"*

The Gang unit all started laughing. Luka smiled, reached to his left and flicked on a light switch.

Luka: *"Have a look, just don't get too close."*

As he stepped out of the way I turned sideways and leaned towards the open door. There was nothing fucking there. A metal hood darkened the view and there was a small platform to the left but directly outside the door it was a straight fall to the ground. I looked down to see that Ramiro had taken a sixteen-story swan dive to his death. He never even saw it coming. His body was splattered on the sidewalk below.

I stepped back and looked at Luka, he just smiled, shut the door, and walked back into the other room. I knew in that moment; one wrong move and I was dead.

Chapter 20

Sometimes, the best thing people can do for us is die.

The door leading to Ramiro's death had been a construction error when the building had been built. The gang unit had used it more than once to see someone out. Claiming later that said person had been trying to escape and falling to their death not realizing there were no steps.

His death would cause a definite increase in attack. I had to put my plan into action soon. I was just procrastinating to be honest. I had to figure out a few of the details still. When you make deals amongst devils, they often come with a heavy price. I'd always known there would come a day when I'd have to pay that price. I just hadn't considered it would be this much or take so much of me with it. I think after the events in Mexico, I was certainly a lot more desensitized to things than I had been. This was different, this was difficult, and hit close to home. It almost made me hate being me as it drew near time to make it happen.

Moving around the city was difficult but not impossible. I didn't get to do much driving lately and it was making me crazy. Working out and driving fast were my escapes from it all. I had to travel in heavily armed convoys. It almost wasn't even worth doing but I'd had meetings with the Mayor, Chief of Police, and the Chief of the Fire department. It went as I had expected but as I'd hoped. I understood so there was nothing else to say. I had to keep my word.

As we drew closer to the Penthouse traffic seemed to slow. I looked ahead to see a semi blocking the road as it apparently was trying to back into a driveway. Then it hit me, that was one of Kessler's trucking company rigs.

Kyl: *"Shit it's a fucking trap!"*

Devin screamed over the radio from the front seat. *"It's a trap! Scatter!"*

Chaos erupted as all the vehicles in our convoy started to point out in different directions with some unloading to take up positions. That's when I saw it, the white streak across the horizon and before I could yell *"Rocket!"* The SUV two cars in front of us exploded.

Gunfire erupted in all directions. It got bad really quickly and there were people caught in the crossfire. Mitch had broken the cardinal rule of never entrapping innocent bystanders in our business. Fucking piece of shit.

I reached under the seat and grabbed the HK G36 machine gun that was there, rolled down the window, and proceeded to start dropping threats as they appeared. Luka hadn't been far, so he and the other three Horsemen had taken up rooftop positions and immediately took out any threats from above. I almost hadn't noticed the car approaching from the other direction.

Kyl: *"Devin brace!"*

I let go of a barrage of rounds out of the window into the driver of the car headed towards us, but it was too late to stop it. Luka saw it from the rooftop and took out a tire in just enough time that it caused the car to violently surge to the right. I braced for impact as it slammed into the left rear of the SUV, spinning us around, and slamming us into a light pole. We were dead in the water.

Devin was working on getting his door open when I heard the familiar whoosh of an incoming rocket propelled grenade. I dove through the window and grabbed Devin right as the RPG impacted the SUV and exploded.

Devin threw himself in front of me as we were blown backwards. He'd taken the brunt of the explosion to protect me. I dragged him to the side of the building and immediately stepped around the corner as I opened fire.

It was him, the Nameless one. He stood there at a distance with his stupid mask on and rocket launcher in hand. I started to run towards him firing but was intercepted by Louis and a couple of Reapers.

Kyl: *"I'll fucking kill you here and now bitch! Let's go, you and me pussy!"*

He had reloaded the rocket launcher and was walking towards me. He'd made the same mistake as I had just made. He'd become oblivious to everyone and everything else around him. He'd taken one step too far forward and as he leveled the launcher to fire, a single round struck him in the arm causing him to fall backwards.

Well played Luka. He'd been waiting for any shot he could get, and he'd clipped him. But before any of us could react, he'd been surrounded by his men and quickly taken away. I knew Luka was pissed he didn't get off a better shot, but he'd saved our asses. Fuck, I'd acted impulsively and nearly gotten us all killed. Oh shit, Devin.

I turned and ran back to where I'd left him. He was conscious but hurt. He'd taken shrapnel from the explosion. There was a chunk of his ear missing, and his back was bleeding.

Kyl: *"Devin talk to me"*

Devin: *"I'm here boss, I'm here."*

Kyl: *"Tell me you're okay, can you stand?"*

I was worried the shrapnel had hit his spine.

Devin: *"You're okay and that's all that matters boss. But yes, I can move."*

Devin was thickly muscled which honestly, had likely been what had saved him from any worse damage. I was relieved he wasn't any worse. This shit was getting too close to home. I had to pull the trigger on my plan asap.

There was complete chaos in the streets surrounding what had just happened. I'd lost four men, and it looked as if only one bystander had been hit by the wild gunfire. Against the advice of my men, I made my way through the street checking on those who'd been caught in the crossfire. I had the names and numbers taken down of everyone involved so I could compensate them for the damage. Most of them were just as glad to see I was okay. Minus one old lady who called me a menace to the city and said I'd go straight to hell. She probably wasn't wrong.

Devin had refused to go to the hospital and wanted our doc to come take care of him. We've been using the same three doctors for about 5 years now. They each had trusted staff we'd vetted also. There was a fully stocked clinic in the Epic Tower building. There was even a fully equipped fallout shelter below as well. I'd had it set up so basically one hundred people could comfortably survive for at least ten years down there. You never know when you might need to survive below ground.

My phone had been ringing off the hook. I looked down at it, this one I had to take.

Kyl: *"Yes Mayor Stephon, how can I help you?"*

Marcus: *"Weird, don't do that. Are you guys, okay?"*

Kyl: *"I lost four street soldiers and Devin took shrapnel from an RPG."*

Marcus: *"These fucks are stupid and brazen. Dare I need to repeat anything from the conversation earlier?"*

Kyl: *"No. You don't need to fucking repeat it, Marcus. Is that why you fucking called me? To make sure your little deal was still a go?"*

Marcus: *"Kyl, please calm down. You know it's not like that. Don't get upset, please. I'm only referencing the clear necessity at this point to get it over with."*

Kyl: *"Fuck you, Marcus. Don't forget your place in all of this. I don't need to be reminded of anything. We chose to be mutual partners in this, but the truth is you're where you are because I put you there. Don't ever forget that. Do not ever feel like you need to remind me of anything. I will pull the lid off this mother fucker and burn this whole fucking city to the ground. You're going to get what you asked for because you and I made a deal years ago. I'm a man of my word and ALWAYS stand by my word. I'm insulted by the insinuation of your doubt."*

Marcus: *"Kyl, I'm sorry. I have to answer to people too. I'm not doubting you and I'm sorry it came across wrong. Please, accept my apology, I do trust you and I know my place. You know I'm grateful. I misspoke."*

I hung up on him without another word. Son of a bitch. The audacity of him to even make that call. He was on the verge of pushing me to go nuclear. No one wanted to see that.

As soon as I was sure Devin was good, I left him to Louis and Pratt. Luka had been waiting out in the hall. He wasn't happy and he didn't hide it at all. I wasn't in the mood for anyone else to come at me sideways at all. I'd had enough of the meeting today, which was completely unnecessary and put all of us at risk. I was well beyond irate, and my emotions were at a boiling point.

As I walked out into the hall Luka turned to me and shit went sideways. He pushed me hard enough that I slammed into the wall.

Luka: *"What the fuck were you thinking? Huh? You think you can just go gung-ho and go off like that?"*

Without even thinking, I moved in one swift motion, grabbed him by the throat, slamming him against the wall so hard it dented the drywall. I was completely vehement and nearly irrational at this point. I was bigger than Luka and still significantly stronger. His eyes were wide with shock and fear. I was the only person in this world who'd ever dare be this aggressive with Luka. Even he knew how dangerous this was for him. Left too far out of control for too long, I'd kill even Luka in a rage.

Kyl: *"I've had enough of everyone's opinions today. The last person I want to be judged by right now is you. What I was thinking was my people were getting killed, the members of this community whom I'd sworn to protect from all this were stuck in the middle of it all and that sorry mother fucker whom I've yet to figure out who the fuck he is took a shot at me with a rocket launcher. Devin could've been killed. The fuck are you thinking putting your hands on me like that. Huh?"*

There were tears in his eyes, the last time I'd seen tears in his eyes was when Gia had been murdered. Suddenly I felt like shit and let him go. Dammit.

Luka: *"I'm sorry boss. I'm fucking sorry. I can handle a lot, but I can't handle losing you Kyl. You're my brother, my best friend, my mentor, and the only reason I'm alive. When I saw you shot up it nearly broke me. I can't do this without you. The only person I've ever loved like family in this world is you. Everything I know is because I learned it from you. All of it Kyl. All of us count on you to lead us. We're fucking lost without you. I'm lost without you."*

The tears were coming in a constant stream. I put my forehead against his and gripped his shoulders.

Kyl: *"Shit is really fucked up right now Luka. I'm under a lot of stress and there's things at play here I've not been able to talk to even you about. I'm doing the best I can to keep it all together. I need you to remember, I'm a psycho asshole like you too. I'm sorry I lost my temper."*

Luka: *"You're fucking scary bro. No one scares me like you do. Your wrath or losing you. Just fucking scary."*

As I stepped back, I noticed that Louis, Pratt, and Devin had seen my blow up. You could see in their eyes the uncertainty of whether to say anything or not.

Pratt: *"Boss...whatever it is. Whatever you are underneath. We have your back and we're loyal to you until the end. Our families know the life we've chosen, and they're set up to be good for a long, long time. We're in this with you."*

Devin and Louis both solemnly agreed.

Luka: *"We live to serve you. We're who we are today because of you. The thought of losing you is enough to break each one of us. We've talked about it plenty of times. The Four Horsemen will die so you can live."*

I stood there in that hallway with the four greatest men I'd ever had the honor of knowing since my Uncle Mac and Lewis. This was what family and loyalty were all about.

Kyl: *"I'm about to do something that you're all going to hate. That everyone will hate. You're the only four on our side that will know it was me who did it. I need you to understand, there are things that have to play out in order to keep the balance between what we do, how we live, and keeping things copacetic."*

Luka: *"Whatever it is, we trust you, boss. Just know that."*

Kyl: *"Devin, you're out of commission tonight. I want you on the radio directing traffic from the top of the Orpheum. Pratt, Louis, and Luka…You're with me tonight. I need all the Reapers and street guard set up as I directed you to do. Tonight, will change the course of things forever."*

No one argued. Perfect, exactly what I needed. I went up to the Penthouse and was immediately attacked by Deedra. She was crying, slapped me, and then hugged me all at the same time.

Deedra: *"No fucking more. Do you understand me?"*

Kyl: *"What the fuck are you talking about?!"*

Deedra: *"You promised me, we do this together. No more leaving me stuck here. I'm at your side through this all. Do you understand me!? I can't do the sitting here waiting, wondering if you're going to come back."*

She had never told me she loved me, but it was in her eyes. I knew because I felt the same. She was it for me and she was right. I wasn't doing her any justice hiding her away. She'd earned the right to be at my side and truthfully, she was just as much the warrior anyone else around me was if not more.

Kyl: *"Okay. You're with me from now on."*

She was stunned I'd said that.

Deedra: *"Really? You mean that?!"*

Kyl: *"You've earned your place with me Deedra."*

She just held me and cried. Today had been such an emotional day already. No one had any idea what I'd been planning, and it was going to be a mind fuck to each and every one of them.

She looked up at me with tears in her eyes.

Deedra: *"I'd rather die standing at your side than waiting to hear the bad news. I'm in this with you, life or death Kyl. I can't live without you. My heart, mind, body, and soul belong to you. I'm not a person without you. I have nothing left if I lose you."*

It had occurred to me just how profound an effect I'd had on the lives of those around me. It's a very sobering feeling. To be the life blood of the hearts surrounding you. It was a lot to take in. Family had a whole new meaning. Which made what I was about to do even harder.

I called everyone I could think of calling in order to get things in motion for tonight. The parking garage I'd chosen was attached to a hotel that had gone bankrupt a few years ago. I knew the buildings well; my company had built them. The parking garage had multiple different entrances into it. It had underground access, mid-level, and access from the hotel. The greatest gang war ambush in history was in the works.

When you added up the BLK's and the Oliver St Three one Sixes, you were still short of the numbers the Latin Crowns had. Sheer numbers are what make them so hard to compete with. My crews were better armed, that was our strength. The Coyote Locos and King's Disciples were equal in numbers. Just over two thousand between them all and they were about to meet in the same place for one hell of a blow out battle.

I'd given orders to all three crews on where to enter and how to set up. I'd had an implanted snitch run back to the Crowns and Disciples and tell them of the "secret meeting" between the other three gangs. Details of how to get into the building undetected were the most important contributions to it all.

I was in the bell tower of the St. Roman Church; it was a massive tower and build like a medieval castle housing three huge bells. They hadn't rung in over a decade at least. Something had happened to the gears below and the church opted not to fix them. The tower overlooked the hotel and parking garage from across a massive parking lot. I watched as the BLK's and Oliver St Three one Sixes made their way through the hotel to the roof. Took note of the Coyote Locos entering through the mid-level entrance. Finally, the Latin Crowns and King's Disciples appeared. I watched as they broke into the lower levels of the parking garage. They'd taken the bait. Part of me had wished they weren't as stupid as they really were. My heart was so fucking heavy that I was about to do this. I felt waves of anxiety and anger all at once. All those years ago, I'd made an agreement. A promise. I'd given my word and now the time had come to stand up to my promises. To honor my words.

In the building just within site, were just over two thousand men, who thought they were about to go to war with their sworn enemies. I turned to Luka, Louis, Pratt, and Deedra. I looked at them and said nothing for a moment. It was time.

Kyl: *"There are times in our lives where we come to a road that's no longer a crossroad. It becomes a solitary path with a single direction to travel. Words spoken in promise, deals struck to ensure the future of this family. A man's word is his honor and his honor what keeps him and those he loves safe. I hope you'll understand someday. I love all of you, just know that."*

I slowly raised my hand to expose the remote I'd been hiding at my side. As those present looked down at the wires attached to it, the sudden realization of what was about to happen hit each one of them almost simultaneously.

Kyl: *"Sometimes, the best thing people can do for us....is die."*

I   braced   myself   and   pressed   the   button.

Chapter 21

Death shook my hand and went on his way

I could feel the sun on my cheeks as I leaned back in my chair next to the pool. The scantily clad girls in bikinis were everywhere. Marcus sure knew how to throw a party. Luka was off flirting and having the time of his life at this moment. I'd chosen to just sit and take it all in. Taking over new zones, setting up rules, businesses, both legal and not, was a lot of work. It had seemed to consume every minute of my day in the months that followed the cleansing. There were certain things you did, things of unspoken honor. I'd not quite understood it when I was younger and had seen Mac doing it. But after having wiped out the entirety of the Cretchfeld family, it was my responsibility to show my honor and have them all properly buried. There was no funeral, and no one dared go near there. Anyone who'd been close to the family, close enough to be a threat, had also met their demise. Most of them ended up ash and poured in the river. The funeral homes had all been so busy and paid so well, no one asked any questions.

The fear in the air that surrounded Luka, Devin, Pratt, and Louis was so thick you could've cut it with a knife. People cowered at the sight of them. They'd earned the street name of Kyl's Four Horsemen of Death. They'd dubbed me the La mano della Morte, or the Hand of Death. When I went anywhere people froze in place for fear of making any kind of mistake. Those who knew me well were even cautious to speak carefully. It was no secret I'd not only taken out the Cretchfeld's, but also the Vonnet family. My family. That tends to strike a deeper kind of fear into people.

Marcus Stephon had decided this was as good of an opportunity as any to make the big jump all the way into politics. The family had been entangled in it for years. Mostly through bribery, extortion, and murder for hire and of course, prostitution. Marcus' father, former head of the Family, Marcello, had no interest in politics other than the money he was getting from them. He'd more than a few times tried to persuade him to take a deeper step in. That they could create a new life and direction for the whole family. He'd laughed at Marcus, but he'd been semi supportive in his efforts to get into it himself. He'd completed law school, the first in the family to ever have a degree.

I remember listening to Marcus bitch that his father would never pull his head out of the Cretchfeld's asses. He'd said the *"Man couldn't get out of his own way."* For that reason, getting further into the political positions he wanted had become nearly impossible. His allies had warned him he'd never get anywhere while Marcello still continued to cause unrest amongst them.

Marcus joined me at the table as I stared out over the laughing women and bouncing tits in the pool, Luka having a great time and getting to let loose, it made me smile. This was a lifestyle I could get use to for sure.

Marcus: *"Great view huh, nothing better than a cold drink and plenty of boobs!"*

Kyl: *"Definitely a nice view, I'm just glad to see Luka having fun."*

I turned to face Marcus, in the midst of all these distractions, we were here to talk business. We'd kept our distance in the months that followed the events of that night. It had been best for everyone for us not to be seen together until the dust settled and he'd had time to do what he needed to do.

You see, this was deeper than anyone knew. Several City council members and even the mayor had been caught up in the constant extortion from Marcello. He'd used prostitutes to entrap them and then forced pay outs to keep quiet. He'd even managed to make several of them party to a murder for hire plot. They'd wanted him gone for a while; he was just too well protected. That is until Marcus decided to become part of the solution. Which in turn meant I'd become part of the solution. On the night of the cleansing, I'd called Marcus and warned him to get himself and his dad away from the Cretchfeld's compound. He paused quietly on the line before saying, "I'm not there. But my father will be, take him with them all Kyl. You'll come out of this unscathed if you do. I'll need to call on you one day for a favor. We'll settle up then."

The powers that be had been bearing down on Marcus to do something about his father. You can't rub shoulders with high positioning people and not expect to be called on at some point to pay for your spot amongst them. He'd been backed into a corner to make the extortion stop in return for a chance to move into politics. In return for making sure we all walked away from it, he'd be extorted by a Judge and other members of the city council for years to come.

Marcus: "*There's going to come a day when I'm mayor, Kyl. You, my brother, and I, we'll run this city together. There's going to be a cost one day though. One day I want all the gangs out of my city. I'll build a Gang unit I can trust, and you can count of for support. We'll work together, but they'll all have to go Kyl. This city has been stuck under violence for too many years and if I'm to keep rising up the ladder, I'll need a couple solid terms as mayor in a city that sees a major change and clean up during my term.*"

As I laid there, that day flashed through my head. That conversation so many years ago, had been the recent conversation I'd had with Marcus. In my current state it floated my mind that I'd been set up, was that right? No, I don't know.

I wasn't dead but it sure felt like it. I might be crazy though; I know I saw the shadowy figure appear and reach down for me. Death shook my hand and went on his way.

I shook my head, my ears were ringing hard, and I couldn't see straight. I rolled over and could barely make out other people laying near me too. What the fuck had happened? Where was I? I rolled to my knees and looked up, the horizon above the walls around me was thick with dust and smoke. There was a fire somewhere. Bells. Bells? It was coming back to me, son of a bitch, it wasn't just my ears. The bells had rung. An explosion? Ya, that's what it was. I looked down, the detonator was still in my hand. It had been me. I caused the explosion. The explosion…oh fuck! The explosion! It all came rushing back and my head cleared. I'd triggered the explosion in the parking garage. I scrambled to my feet and looked over the wall of the tower. What I saw before me was absolute carnage. I'd never seen anything like it.

Luka appeared next to me, then Deedra, followed by Louis and Pratt.

Luka: *"I think you might've overdone it."*

I looked at him and I had nothing to say. I just shook my head.

When I'd pressed the button, the parking garage and half the hotel had disappeared almost instantly. The shockwave had been so violent and powerful, it shook the bell tower and rang all three bells. Knocked out nearly every window for a block in every direction and left a crater where the building once stood. I had no doubts there were any survivors. The realization of what I'd just done hit me hard as I looked over the carnage. My heart felt heavy, but it was done. I'd lived up to the deal I'd made so many years ago.

I turned around and sunk to the floor of the bell tower. Deedra was at my side; she'd been trying to talk to me and looking me over for injuries. She leaned in and kissed the side of my face; in my ear she spoke softly. *"Whatever it is, we're here in it with you."*

I had not expected what happened. I'd well past over done it on the

C4, my chest hurt from the percussion of the explosion and my ears were still ringing. I looked up to see Luka reaching a hand towards me to pull me up.

Luka: *"Let's get down from here and inside boss."*

I could tell they all had questions, but they knew I'd tell them when I was ready. No one pressed me. They were the best crew, friends, and family I could ever hope for. I felt like I owed them better. I think that was the point in all this, I'd lost sight of exactly what I was doing here. All those men down there…so many who'd loyally stepped in to fight with us. Granted most of them were in it for their own benefit. But the BLK's had been my own creation and they'd done everything I'd ever asked of them.

As I sat there gathering my thoughts, I'd not even noticed the sounds of sirens. The whole area would be crawling with police and fire fighters. I heard the door open slowly and looked up to see the Fire Chief leaning in. Alvin was Marcus' cousin and had been just as much in on all of this as the others were.

Alvin: *"Hey Kyl, you got a minute? You, okay?"*

Kyl: *"I'm good Alvin, you can speak freely here."*

Alvin: *"Holy shit man, that explosion rocked my house in Westborough. I'm glad you're okay."*

Kyl: *"Ya, any idea what happened?"*

Alvin: *"Well, aside from the obvious massive amount of C4, there was a giant propane storage tank in the basement. It basically recreated the same effect of dropping a one-thousand-pound bomb. It's safe to say, no one would've survived that."*

I just looked at him. I could tell he was uncomfortable and nervous.

Pratt: *"Thanks Chief, we appreciate the information."*

He took that as his queue to leave, he nodded and was gone.

I searched for the right words and concluded there weren't any. Just had to say it like it was.

Kyl: *"Everything has an order to it and price…We have enjoyed the spoils of our business and the freedom to act in our wild and violent ways while those who shouldn't, looked the other way. Years ago, I'd entered into an agreement with Marcus. He'd been pushed into a corner about his father, the powers that be in the life he wished for wanted him gone. As we entered the Cretchfeld's compound, I fired two shots into a car outside killing Marcello Stephon. That got Marcus into the position to enter politics. In order to get those same powers that be to look past what I'd done; Marcus paid the price of doing the dirty work of Judges and City council members. In return for that, he asked me to promise I'd make his city gang free one day. There was no better time than during a gang war that was tearing the city apart. If you go outside now, there's a massive presence of Swat and the Mayor's prized gang unit. They'll take credit for the attempt to take down the city's gangs, when something went wrong, and a bullet struck a propane storage tank. The city loses its gang problem, and the mayor looks like the saving grace with an upcoming election next year."*

Luka: *"Why the secrecy? You don't trust us?"*

The look on my face must've said plenty, he looked down ashamed of having said that.

Kyl: *"Because it was my deal. All those lives are on me because it was my deal. I'm not even going to respond to the second part of that question mother fucker. I gave my word to Marcus; I'd handle it personally. I was personally responsible, and I made sure it happened."*

No one said a word. I hated being so abrasive to Luka but damn, this is more than point and click. I have to do shit sometimes that requires me to be the one who executes it.

Kyl: *"What happened here tonight and what was said here tonight, stays here. Take me home please."*

I'd just blown up a building to execute the five largest gangs and then shook hands with Death. I was tired, I needed a drink and sleep.

Chapter 22

Money, Power, a dash of Mental illness, and a splash of good looks.

I knew I wasn't completely crazy. Right? I laughed at the idea of asking and answering that question myself. I stared into the mirror and imagined myself smiling. A happy smile. I sighed and shook my head. The truth is, I'm not as mentally stable as I come off to others. But I also didn't require the continued amounts of death that seemed to surround my every decision lately. I appreciated the power I had gained. I respect the place I have earned myself and this family. I hadn't ever considered it would go this far. There was a heavy debate in my head on necessary versus chosen. I didn't feel I had chosen this; it was pushed onto me.

I was shaking. Was I angry? What was my problem? I slammed my hand into the mirror shattering it into pieces. I was far too analytical to be dealing with this. I have to make sense of things in my head. It's not even really about justification. It needs to make sense to me. Clearly it fucking made sense up to this point. I'd planned the complete extermination of the Sonola Cartel. That was a necessary side effect due to their constant disregard and disrespect. Being the orders behind thirty thousand men dying is different than ordering a couple hits or a room fool of idiots. I was laughing now, that's what it is. I'm affected by the prospect of mass murder. I drained the rest of my drink and walked to the window. The site of the explosion was still smoldering. There was a dark cloud over the whole city. I thought back to the moment I saw Death standing there. I wasn't fucking nuts; I know what I saw, and I remember the feeling of shaking the cold boney hand. It was as real as I am standing here.

I'd banished everyone from the Penthouse for the time being. Even Deedra, and she'd been quite upset about it. Luka literally had to carry her away. That woman was so deeply devoted to me, she'd fought and cried while being taken away. I needed some space from everyone. I knew she didn't understand and I'm not even sure Luka understood, but he didn't argue. We'd spoken about things before, he knew I wasn't completely right in the head. Who would be after what had been done to me and what I'd done.

This is what it is, the massive loss of life was a necessary part of the lifestyle I'd build and chosen to live. It weighs on the soul; I could handle that. What I'd done for Marcus was also a necessary product of this lifestyle. I'd been close and personal with a lot of those people and their families. That's what bothered me. Part of those killed were my people. They had families in my zone and had for a long time. I'd console them, I'd help them in their times of need. I'd pretend I hadn't pushed the button that killed their loved ones.

As I poured another drink my mind kept floating back to the attack and the four men I'd lost. When I was shell-shocked after the explosion, it had crossed my mind that I'd been set up. The timing of Marcus' meeting, the convenience of me being out in the open and the way the attack had been coordinated. Even if they'd been watching, it would've been difficult to coordinate with such precision the exact time and perfect place to hit us. At this point, I'd kill Marcus on even the premise of suspicion that he'd set me up. Our agreement was a two-way street. He was where he was because of me, and I was where I was because of him. I honored my promise.

I'd decided to pay Marcus a visit. Catching him off guard and without a predetermined meeting would serve me best in this moment. I loaded my pistol and slid my ankle piece into the holster. I was about to do some stupid shit, but I was less worried about it since I'd killed all of Nameless' crew. He'd have to come get me himself.

I opened the door and Taska was sitting there. He looked at me and I think he must've known what I was thinking.

Taska: *"Boss, you know I'm not supposed to leave your side. I know you could kill me for not following your orders, but I've also been threatened by Luka, Deedra, Pratt, Louis, and Devin. Kind of feeling like I'm going to fuck this up no matter what I do."*

Kyl: *"Let's make it easy Taska, you're coming with me. But I'm driving."*

He smiled and looked like a little kid in that moment. Taska had been one of the most loyal people in my life for years and years. He'd been assigned to the Epic Tower for most of his career with me. I just knew I could always count on him to run things properly here. He was from Germany, had come here as a fugitive from justice. His father had been an abusive piece of shit that frequently beat on him and his mother. Taska had gotten sick of it and beaten his father to death with a brick. I found him in England while on vacation and I had paid for his freedom, and they dropped the charges. He was free to move around finally and chose to follow me back to America. I'd put him through all the appropriate training to make him a proficient guard and killer. One of these days I'll tell you about that. There's more to the story of the Reapers than has been spoken. There's a reason for that.

Being that I was being brazen and, in the mood, to say fuck the world, I chose my custom build Nissan R34. It was imported from Japan, right hand drive and fully build motor with everything you could think to do to it. Taska worked his big ass into the racing seat on the passenger side and buckled in. He knew I was all gas, no brakes.

I left the parking garage and lit the throttle all the way wide open. Tires smoking, sideways, one violent shift after another, I made my exit epic and my presence on the street known. I made my way into the interstate so I could open Skyline's very capable motor wide-open. I needed to feel the freedom of the road. This was my happy place.

As I pulled off the interstate, I turned towards the Westborough Edition. I hadn't been to Marcus' house in a long time. He liked to keep business and home separated. I knew more about him than most though. Like that he sent the wife and kids on exclusive trips so he could have his little get together parties with any women he could round up. I had a feeling about today though. Don't ask me to explain that I couldn't do it I'd have wanted to. It was just a feeling I couldn't ignore.

As I rounded the corner, it had been as I'd expected. There were cars all the way around the circle drive of his giant house. There was one car out of place to me though. It was one of the unique black with green accent Range Rovers that were exclusive to the former King's Disciples. I looked at Taska who'd already picked up on what I was seeing. We both knew what that meant.

Kyl: *"Taska run perimeter."*

As I walked through the side gate, I slowly peaked around the corner. There he was, standing right there talking to Marcus. Mask and all. This mother fucker was bold. Marcus I meant, how cocky do you have to be to have anything to do with the piece of shit that killed my loved ones and tried to kill me?

I wasn't rational at all. I walked straight through the gate and directly towards them. They hadn't noticed me at all at first. Then he saw me and reached for his gun. Too late, I'd already drawn mine. I had him dead to rights, I looked at Marcus who was in complete shock and had utter fear on his face.

My masked friend stood there, posed to draw his weapon but knowing I'd put him down.

Marcus: *"Kyl, you need to be smart. There are too many people here to do this right now. You know that. Killa was just leaving, we'll have a conversation once he does."*

Kyl: *"I will fucking kill you. If you hadn't figured it out by now, I will find you, I will fucking kill you."*

He put his hands down to his sides, then raised them as if to surrender. He held them there and he turned and walked away. I heard him laugh, I'd nearly lost it and shot him in the back of the head.

Nameless: *"You going to shoot me in front of all these people Kyl? At the Mayor's house? Not a very good look if you ask me."*

Marcus: *"Kyl, what are you doing here?"*

The question alone made me angry. It made me grind my teeth and I had to abstain from just hitting him.

Kyl: *"Don't fucking question me Marcus. You sorry fuck, I know you set me up. What the fuck is he doing here? What the fuck are you doing?"*

Marcus: *"I think it's time you made an exit before we all end up dead."*

Nameless: *"Our conversation isn't over Marcus. I will be back, count on that. Kyl, I'll see you soon too."*

As he backed away towards the gate, I considered just killing him and suffering the consequences. Before I could react, Taska appeared at the gate blocking the exit. I could see the nervousness in the eyes behind the mask. I let him stand there for a few moments before nodding to Taska to let him go.

Kyl: *"I will walk you into your own house and shoot you in the fucking face if you don't have a really good reason for all of this."*

Marcus: *"I did not intend for what happened to happen. They lied to me, they were supposed to run up on you and fire a few shots at you. I had hoped that would push you a little and you'd get angry and push forward with our plan. Look, I'm sorry. I felt like I needed to get this done and I had to do something. You were procrastinating getting it done."*

I'd heard enough to lose my temper. I step forward and bitch slapped him out of his chair. As he hit the ground he rolled over, his lip and nose bleeding. The fear in his eyes is what I needed to see.

Kyl: *"Let's get something straight you slack jawed piece of shit. I made you. No matter how you spin it, you're here because of me. You didn't have the balls to take your father out. You were stuck under the Cretchfeld's thumb like a bitch. You begged me to kill your father. You remember that? Begged me Marcus, and I made it happen. I took out the people who made you their bitch and then had to follow behind you all these years later and take out the new people who'd made you, their bitch. Don't you dare EVER talk to me about what time frame I get something done in. You fucking pussy. I've stood by you for everything you've needed so you could have all this. I lost four men and one of my closest personal friends was hurt."*

I stepped closer to where he was laying on the ground and he flinched, and a puddle appeared and began to run out from under him. He was so scared he'd pissed himself.

Kyl: *"Why the fuck was he here?"*

Marcus: *"He just showed up. He's pissed his whole gang is dead. I didn't tell him what happened! I didn't even make the deal with him; I paid Ramiro to set it up before he ended up dead. When someone reached out in his place, I didn't know it was masked psycho. He's threatening to hurt my family if I don't fund getting him a new crew and apparently someone took out the entire Sonola cartel, so he's got nowhere to turn now."*

I smiled as I squatted down to meet him closer to eye level. He looked into my eyes and the realization hit him and the look on his face went from fear to absolute panic.

Marcus: *"Oh my god Kyl, it was you."*

He'd begun to softly sob. The tears mixed with the blood on his face and began to leave red spots on the concrete.

Marcus: *"I fucked up Kyl, I don't want to die. Please, whatever it takes to make things right, I'll do it."*

I pondered on things for a minute. I stood, pulled him up off the ground and sat at the table with him. Mostly for show as I'd realized how many people had watched me slap the shit out of him. I stared at him for a few minutes as he cleaned himself up.

Kyl: *"Family is everything Marcus. Absolutely everything. You have a beautiful family. Paige is an amazing woman the fact that she puts up with your bullshit is admirable. You have two very bright children. You're a lucky man Marcus. I had that taken from me before I ever got to know what it was like. You squander it like it means nothing. Ya, you're going to make things right. You're going to start by getting right with your wife and kids. No more of this. The rest of what you're going to do, I'll figure out."*

He stared at me in genuine confusion. There were still tears in his eyes.

Marcus: *"I don't understand you at all Kyl. You're the most dangerous man I've ever met and likely one of if not the most dangerous man in all of North, Central, and South America. Yet, when met with an opportunity to take whatever power you could get, you lean on moral value and ask me to be a better man."*

Kyl: *"The option is I just give up on you and kill you. Aside from what's been done in the shadows, you've brought this city to a place of greatness it's never seen. Even if that meant deciding to look the other way on certain things. We've done a lot together, but if you ever even think about crossing me again Marcus. I will kill you in the worst possible way I can find. It will take days for you to die. Are we extremely fucking clear?"*

He nodded repeatedly. He'd forgotten his place, but I was sure he was in tune with where that place was now.

Kyl: *"I need your gang unit working overtime to find out where that piece of shit is hiding out."*

My brain was on overload. It's been one thing after another constantly. I didn't feel like I'd had a break too long enough to relax from one issue to the next. I always drive when I need to blow off some steam and I hadn't been able to do that even.

Taska looked at me as I drove. I caught his gaze and gave him the "What's up" head nod.

Taska: *"I don't know how you do it. Any lesser man would just crumble."*

Kyl: *"Money, Power, a dash of mental illness, and a splash of good looks."*

He laughed and just shook his head.

I turned on my blinker and headed towards the highway, I'd certainly take advantage of this opportunity. I downshifted and pounced on the throttle sending the Skyline sideways as I entered the highway. Everything became nearly a blur as the car surged past one hundred and fifty miles per hour. The few miles between getting the highway to where I needed to exit passed entirely too fast. I wanted more, but I had things to address, and I needed to get the Nameless thing figured out quickly.

Chapter 23

The price of war always ends up paid in the lives of men.

No matter how you spin it, there's always a cost to this lifestyle. Most of the time it feels more distant and disconnected. There comes a point though when it gets closer to home. Whether it's people you love or care about. Those you call friends or family. Money and power don't make the man, it's what's in his heart and soul that determines what and who he is. The heart has a powerful presence over the mind sometimes. Manipulating feelings and ideas. I've seen men give up over things like break ups and divorce. In my line of work, my chosen lifestyle, you knew death. You accepted the path you'd chosen to get where you were. Death was as much a part of it as life. Taking a life becomes necessary to living your life.

I wasn't sure I'd ever really trust Marcus again. At this point, it didn't even fuck with me enough to be overly bothered. The absolute truth is, I could kill everyone I even slightly doubted, burn this city down, and walk away from it all. I was starting to care less and less every time someone betrayed my trust. To be completely honest, I'm usually a humble person but there's no way you eliminate a whole cartel and five major gangs and not end up being more deeply twisted than you were before. It affects you in ways most will never understand. I'm no serial killer but, it's possible I could be worse. Mass murder by an incredibly detailed and coordinated plan. The problem is, I'm a compassionate person on top of having the ability to kill and order death. It was more of an internal struggle than anything. I wasn't all bad, I had the heart to do good and help others. But I had no problem doing bad shit either. I think this is why I'm still a mostly rational person. Or was I? This is what goes on in my head. This is why I struggle with my sanity.

I knew at some point there would be questions about the unexpected and untimely death of the gangs. Losing the Coyote Locos was a huge loss for the Tierra Caliente Cartel. The Coyotes were the street soldiers for their drug trade, street enforcement, and multiple other businesses. I'd kept it so close to chest that no one had even had the inclination I was planning anything. The Stephon's knew but I felt I had to worry about them keeping their mouths shut since my issue with Marcus. I knew that my Horsemen and Deedra wouldn't say anything. Maybe I will make Marcus write me in as deputy mayor and then eliminate all of them.

I chuckled at the thought of myself as mayor. Not that I couldn't do it, just a wild thought. Talk about running the system. My head was all over the place today, I needed to focus.

As I looked down at the blood all over my hands it came to my attention the absolute mess, I'd just made carving up Marcus' personal snitch and errand boy. He'd told me all I needed to know a while back, but this was more about sending a message. There's just something about finding one of your people cut up and choked to death with their own intestines. Probably excessive but I needed to be sure he remembered exactly what I was capable of.

I washed my hands in the bathroom and wiped a few things down before leaving. Not that I was worried about it, just a good practice to keep active. I closed the door behind me and stepped out. Taska had been waiting and keeping an eye out. He looked at all the blood on me and shook his head.

Taska: *"Let's get you home so you can get cleaned up boss."*

He was a great guard and close friend. He'd devoted his life to this family and protecting me. When I thought about the people around me that I trusted without question, Taska ranked in line with Luka, Louis, Pratt, and Devin. I'd become increasingly paranoid after the list of betrayals that had emerged as of recent. I had legitimately considered killing everyone I wasn't one hundred percent confident in. Luckily, I'm still rational enough to consider that excessive.

As I walked into the Penthouse, Deedra looked at me with a concerned and inquisitive look. I motioned to her to sit back down.

Kyl: *"I'm fine, it's not mine. I'm going to shower. Alone."*

The look on her face was pure hurt and disappointment. She hated when I put her at a distance. I felt it necessary though. I had grown to deeply care for Deedra. She'd become someone I felt like I needed and right now, I need people like that to keep their distance. She looked back at Taska, and he just shook his head and closed the door.

I took a long shower; I stood there leaning against the wall and just let the hot water wash away the day. I was tired. Mentally, emotionally, and physically. All this shit that's happened and somewhere in it, I'm supposed to be dealing with Mitch Kessler and had really not even been able to give him the attention I needed to. How fucked up are things when the guy you're at war with is literally the lowest on the priority list.

When I stepped out of the shower, I could see Deedra sitting on the edge of the bed. I felt a little bad for how cold I'd been to her when I came in. She was legitimately a good woman and was taking good care of me.

Deedra: *"Can we talk? Please?"*

Kyl: *"Ya, I'm sorry for being cold. I have a lot going on."*

Deedra: *"I know you do. I'm worried about you, we all are. You're different Kyl. You're scary. Even Luka said so. I just want to know you're okay."*

Kyl: *"I'm fine. I think so anyways. I have my moments and my days. But I think I'm okay."*

Deedra: *"Kyl…. you're fucking scary. It's not just what you do, it's how you do it. You're almost self-destructive in every way right now. Please don't be upset with me, I just want to help. If I can."*

She was looking at the floor and I felt a little ashamed that she felt like she couldn't even look at me while she spoke. Maybe I had been off the deep end lately. I knew my own struggles in my head, but I guess the outward appearance was far different than what I was seeing.

Kyl: *"Hey, look at me. I'll be okay, I struggle with certain things in my head. I'll admit…I'm not as mentally stable as I pretend to be. I know that. Just keep checking in with me and if you need to push to get my attention, you have my permission. You're a good woman Deedra, I need you here with me."*

That was all she needed, she collapsed to her knees and wrapped her arms around me and began to sob. I pulled her up and laid on the bed pulling her onto my chest. I just held her while she let it out until we both fell asleep in each other's embrace.

As I woke and started my morning, it occurred to me that I hadn't heard from Louis in a couple of days. The guys checked in every day, which was a rule. I called Luka immediately.

Kyl: *"Good morning brother, have you spoken to Louis?"*

Luka: *"Good morning boss. No, not for a couple of days? What's up?"*

Kyl: *"He hasn't checked in for days. Something feels off to me."*

Luka: *"I'm close, I'll swing by and see what's up. I'm sure it's nothing. Probably just getting some family time in."*

Kyl: *"Ya, maybe so. Do it and let me know asap."*

I had a bad feeling, and I wasn't often wrong. I quickly got dressed and filled Deedra in on my thoughts. She was up and ready to go in no time. I was pacing the room when my phone buzzed. The message said, "You should get here asap." My heart sank, Deedra read the look on my face, handed me my pistol and we were out the door.

Taska and some of his team did their best to keep up with me. I was not in the mood to be driven and I wanted to put power to the road in my own way. I drove like a man possessed and Deedra never once flinched. I loved that she trusted my driving. Two things in this life I was really, really, good at were fucking and driving.

We pulled up outside of Louis' house. Luka had already pulled in a team and set a parameter up. I knew that meant bad news. Fuck.

Luka: *"It's really fucking bad boss, I'm not sure she should go in. Fuck, I'm not sure you should go in."*

Kyl: *"Deedra, why don't you wait here. Taska, stay glued to her."*

He nodded and I moved towards the house with Luka. I took a deep breath and prepared myself for what I was about to see.

Inside of the house was something out of the worst horror movie you'd ever seen. There was blood floor to ceiling. As I moved through the house, it got worse and worse. His wife had clearly been raped and then dismembered. Nothing could prepare me for what I'd see next. Louis' two kids had been murdered and beaten so badly their heads were smashed in. They'd been then hung from the ceiling fans by the feet in each of their rooms. I walked into Louis' bedroom where he'd been dismembered and nailed to the wall like some sort of fucked up artwork. His fucking dick had been cut off and shoved in his mouth. There on one of the walls, a message written in blood. "I'm coming for you Kyl. Your friend, Nameless"

My blood began to boil. I was about to lose it completely. I took out my phone and made a call.

Kyl: *"William, if I don't have information on where to find this Nameless mother fucker by the end of the day, I'm going to start killing people and I'm going to start with Marcus. Understood?"*

William: *"Understood Kyl, I'll make sure of it myself."*

I hung up without another word. I felt myself getting close to snapping. The price of war always ends up paid in the lives of men. But this, this was more than enough for me to start burning this city to the ground to find where this piece of shit was hiding. I was going to do things to this man God might never forgive me for. I'd just have to take that chance to avenge the deaths of this beloved family.

Chapter 24

Dead man walking

There's a lot of reasons to kill someone, one of those reasons being, so they can't fuck with you anymore. An important part of the process is to be sure they're dead. So far, I'd been lucky enough not to end up on the dead side myself. The caveat to this is when you don't make sure they're dead, they tend to come back after you. The attempts on my life had fueled the firestorm and death march that was currently steam rolling through the ranks of the crime world.

Something about this whole thing with Nameless had been working my brain in overtime. If his goal this whole time has been to take me out, why not team up with Kessler? I mean he'd aligned with the Crowns but there had always been a silent agreement between them and the Disciples. So that part wasn't unusual to me, the fact he completely avoided any contact with Mitch was. What was I missing?

I'd gone to check on Diamond and spent some time there. It broke my heart to see her just lying there. She hadn't deserved this at all. I needed some windshield time, so I'd been bouncing around driving different cars every time I came by one of the places I had them stored. I ended up back in the Viper, it was just a violent car and with power upgrades, it was even more so. I'd been thinking about Louis and his family. Apparently, Louis had dismissed the guards I'd posted there earlier in the day. He'd said it made life seem tense for the family. It wasn't their fault; they were following orders from a ranking member. I'd made it clear that no one leaves their assigned post without my approval from here on out. I'd even doubled up on the numbers at each location. One of my fabled Horsemen had somehow met his demise at the hands of some Nameless shit stain. I was almost completely numb to loss by this point. I was hurting inside but I couldn't even shed a tear anymore. I was so fucking angry.

I had ended up sitting outside of the burned-out remnants of the gas station. One of my crews had started the teardown. It was best to knock the whole thing down and start over after what had happened. As I sat in thought I noticed multiple cars pulling up around me, Gang Unit. I also saw amongst the dozens that had arrived was Agent David Lewis. I considered that I should grab my AK-47 that was behind the seat, but no one seemed to be threatening anything. It looked very casual. Well, here goes nothing, I stepped out of the car and was met by the Captain of the Gang Unit, Horatio Gutierrez.

Horatio: *"Hey Kyl, sorry to pull up on you so deep, we come in peace."*

He held his hands up as to say he surrendered and I noticed several uniformed officers pull up I shot him a concerned glance to which he immediately replied, *"Just hear us out."* I looked at Agent Lewis and he nodded as if to say hear them out.

Kyl: *"I'm listening Horatio, what's on your mind."*

Horatio: *"I'll keep this simple, first off, our condolences on Louis. We all liked him; he was good man. We heard about what Mayor Stephon did to you and your message was heard loud and clear. What we all want to say here, is we stand with you Kyl. We're not going to follow any given command to come at you if they try that. The Chief knows where we stand too. No one is interested in going to war with you. Just want you to know that."*

Kyl: *"I appreciate that, just a side note for you, Marcus handed over everyone's addresses, family addresses, kid's schools, and about anything you could think of a couple years back. As a security blanket, so I know where all of you live."*

He shifted uneasily and looked around at his team.

Horatio: *"You have our word, Kyl."*

Agent Lewis: *"We have information on the whereabouts of Nameless. Horatio's team has a snitch that has been working with Nameless. We can use him to draw this guy out. You just give us a plan."*

Kyl: *"I'll give you a plan, but I don't want any of you involved. What I'm going to do to that piece of shit, you don't want to present for it. If you'll just run the perimeter. I need sharpshooters in at least four locations. I have a plan he won't be able to resist. I'll be in touch."*

As I shook hands with Horatio and a couple other members of his team, I nodded to Agent Lewis to follow me.

I wanted to switch cars about, so I had Agent Lewis follow me to the storage building nearby. As I pulled into the building, I motioned to him to follow. I had questions but I wanted them away from prying ears. No mistakes could be made here, and I needed to know Agent Lewis thought of it all. I could tell first we were going to have to talk cars, the look on his face was pure excitement. I didn't mind, I loved talking about these cars. Most of them here were classic and pure race cars.

Kyl: *"What do you think David?"*

David: *"Holy shit Kyl, I had heard you had quite the car collection, but I had no idea you had this many and so many classics. Wow!"*

He excitedly shuffled towards the line of Mopars against the far wall. I loved the old Chargers, Challengers, and several others. He'd made a beeline straight for one of my Plymouth Road Runners.

David: *"Man this is fucking stunning. I've dreamed of owning one of these my who life."*

I tossed him the keys.

Kyl: *"Fire it up. It needs to be started anyways."*

I didn't own much in the way of cars that weren't modified to be faster in some way. As the engine cranked and fired up the supercharger began to whine. He was smiling ear to ear just like a little kid. I motioned to him to flex the throttle a little, I didn't think he could possibly smile any bigger, but he was.

David: *"Man this this is a dream. Thanks for that Kyl. Best moment ever."*

Kyl: *"I think I can beat that, keep it. It's yours now."*

His jaw dropped and he was completely dumbfounded. His eyes welled up with tears.

David: *"Kyl, I couldn't. Man this is a really expensive and beautiful car."*

Kyl: *"Look, you've been loyal, and you've put everything in the line for me and this family. You didn't have to do that, but you did, and you deserve this. You can park it here and come get it any time you want. When this is all over, you take back home with you."*

He gripped the steering wheel and just looked around the car. I could tell he was very emotional and trying to keep from breaking down.

David: *"This means more to me than you'll ever know. Thank you, I will do everything in my power to protect you and this family."*

Kyl: *"Good, I need people like that around me. Let's talk about what went on today. What's your gut tell you? Can they be trusted?"*

David: *"I say they're all legit. It caused quite a ruckus when Chief William mentioned there could be some blowback from the whole incident. Horatio stood up and immediately said his team would have nothing to do with it. They'd quit first, and the mass of the uniforms echoed that. William told me that without his team and the force standing behind Marcus, you had him and this city by the balls. I don't get the feeling he agreed with what Marcus had done. I also don't think he knew about it."*

Kyl: *"You feel a solid one hundred percent on that?"*

David: "I really do, I took the Profiler Master's program at Quantico. All my federal spidey senses say I'm right on this."

I smiled, the more I spoke to David and had him around, the more I liked him. I was glad to have him on my team.

Kyl: *"I need you to set up a meeting with William, have him meet me at Natoli's. I have some other business there anyways. We also need to talk about how to handle this plan I'm working on in my head. I want you a part of both."*

David: *"Copy that. Hey Kyl…Thanks again. This car will mean so much to me always. I'll tell you a story one about why I love them so much."*

Kyl: *"Deal. Now get out of here and go drive it. Ease yourself into the power. That bitch is nasty powerful."*

I watched as he took off down the road getting a little sideways. It made me smile thinking about how happy he'd been. As much of a monster as this all required me to be, I still preferred to help anyone I could. I liked the feeling of knowing I made life better or easier for someone. It was the trade off for me. Doing bad shit to be able to do good things for good people. Speaking of good people, I'd been distant from all my people since Louis's murder. Deedra has been genuinely upset. Luka said she's done nothing but pace and bitch about not being able to talk to me. That woman had done enough earned her place at my side. More so than ever and she genuinely cared, and I think loved me too. I've struggled for so long to really let any woman close to me. Diamond held a special place with me too, I think if I'd have ever really given her the chance, we could've grown into something good. I'm just a closed off asshole and I push people away who deserve to be closer. Deedra was different, she kind of forced herself on me. Not like in the conventional way you're probably thinking. I mean that she was in a position that required me to keep her close and then we nearly died together. She could've walked away at any time. I offered her the money to escape to a new life. She chose to stay and specifically asked to be at my side. She's loyal. I like that. I needed that. I wanted her there. Which made the plan I was working on even harder. I'd be throwing her to the Devil himself and I didn't doubt she'd even question me on it.

I called Luka and told him to gather up the remaining Horsemen and bring Deedra back to the Penthouse. I'd had both Pratt and Devin's families relocated to the Epic Tower building until this was over. The floor below me was split into two apartments. Both are still very sizeable, so the kids had plenty of space to play and get wild. I wasn't going to lose anyone else and yet I was about to put two of the most important people to me right into the fire.

When I got to the Penthouse, Luka met me in the lobby. The look on his face was pure worry, I hadn't seen him look like that I could ever remember. He embraced me in a strong hug and held me by the shoulders at arm's length.

Luka: *"Kyl, I'm worried about you. I haven't seen you this way since…well since things happened back then. Just need to know you're okay."*

Luka, he was my brother. No one was closer to me. No one would ever be more family to me than him. We'd both give our lives for each other and ride together until death. You can't replace that.

Kyl: *"I'm okay. I promise. I'm just trying to get a grip on being who I chose to be so many years ago. I haven't had to be that ya know. I've been a version of myself that was easy going and happy. I'd almost forgotten there was a price to this lifestyle. A requirement of me that couldn't be cut short or half assed. I'm exactly who I need to be right now Luka. When the bodies stop falling, I'll see if I can check back in with that other part of me again. But, right now, we have a family to protect and business to run."*

He smiled and squeezed my shoulders.

Luka: *"And here I thought you were losing your shit. Stupid me. Let's get this fucking war moving."*

I walked in and Deedra nearly knocked over her chair jumping up as she saw me. She paused and collected herself so as not to act out of order in front of everyone. It wasn't a secret how close we'd gotten, and everyone here knew. I motioned for her to come to me. I didn't know she could move that fast. She was instantly wrapped around me. I think she might have flown across the room! I could feel her tears on my neck, I felt guilty for making her feel this way. I peeled her off me and stood her in from of me. I looked down at her, tilted her chill up, and kissed her. She blushed for the first time I could ever remember seeing. She looked around nervously, everyone smiled, and she instantly seemed at ease over it.

I greeted Pratt and Devin. We hadn't gotten to speak in person yet. They were both trying to be so tough. I told them it was okay; we didn't need to be at that moment. We shared tears, memories, and spoke our condolences through prayer. I don't know if there's a place for gangster in heaven, but we prayed for his acceptance none the less. We were all God-fearing men, it's just a strange balance with where we choose to stand. We definitely weren't doing God's work I felt like, but we all kept our faith close to heart. I'd struggled with it for years. Whether I was even worthy of His mercy. We all had. The church told us were forgiven but they didn't know what we really had done or what we really were. Certainly not who and what I was. I'd orchestrated the murder of the equivalent of a small town. A whole cultural community completely wiped from the future pages of life's story. On top of all the unsuspecting lives lost in the explosion. I struggled to think I could ever be forgiven. More of the shit that goes on in my head.

Kyl: *"I want to start out by addressing the Four Horsemen. Louis will never be able to be replaced but the truth is, we need to make a decision on who we want to try and fill his shoes. The Four Horsemen must live on and operate in full capacity. I'd like to nominate Taska as the next generational addition to the crew."*

Pratt: *"This is why we work so well. Why were the family we are. We all had literally just talked about asking you if we could have Taska before you got here. Taska has my vote."*

Devin: *"Taska has my vote."*

Luka: *"Taska has my vote."*

I turned to Deedra. Her eyes went wide, and she was completely caught off guard.

Kyl: *"The Horsemen of Four requires a vote of five to seal and accept their place. It's your vote now."*

Deedra: *"Taska has my vote."*

Kyl: *"In final, Taska has my vote. It is decided, Taska will be the Fourth Horseman. Someone call him up here."*

Taska had shed the only tear I'd ever seen him shed when we told him. He'd always looked up to the Horsemen and I think secretly he'd always wished he could be one. He would never disappoint or dishonor the position. That I was certain of.

We'd lightly celebrated the evenings event and paid memorial to

Louis. Losing him and his family was hard. To have seen them murdered, how they had been, it changes you. You break a little more. You can keep the crazy put away a little less. I was the only one who knew exactly where I was in my sanity. When you start to question yourself about your sanity it's worrisome. When you stop questioning yourself in your sanity, it's even more worrisome. I had started to stop questioning myself.

Kyl: *"Let's talk about how we're going to draw Nameless out of hiding. I've taken into account the dangers involved in this and I apologize that I didn't consult anyone before I chose this plan for a reason, and this is how it will be."*

I looked at Deedra as if to preemptively apologize.

Kyl: *"At this point, Nameless is looking to get his next shot at us as soon as he can and he's looking to make it hurt even more than what he'd just done. That's why it has to involve Diamond and Deedra."*

The look on everyone's faces was almost the same identical sick look. Deedra was the only one who stood up and immediately owned her spot in it.

Deedra: *"Whatever I have to do. You order it and I'll do it boss."*

I had so much admiration for her. Fuck, this was going to be hard. I trust my team though; she'd be okay and so would Diamond. I just had to be sure all angles were covered.

As the evening drew to a close, I looked around at my closest and most loved people sitting before me. I had to make sure no one else was lost in this shit. I'd had eyes on Kessler through everything, I hadn't forgotten about him, and he certainly hadn't forgotten about me. Taking out the Sonola cartel and all the gangs in the area had certainly slowed things down for them. Mitch had relied on the street gangs heavily for support and action. I will give him credit for how tight lipped they had kept things. There wasn't much at all picked up off the street chatter. Surveillance had shown several trucks entering their compound and cases unloaded; I had to assume were weapons. I had a pretty tight grip on the weapons trade so my guess would be he had to branch out to someone on the East coast and I was willing to bet it had cost him a fortune to acquire whatever he'd bought. This was going to come down to old school family on family violence like it had been so many years ago. We'd be ready when it was time.

I felt much better having everyone staying here in the Tower. I'd tried to get Luka to stay here too but he was just as well protected as I was having the Reapers as his personal guard. You'd need an army to get through them. What I'd put in place months ago would push their ranks to new levels and make them more dangerous than they had ever been. Trust me, no matter how overwhelming things get, I'm always making moves that keep us ahead of the curve. I'd learned my lesson about thinking we were untouchable.

Luka: *"Everyone is secure, and my guys are waiting on me. Thank you for tonight bro, we needed this. We've all been worried about you. Especially that one over there, I think you got a real keeper there. She paces and is a wreck when you're gone. She cares like…ya know."*

Kyl: *"Like Gia did, I know. I see it. I think you're probably right. But hey, I appreciate you too. You and I brother, we've come a long way. It's been quite the story, hasn't it?"*

Luka: *"It certainly has, and I think it's time to bring this chapter to an end."*

I saw him out and closed the door behind me. I made my usual rounds to shut off lights and check locks. When I turned to head to my room, there she stood. Completely naked, her perfect curves illuminated by the light behind her. I made my way to her, grabbed her by the throat and pushed her back towards the bed. I loved how she smiled as I squeezed tighter.

She was mine, and I was finally accepting that.

The next morning I'd gotten up early enough to get my workout in and have breakfast with Deedra before we headed out. I had to make rounds to check on all the different projects I'd felt like I'd been ignoring. I had plenty of people in place to keep things going but I still felt better being a part of it all. Deedra enjoyed getting to see the complexity of my real estate and construction businesses. When you look at it all, how it ties into the family part of the business, it makes sense. If you didn't know it was all run by a crime family, you'd never know.

I headed to Natoli's early so I could handle some business that had gotten put on the back burner with everything else going on. I had a certain son I had yet dealt with.

I pulled into the parking lot and headed towards the black SUV sitting towards the back of the lot. When I stepped out, a couple of Reapers exited the vehicle and removed a not so happy and very drugged out Matteo Natoli from the back. Looked like he'd had to be restrained. It broke my heart to see him so far gone in this moment. When he saw me, he instantly stopped struggling and tears filled his eyes. He knew that his life was likely about to end and in front of his own family.

I'd sent a Reaper ahead to get us a private room ready. When I entered through the back door, I was met by Francesco and his wife. She was already crying, I hugged her and whispered in her ear. She looked up at me wide eyed, burst into tears again and hugged me. Then she hurried off towards the kitchen. Francesco raised about eyebrow but didn't say anything.

We entered the room and Alessandro stood to greet me. The man had stopped time in his seventies and never seemed to get any older. He'd always been like a grandfather to me. As much respect he ever paid me, I gave in return.

Alessandro: *"My boy, come see me. I haven't gotten to look at you much since you tried to die."*

Kyl: *"Speak no more of it. I'm not going anywhere. Thanks to you, of course."*

His eye twinkled and smiled the biggest smile.

Alessandro: *"I'm grateful I finally had the opportunity to do it. I've waited for years. What brings us together today."*

He leaned to the side to look behind me, his brow instantly furrowed, and the smile left his face as he sat back down. Francesco joined him at the table and started to say something until I raised my hand and stopped him.

Kyle: *"This is simpler than you think. I have made my decision, and I will relay that decision here in front of you."*

I motioned to have Matteo brought to me. As he approached, I drove my knee into his groin and then plowed my fist into his nose. The blood immediately began to pour from his freshly broken nose. He sunk to his knees in pain. I pulled a chair up in front of him and sat down.

Kyle: *"Let's be one hundred percent clear, you're alive because of who your father and grandfather are. I should still kill you for what you did. Fortunately, I love this family, so you get a pass on death this time. Instead, you will go to a private treatment facility where you will start your journey to recovery. If you fail, I will kill you. This will be your reminder every day of the rest of your life."*

I reached out, grabbed his face, and sunk my blade deep into the soft meat next his eye and sliced him down the cheek to nearly his mouth.

Kyl: *"You betray and disgrace your family with your addiction. This will be your only chance."*

I stood and turned to the Natoli elders, Alessandro nodded in approval and Francesco had tears streaming down his cheeks.

Kyl: *"I stand by my statement; this is my gift to you. Now, I have other business to address here today. My usual please."*

William was already here waiting so I made my way to his table. He stood and paid his respects to me, and we both sat as Agent Lewis came through the door. He promptly joined us.

Kyl: *"I want to keep this short and sweet, William. I need to know where you and I stand. I'm not here to judge you for standing with your brother, but if that's your choice, I just need you to be man enough to tell me so. We have far too much history between us to not just be honest here."*

William: *"So, I'm not sure how much you know. But Marcus and I have been at odds for a while. I never wanted to be in the family business. I hated it and my father and brother made me do it. They made me do things I didn't want to do, and I never forgave them for it. When Marcus said he wanted to make a run at politics and bring our family out of the crime life, I was excited. I was all in. Clearly, we're still dirty, but according to the norm in the political world, we fit right in. The thing was it didn't make Marcus a better man. In fact, it made him worse. The way he treated his wife and kids, the way he acts, the things that he's done behind my back. What he did to you. I don't stand with that and neither does my force and I stand with my officers. I don't know what you're getting at or why you came today, but I'm not standing with my brother if he's coming after you."*

Kyl: *"I don't know if he is either Will, but if I find out he does one more fucked up thing, I want you to know I will kill him myself."*

William: *"I understand. I'm devoted to you and the family. Just promise me, you'll protect me and my wife and kids. Please."*

Kyl: *"You have my word."*

The fact that he didn't know what his brother was up to told me all I needed to know. I could no longer trust Marcus.

This had to be performed flawlessly or I could lose both Diamond and Deedra. It wasn't exactly a gamble because of the way everything was set up and planned but you can never ever discount that shit can go sideways in an instant. Nameless was resourceful and had surprised me a few times already. I'd need to be extra cautious this time. I planned to shed the last bit of humanity I had left to exact my revenge.

I had Diamond moved from the secure floor she was on to a room next to the stairwell. To this point, no one had known where she was except a few of my personal guards, the medical staff, and doctors I'd hired to care for her. So, no one would know from the outside I'd intentionally moved her.

The room she was in was on the corner of the building directly attached to the parking garage. There was a large window into the room, and I'd set up sharpshooters in three different positions. There were no blind spots in this room, so it was perfect. I'd also had two of the closet cabinets modified to comfortably hold a person inside. Luka and Devin would be in the room waiting. I had no real idea how he operated. Something told me he took pleasure in the killing, so an immediate kill would seem out of character. But, on the hand, it was a hospital, so he'd not have the time and privacy of someone's home or a random location. Dammit, no negativity. Precision. No mistakes. Why the fuck was I so nervous? Diamond and Deedra. That's why. I'd never forgive myself if this went wrong and something happened to either of them.

I had William and his Gang Unit in place in the building, parking garage, and spread over a three-block radius. Reapers spread over six blocks in every direction.

At minimum, he wasn't getting away even if he got spooked.

I checked on Diamond and kissed her forehead as I said a prayer to myself. I didn't know if God listened to me anymore, but I had hoped he'd at least listen to my pleas to keep those around me safe when I asked. It's not that I wasn't God fearing or faithful, it was more that I couldn't understand how He could possibly ever smile upon me for the things I'd done in my lifetime and continued to do. Right now, I don't care about me. I'd endure his wrath if He'd just keep these two women safe.

Deedra hugged me and smiled. She was so confident and sure of herself. She said it was all because of me, that she knew I'd keep her safe and take care of business. I kissed her and sent her off to wait to live or die. I was sick to my stomach for the second time I'd ever remembered in my life. I took a deep breath, time to man up. Game time.

In order to set up the perfect operation, your people need to have been in place for at least eighteen hours prior. I sat in the adjacent room; I'd caught a few hours of sleep but had been awake to watch the sun come up. The morning passed by as if time had stopped altogether. I think it was around ten a.m., I'd closed my eyes and started to doze off when those words pierced my ear like a knife. Loud and clear, "Dead man walking."

My heart was thudding in my chest. I had to take several deep breaths. I was almost dizzy, the adrenalin started pumping. Shit, get control of yourself Kyl. My senses were heightened to the point I felt even the slightest breeze on my skin. Another call over radio, "He's in the stairwell." It was almost here, the moment I'd waited for. I stood next to door listening. Waiting. Another deep breath. I felt like he'd hear my heart beating. Footsteps. Why were there footsteps in the hallway? Who the fuck was out there? Nameless should've been coming up the stairwell.

I heard the steps stop by the room next door. A pause, then more steps and I could hear the stairwell door open. He'd somehow gotten an accomplice past all of us?! I was sick from the adrenalin and ready to run from the room. I had to wait. Don't blow this now Kyl. Who the fuck was here? I squeezed my eyes shut tight trying to control my breathing and lower my heart rate. Please, someone say something. I heard the closet doors bust open and Luka belt out *"Don't fucking move!"* followed by *"What the fuck?!"*

Chapter 25

When dead men aren't really dead

My heart was beating so hard I couldn't see straight. I nearly went down trying to get out of the room and I slammed into the door frame going into the room next door. I was just as caught off guard as everyone else in the room had been. Luka, Devin, and Deedra stood with weapons drawn. All three nervously shifted their gaze between the two men in the room, then to me. My stomach tightened, my throat seemed too dry to speak, and in my head, I was ready to burn down the world. What was he doing here? Had he completely lost his mind? After all these years, all the things we'd accomplished together, all the hard work, and so many hours of conversing through every detail to make sure nothing could ever get in our way. This is where we were. I was heartbroken and yet angry enough to throw him out of the window so I could watch his head explode on the sidewalk below.

I trusted him for so many years, he was more than a friend. He was family. I wanted to scream and cry.

Charlo: *"Kyl…It's not what you think bro. I thought it was just Diamond here. He had my daughter. I had to agree."*

Kyl: *"Charlo Mardechi, your father would roll over in his grave. You bring shame to both of our families. I should kill you here. Fuck Charlo. You need to go now."*

Charlo: *"Bro…"*

Kyl: *"Shut the fuck up and move!"*

There were tears in his eyes. I knew he was telling the truth. Nameless had used him to ensure he could get in. No one would question Charlo being here. He didn't even look at me as he walked past and out of the room.

Nameless began to chuckle.

Kyl: *"You shut the fuck up too. Move your ass."*

I motioned to Luka and Devin to move him out of the room. We'd already pre-designated the room where we'd be taking him. I wanted him away from Diamond and Deedra.

Kyl: *"You're not going to want to be here for this next part. You should go back to the Penthouse."*

Deedra: "*No. You're not just going to use me and send me home. Fuck you. I'm in this with you.*"

I couldn't really deny her after I'd just used her for bait. I hope she had a strong stomach.

Kyl: *"What you're about to see, is going to change you. Just be prepared."*

She didn't say a word. She looked me in the eyes, kissed me, and followed the boys. This woman, I think Gia would be proud of her loyalty to me. She made me want to leave all this behind and now Deedra had me feeling the same way. Maybe I would, one day, sometime soon. Maybe.

As I walked into the hallway Charlo quickly turned to me with a look in his eyes I hadn't seen since the day his father was murdered.

Charlo: *"You listen to me Kyl, it's not him. Marcus took my daughter, and the masked shit stick was hired by him also. It's not all as you think though. There's something with this guy, I can't pinpoint it. But I know him. Marcus is not in charge like he thinks he is."*

Kyl: *"I'm sorry you and Selah were drug into this. Do you know where he's keeping her?"*

Charlo: *"She's with his wife and kids. They don't have a clue what's going on."*

Kyl: *"I want you to walk out the front doors. Hold up six fingers and there's going to be a team that grabs you. Go with them, tell them to take you to get your daughter on my orders."*

Charlo: *"Thank you Kyl, I love you brother. Finish this once and for all. You hear me? For our families, you finish it."*

I turned and walked away without another word. There was a commotion coming from the operating room where they'd taken Nameless.

Luka: *"Boss, he's claiming there's a bomb and if we don't let him go, he'll detonate it."*

He stood there with a cell phone in his hand. Finger on the call button. There had been eyes on this building for the last two days. I knew he hadn't been able to get in to plant a bomb. He was bluffing.

Kyl: *"Fuck you dickless."*

As I watched him press the button on the phone, an explosion rocked the building. It had come from the parking garage. He wasn't bluffing, I'd been wrong.

He was laughing.

Nameless: *"You just killed your city's fine mayor. I was never going to let him live. He was just an insurance policy. Doesn't look like I'm getting out of this one. He was my ride here. I ain't leaving, neither is he."*

My phone rang.

Horatio: *"Kyl....It was Marcus. He's dead."*

I just hung up. Before I could even get in my heart about this I stopped and let my head take over. This mother fucker, both of them. He'd betrayed me. But Nameless had killed him. The upside was I didn't have to do it.

I slid my phone into my pocket. I looked down and noticed a small oxygen tank sitting there. Before anyone could react, I grabbed it and in a fluid motion, I smashed it into that stupid ass mask he was wearing. To my surprise, it held up surprisingly well. It was still on his face, broken, but still there.

I stepped back as he tried to get his bearings to get back up and soccer kicked him right in the face. The mask flew off and as his face became exposed, my knees became weak, and I nearly collapsed. I was sick to my stomach, I wanted to vomit. Why was I so dizzied suddenly? How the fuck was this even possible?

Luka and Devin both looked at me in pure confusion. Luka lunged forward ready to fire.

Kyl: *"STOP!"*

He immediately withdrew. He was in shock, breathing heavily, his jaw was clinched so hard I could hear his teeth grinding. Devin was shaking. I was shaking. When dead men aren't really dead, they come back to haunt you in a different way.

My heart was beating so hard I was still dizzy and couldn't see straight.

He was leaking blood from his face, but he was laughing hysterically. He'd rolled to his knees and then settled for falling back against the wall. He took a deep breath as he wiped his face and rested his arms on his knees. Nameless, wasn't without a name anymore.

Chapter 26

Blood of my blood, Vengeance is served.

I stood there shaking. How this was even possible was so far beyond my understanding. The longer I stared at him the more my rage grew. It took everything I had not to just smash his face in and beat him to death. He'd taken people I loved from me. Tried to kill me. I was going to make him suffer the worst possible fate. I wasn't anything close to mentally stable in my head right now, I was about to do something that might make even the devil himself cringe.

Behind me, I could sense the pure hatred boiling from Luka and Devin. I could see Deedra was completely lost for what was happening right now. I didn't want her here for this, but she insisted.

Deedra: *"Someone fill me in here please. Who is this shit bag?"*

Luka looked at me, I nodded my permission.

Luka: *"This shit bag is a former enforcer for the Cretchfeld Family. He murdered our mentor Lewis, Charlo Mardechi's father, and Kyl's fiancé' and unborn child. Kyl stuck a knife through his neck, but it appears somehow, he survived. His name is Hudson."*

Hudson began clapping his hands as Luka finished speaking.

Hudson: *"Wonderful introduction Luka. The best part of it all, I beat that little bitch of yours Kyl. She was quite the fighter, what was her name? Oh yes, Gia. I slid my knife into her slowly over and over as Bash held her. I watched her take her last breath."*

I felt like I'd lost consciousness. I couldn't move, my arms felt so heavy. My chest was heavy. It felt almost impossible to breathe. My ears were ringing, and I could barely see straight. I hadn't ever put much thought into who had killed her and my unborn child. I'm not sure I had ever felt the way I did in that moment.

If there wasn't enough going on already, William Stephon burst into the room with tears streaming down his face. The second he saw Hudson his face contorted into pure anger, and he lunged forward before anyone could grab him and landed a solid kick right to Hudson's face. Before he could collect himself to throw another one, Devin picked him up and headed out of the room with him. I followed him out to the hallway.

William: *"He fucking killed my brother Kyl!"*

I reeled back and landed a hard open-handed slap to his face. He fell back and looked up at me in shock.

Kyl: *"He did, Will. But your brother signed his death warrant by working with Hudson. Did you know he fucking kidnapped Charlo's kid? Ya, I'm sorry for your loss but the truth is he was dead already."*

He settled to his knees and started to sob. I knew he was in pain regardless of what Marcus had done. I knelt with him and pulled him close to console him.

Kyl: *"Listen to me Will, things are about to get even more serious. I need you to pull it together right now. Your brother's Deputy Mayor was in on it all. He was planning to have you taken out. You need to make him disappear. Do you understand?"*

His eyes went wide in disbelief and then to anger.

William: *"Are you telling me my own brother and his bitch made underling were planning to drop me? Say it ain't so Kyl!"*

Kyl: *"I'm sorry Will, it's true. You know what needs to be done. You'll be next in the order to take control."*

William: *"Consider it done. You make that mother fucker in there pay. You hurt him in the afterlife."*

He stood, wiped his face and was gone. I'd completely lied to him. The truth was the Deputy mayor knew very little about most of our business dealings and wasn't much more than a political place holder for the process and public eye. That in itself was an issue though. I needed William to take control. This was how I made that happen, collateral damage. Sorry, not sorry.

I turned my attention back to events that had just unfolded in that room. We'd been so busy and so enveloped in our murderous rage, we had never considered counting bodies. Honestly, I didn't notice he was even gone, nor had it even crossed my mind. Thinking back, I hadn't even thought about Hudson at all. I'd stabbed him in the neck. This was my mistake, I had to own that. I was about to make things right with those who'd suffered because of it.

I ordered Luka and Devin to get him up onto the surgery table. As they stood him up, I drove a knife into his spine. He let out a scream in pain and collapsed. My intention had been to sever his spinal cord in order to paralyze him. Apparently, I'd missed severing. But, clearly, I'd at minimum nicked it. He was struggling to move his arms and legs and couldn't stand.

Luka looked at me slightly puzzled. The smile that creased my lips told him all he needed to know. He picked Hudson up and slammed him onto the table. Things were about to get very twisted and sadistic.

When you're in my position, you acquired all sorts of people within your payroll. I kept a full staff of medical professionals at hand for a lot of different reasons. Dr. Wistick and Dr. Mahmoud were both very skilled doctors. Both were also well versed in alternative practices. As they entered the room, they both paused to look at me.

Kyl: *"It's as we planned."*

They both nodded and looked around the room.

Dr. Wistick: *"If anyone has even the slightest of a weak stomach... You're going to want to leave now."*

Kyl: *"Deedra, what you're about to see will be burned into your head forever. We're all seriously fucked up and this is just another day for us. You have the chance to walk out now."*

Deedra: *"I'm all the way in Kyl. Let's do this. I want to see him scream."*

I'd created a monster in her, and yet it made me smile.

A lot more made sense to me now. Like why he hadn't gone to Mitch Kessler for help. The Kessler family hated the Cretchfeld's. He hadn't fucked with Charlo because he didn't know they were still around. Charlo had been so far removed from everything; most didn't even consider them as having a player in the game. Which is why Marcus had pulled that card. No one would ever expect him to do what he'd done. If I had learned anything, it was to keep my eyes wide to all things and everyone.

Kyl: *"Fucking Hudson. The piss ant who'd not even been important enough to give a thought to after I'd stabbed you. I give you the credit you deserve for dragging yourself out of there and surviving. Unfortunately, you're about to wish you had just died back then. You killed my woman and my child you piece of shit. I'm going to take your soul and make sure you never find peace."*

Hudson: *"I didn't know about the fucking kid but fuck it. One less of you in the world. Fuck you Kyl, you don't scare me bitch."*

Kyl: *"I don't want you to be scared Hudson. I want you to be terrified and I want you to suffer every breath."*

I nodded to the doctors to start. They had come up with a method to exact the revenge I sought. They began to pierce his skin with a large needle attached to an air gun. By injecting air under the skin, it made it possible to cut the flesh away from the muscles.

As the process started, Hudson tried to squirm. He began to strain and scream as he realized what was happening. I wanted it cut away as completely as possible.

I want to really impress upon you the depth of what was happening. They'd started on his hands. At current, the skin from his fingers and hand had been peeled away. The forearm and upper arm to the shoulder now exposed.

Because of the way I'd stabbed him, he couldn't use his limbs but could still feel the sensation of pain. He felt every injection of air and each cut as he was being skinned alive. I knelt beside him as he writhed in pain, he was begging me to make it stop. I spoke in a low even tone, I wanted to be clear he'd understand every word. I reminded him of every life he'd taken from me. I asked if he thought Gia had suffered this much. Did my unborn child feel the pain of what was happening outside of the womb? Had my child felt the pain of being stabbed? Each time I felt the anger welling up inside of me, I took a deep breath. I wanted to be calm and composed for this.

I stood and reached for a scalpel as Dr. Mahmoud inserted the air gun under the skin behind his ear. He began to strain and was making small movements with his head. Luka grabbed him by the throat to keep him still as I began to carefully cut the skin away from his face and skull. It was impressive just how far the doctors had gotten already but the real treat for me was the last cut that removed his face. I'd let the good doctor make the cuts near the eyes so as not to injure them. I wanted Hudson to see his face dangling in front of him. The feeling of horror must've been immense, I could hear his heartbeat.

It took just under an hour to completely skin him. I'd see my fair share of bodies in many different forms over the years.

This was a first. Seeing someone skinned alive. He'd blacked out multiple times throughout the process. The inability to close his eyes alone must've been such a mind fuck. To be clear, this served no real purpose other than pure revenge. Even this felt like it fell short of what he deserved. It was, however, time to end this.

We took him to the hospital basement where the incinerator was. Normally, you'd just slide the special tray in and close the door. Wham, bam, business done all is ash. What I liked was that I could slide him in slowly. He'd be burned alive a little at a time. Incinerators run roughly 2200 degrees and typically it takes a couple hours to burn down a body. But the agony of being burned alive was the effect I was after here.

Watching him scream and suffer had been satisfying. But it was time to move on. I slid him the rest of the way in and locked the chamber door.

Kyl: "Blood of my blood, Vengeance is served. Let's see you come back from the dead this time mother fucker."

Chapter 27

When it comes undone

As I made my way towards the parking garage, I had to just sit down. I looked at the bloody face in my hand I'd removed from Hudson. I was okay but wasn't okay. If that makes sense. Was I impressed with who I'd become? Or was this really just who I've always been? The money, the power, the clout, none of it seemed worth any of this. How did we even get here? Was this all simply from my trauma and heartache from all those years ago? Had I created the whirlwind of death that had swept through this town and even into another country? What was the point again? Why was I doing all this? I'd done some fucked up things over the years, but this past 8 months has taken the cake. Thousands of lives were lost by my hands and at my feet, all for a crown I never knew could weigh so much upon my head.

Here I sat after skinning my enemy alive and then watching him scream as he burned. I think it bothered me more that what had just transpired, didn't really bother me. It bothered me that all this had dragged my long-time friend back into this life. Charlo had done such a good job of separating himself from this life and because of me, his family had been put in danger. It was just sinking in that Marcus had ultimately betrayed me and was fucking dead.

I sensed eyes on me, I looked back to see Luka, Devin, and Deedra all staring at me. Shit, I'd forgotten they were there. I looked down and shook my head.

Luka: *"Boss…Are you okay?"*

Kyl: *"Ya Luka, I'm okay. I just needed a minute to collect my thoughts."*

Devin*: "We got your back boss. No matter what it is. We're here."*

Deedra: *"What can we do right now to help?"*

Kyl: *"I don't know. You should probably all get away. As far away as you can. I feel like I'm becoming a poison. People I love dying. People I love and trust betraying me. I just don't know."*

Luka: *"I can't speak for everyone, but you know us three and Pratt, Taska, the Reapers. You know you can trust us. Right? We're in this until the end Kyl. We live and die in this."*

Kyl: *"I know Luka. I don't question any of you. This is about me. This is not where I ever intended us to be."*

Deedra: *"Tell me how any of this is your fault. What you've done is eliminate every enemy and every risk that put us all in danger. This family grows stronger for everybody that drops of those who stand against you. Stop doubting yourself."*

I nodded and stood up; she was exactly who I needed in those moments. All of them. It wasn't so much that I doubted myself, it was that I had a fear of completely losing myself in this. If my sanity slips any further, I would burn this city to the ground just because I could. No one needs that.

Kyl: *"We need to go check on William. We have a whole other issue with Marcus being dead."*

The explosion had ripped the car nearly in half and damaged every car within the blast radius. It had even damaged the wall and nearest support pillar. You could've achieved the desired result with half the explosives that had been used here. It seemed excessive, even for Hudson. The parking choice seemed odd to me too. Why park so far from the door if you're the getaway car? I looked around for cameras. There was one down the way that he'd have had to pass. I surveyed the car itself, something felt off to me. I couldn't put my finger on it yet.

The bomb had been directly under the driver's side. It had literally blown him to pieces with such a force that the pieces were basically unidentifiable. There was, however, the lower part of his leg lying about twenty yards from the car. The tan loafer was still on the foot. Now I knew this was all wrong. Mother fucker.

Kyl: *"Detective, I'm sure you've checked the cameras. Anything?"*

Detective: *"I'm sorry Kyl, there's not much to go off. It shows Mayor Stephon and a masked man drive in, but because of the angle, you can't see the car once it's parked. But the strange part is, someone cut the feed shortly after. There's no more footage."*

I thanked him and walked off to look around. Across the street was a jewelry store. He had an external camera.

Kyl: *"Devin, reach out to the jeweler. Tell him I need to see his camera feed asap."*

He was on the move and so was my head. I had to figure this out. I was missing something, but I knew it was there.

Kyl: *"Luka, get a tail on William and eyes on the Stephon home. Have Taska take a team to Benton Airfield and check hanger Twelve and the flight manifest. Deedra, you're with me."*

That loafer was about to blow things completely out of the water.

I needed to make a call, but it had to be from a landline. There was a pay phone just around the corner. The line rang a few times, "hello?" "Meet me at the Road Runner." I hung up without even waiting for a reply. I knew he'd be there shortly. I had a feeling things were about to get even more messy on a whole different level. A simple phrase I'd remembered hearing a few years back, suddenly made a lot more sense to me.

Deedra: *"Care to fill me in on what's going on in your head. What are we doing here?"*

242

Kyl: *"I don't have it all yet, just give me a few to work this out. You'll know when I know."*

With the absence of the stress about being noticed gone, I wanted to drive my Viper. It happened to be parked in the storage with the Road Runner so I could swap cars while there. Within a few minutes of pulling, Agent Lewis walked in. He smiled and paid his respects to me.

Agent Lewis: *"What's going on Kyl? I heard Marcus was dead, I knew you guys were having issues, but I also know you had a lot of history. I'm sorry for your loss."*

Kyl: *"Thanks, I appreciate your concern. I have a pressing issue I need you to tackle as soon as possible. I need you feel out the other agencies for activity. Specifically, the FBI. I think we may have an issue."*

Agent Lewis: *"You think Marcus might've been working with them?"*

Kyl: *"I think Marcus had a contingency plan in the event things went sideways. I need to know for sure though. I can't afford to be blindsided by anything right now. Especially the FBI."*

Agent Lewis: *"I have a solid insider there. I'll see what I can find out. Stay safe Kyl."*

Kyl: *"Don't I always? Thanks David."*

He half smiled but rolled his eyes as he turned to walk out. I hoped I was wrong about all this bit my gut told me I wasn't.

As the door closed, I heard Deedra clear her throat and when I turned, she was right there. Completely naked. She kissed my lips and whispered in my ear, *"You need a good release and I've never been fucked on an exotic car."*

She had my belt undone for I could even say anything. My body was so reactive to her that I was hard just because she was near me. She dropped to her knees and took me in her mouth. The way she looked up at me as she slid me down her throat, made me weak for her. She had the touch that set me on fire. Not just because she was beautiful or absolutely sexy. Not even because of our sexual connection. It was the everything about how electric it felt when she touched me and kissed me. There was a passion you couldn't put in words. I felt her loyalty in her desire, and it was a mutual desire.

I peeled off the rest of my clothes as she continued to suck my dick. I needed to feel her, and she was waiting for me to take her. She liked the aggressive nature of how I would take her. It made her almost cum just feeling the dominance of my presence over her. She whimpered and her legs began to shake as I pulled her to her feet by her hair. She wanted me so bad she told me "Take me now, I need you inside of me. I have to feel you."

I picked her up and lowered her down onto my rock-hard cock. She let out a moan as I penetrated her and instantly, she came. Her nails dug inside my back as her body went rigid. I could feel her almost convulse as I continued to drive deep inside of her. I lowered onto the good of the Viper, putting her legs over my shoulders I drove deeper into her.

She wanted to scream but nothing came out, her eyes rolled back, and her soul exited her body temporarily as she let out a pleasure driven moan that I'm certain could've been her last.

At least forty-five minutes had passed, and she was barely conscious by the looks of her. I was exhausted but it felt so good. She'd wrapped her legs around me so I couldn't get away. The way she was looking at me, I knew she was mine and I wanted to tell her so. But before I could say anything, she started speaking.

Deedra: *"I'm not going to wait anymore. I don't need to, and I* understand what you've been through, and I see you. I'm never going to want to be anywhere but at your side. Kyl, I'm in love with you. I love you."

And just like that, everything I felt was right there. She'd said it all before I could. For the first time in years, I didn't feel guilty about having feelings.

Kyl: *"I love you too, Deedra. I want you at my side forever."*

She pulled herself to me and began to cry. Life felt right for the first time in a long time, aside from all that had occurred, and all the bullshit that had filled our lives recently. I needed this; I needed us. This was the ray of hope I had needed to keep going. If this woman could love me through all of this, she was everything I could ever need. My heart felt full finally.

We stayed curled up together for awhile. She didn't say a word, but she touched me and ran her fingers across my body. Touched my face and kissed it more times than I could count as if to claim every spot she'd touched as hers. She gave me a peace that I'd not felt in so long. I had to end this war and focus on giving her the life she deserved.

I'd ignored my phone the last four times it had rang my pager had gone off multiple times too. No one knew where I was, so I'm sure they were starting to panic. I called Luka first.

Kyl: *"Luka, what's the word?"*

Luka: *"Man, don't scare me like that. I was about to fucking panic. Anyways, William is a mess. He's been to Marcus,' the office, the Deputy Mayor's place, and he's currently at some spot on the east end of town, nice place."*

Kyl: *"So he doesn't know what's going on. Hmm. Okay, well that's comforting. East end of town huh? Brick house, green tile roof?"*

Luka: *"Yes. How did you know?"*

Kyl: *"That's his long-time mistress. He fucked around and got her pregnant about 4 years ago. He's been paying to keep her quiet all this time but has still been fucking her."*

Luka: *"I didn't know he was such a piece of shit."*

Kyl: *"I did, it's his life though whether I agreed or not. I've always hated how he treated the wife and kids. But he was a necessary part of all things in the grand scheme. What did Taska report?"*

Luka: *"His plane is in the hanger, but an unregistered jet landed without prior notice and left headed for Brazil. They fueled, one person boarded, and they took off without checking in or clearance from the tower. What are you thinking boss?"*

Kyl: *"Get William and meet me at the quarry. We need to have a conversation and it needs to be in private. Have Taska and his team head over there and set a perimeter."*

I hung up and looked at Deedra. "It's time to get back to work, but when we get home, I'm going to touch your soul with my dick and my name will be your every breathe." She drew a sharp breath and I saw her body quiver. She smiled and blushed. I'd never seen her blush like that.

As I drove towards the quarry, so many things were going through my head. I had just told the first woman since Gia that I loved her. It was a lot. Not in a bad way, just bad timing. I had to focus on what had just transpired and how to deal with it.

As I pulled in, Taska signaled an all clear. I got out and took a breath. Things were going to go one of two ways here. I was going to tell Will what I had figured out and he was going to be genuinely shocked, or he was going to fake it and I'd have to kill him. I really liked Will, I hoped it didn't have to be the latter of the two. But, when it comes undone, all you can do is prepare for the flood.

Kyl: *"Hey Luka, just a fair warning, this could go south really quick."*

Luka: *"I know you well enough to know that if we're meeting at the quarry, it's a real possibility shit is about to be fucked up. Care to fill me in?"*

Just as I was about to answer him, William pulled in. He had Horatio with him. I'd expect nothing less. After all, he wasn't stupid. Meeting me at the quarry was the equivalent of the door to nowhere in the gang unit headquarters. William knew that.

William: *"I don't like that we're out here Kyl, it makes me uneasy. What's this all about?"*

Kyl: *"You sure you don't want to clear the air about anything before I get into this? Now is your chance."*

William: *"I'm not sure where this is going or what you're insinuating Kyl. But I don't have anything you don't already know. Marcus clearly kept me in the dark about a lot. So, if you think I have something to tell you, I don't. I just lost my brother and I'm trying to put all that together."*

He was telling the truth. I could always tell when Will was lying. He had an unconscious nervous tick when he lied. He'd look down and scratch his head with his right hand. I could bet a million dollars on it. He really didn't know.

Kyl: *"I believe you Will. Here's the thing, I want you to think back over the scene at the parking garage. There was one thing out of place, one thing that didn't belong."*

He looked at me puzzled. I could tell he was going over the scene in his head trying to figure out what he'd missed that I hadn't.

Kyl: *"You know who wore loafers Will?"*

William: *"Loafers? What the fuck are you talking about? My brother hated loafers; he'd never wear them."*

Kyl: *"That's exactly my point. The leg in the parking garage was wearing a loafer. Just like the Deputy Mayor wore. Marcus isn't dead, he's on his way to Columbia."*

Chapter 28

Loyalty is like laundry to some people. When you dirty it, just wash, rinse, and reuse.

The look on William's face told me that he genuinely had no idea what his brother Marcus had been up to. There was pain in his eyes, his body language spoke discomfort and betrayal. I knew this feeling well, so I easily recognized it. But I'd been fooled a lot lately by people I trusted and cared for. Maybe he was just a really good actor. Could I really afford to make any more mistakes in trust?

William: *"I don't understand.... Why would he do this? Wouldn't he tell me?"*

Kyl: *"I'm going to be honest Will, I'm having a really hard time with all of this."*

I handed him the bag I'd been holding. He looked at me puzzled but proceeded to open it. He let out a yelp as he quickly tossed the bag away and stumbled backwards, falling to the ground.

William: *"What the fuck Kyl!"*

I knelt so we'd be eye to eye.

Kyl: *"I just took the time to have a man skinned alive. I partook in most of the process of cutting his face off. Clearly, I'm not in a mental state that's all that safe for anyone around me. I'm going to give you one chance to tell me anything you know about what ever the fuck is going on. I'm already on the fence about just killing you right here to avoid having to see another betrayal down the road. Speak with intent and think carefully before you do."*

Out of my peripheral vision, I saw Horatio make a movement.

Before he could even take two steps Luka had drawn his gun. But it was Deedra who'd gotten to him first.

Deedra: *"I will remove you from this life if you take one more step."*

Horatio: *"Holy shit. Kyl man call them off. I just wanted to say I genuinely believe Will didn't know anything. My guys had been tracking the movement of some Columbians that came through town a few months back. We didn't follow up because they met with Marcus at the club. Just seemed like business."*

Luka: *"Knowing we're the only ones who deal with the Columbians, why didn't you say something?"*

Horatio: *"To be honest, I didn't think Marcus was keeping shit from you guys. I thought y'all were tight, ya know."*

Kyl: *"I don't know how I feel. Maybe just take both to the bottom of the quarry."*

William had tears streaming down his face. He crawled to his knees and put his face in the dirt.

William: *"Kyl, I've never been more humbled and absolutely terrified than I am right now. I don't know what Marcus was doing. I'm telling you the truth. I don't want our families to suffer any more. Horatio doesn't know anything either. Please...."*

I stood up and reached down to offer him my hand. He looked up at me and reached out. As I pulled him to his feet, I looked him directly in the eyes.

Kyl: *"My heart says you're telling me the truth, but my heart has been wrong a few times lately and the betrayal has run deep this last year. If I find out you're lying, I will kill your whole family in such a way no one will know a Stephon family ever existed."*

William: *"I give you my word, I'm telling you the truth. What the fuck am I supposed to tell the family. His wife and kids?"*

Kyl: *"You tell them he died in an explosion Will. Because when I find him, he is going to die."*

William: *"I understand. I didn't expect anything less. He's my brother but he betrayed us all. If given the opportunity, I will kill him myself. God as my witness, I will."*

I stared at him for a moment. I could feel him shaking as I held a tight grip on his hand. This was my turning point. From this point forward, the notion of mistrust or betrayal, and I won't ask questions. They will lose their life.

Kyl: *"Horatio, I still have an impending issue to deal with in the form of Mitch Kessler. I need up to date intel on what they've been doing, why they've been so quiet, and what kind of numbers they've got. William, dig into your brother's life through the last few months and see what you can find."*

I turned and walked off without waiting for a reply, I'd had enough of this conversation, and I needed to leave before I changed my mind. I wanted a drink and to bury my face between Deedra's tits.

As I drove back home it was starting to really sink in that the world, we all knew had shifted. It wasn't the same at all. It was becoming very clear to me that loyalty is like laundry to some people. When you dirty it, just wash, rinse, and reuse. For the second time in my life, I was in a place where I had to consider cleaning house. At this point, the body count didn't even matter. Stack them up and send a message to everyone around me. Then what? To be completely honest I was running out of bodies to stack. Now I had to question my relationship with the Columbians.

I'll be having a conversation with Oscar tomorrow. I was certain he had to be involved in getting Marcus out of the country. There weren't many Columbian cartels that had the resources he did and certainly wouldn't have the resources to fly in unannounced and pick up one unregistered person and just leave. Things were certainly going to get interesting.

The days of peace and easy living were gone. Life was about to turn completely inside out and upside down. Tomorrow the city would know its Mayor and Deputy Mayor had been murdered. What I didn't know was that I was about to be implicated in the whole thing.

Chapter 29

When you want to make an example of someone, shoot them in the face.

When I'd gotten home that night, I had kept my word and put Deedra into state of dickmatized she'd never forget. I slept so hard I didn't even hear my phone or pager going off the next morning. It wasn't until I heard the doorbell repeatedly and the beating on my door that I finally woke up. I slid into my pants and subconsciously grabbed my pistol.

I looked through the peephole to see a very agitated Luka pacing. I was certain this wasn't going to be a good start to my morning. I opened the door and let him in.

Luka: *"Fuck Kyl, were you dead or what? I've been calling and paging for a couple of hours."*

Kyl: *"Damn, I was exhausted bro. I needed sleep. What the fuck has you beating the door like a psycho female stalker?"*

Luka: *"The media is reporting on Marcus' death they're saying you're suspected of being involved. This is fucking bad Kyl; I can't get a hold of William either."*

I just kind of stood there. Had I really just let that son of bitch live and he turned right around and threw me under the bus? I almost laughed but before I could even say anything Deedra came sliding up behind me. "It's Will."

Kyl: *"This better be fucking good."*

William: *"Kyl I swear to all that is holy this wasn't me. Some rogue reporter has been poking around and spouted off without any evidence. The only thing out there is a picture of you leaving the hospital after the explosion. I'm headed to City Hall to do a news briefing. I'll fix this."*

Kyl: *"If you don't, City Hall will be your final resting place."*

William: *"That won't be necessary. I've got this."*

Kyl: *"Luka, put a Reaper there and find out who this reporter is too. I want details down to who their cousin's best friend is."*

He nodded like he always does when things are critical and was gone. I turned and looked at Deedra, I could tell she was waiting for my direction. I loved that about her, she knew when to be in a relationship and when to be a soldier. I felt a certain peace with her around. I was still on edge, but she made me feel like I didn't need to be. I had to protect this feeling; she had become what made me feel alive again.

Kyl: *"Set a meeting with the Horsemen and I want you to lay out the Kessler compound. It's time to get that train rolling and get this over with."*

Deedra: *"Where are you going?"*

Kyl: *"I have business."*

She looked as if she was going to say something and stopped before the first word came out. She sensed I wasn't going to argue, and she took her place in that moment.

I needed to go see a friend and I needed to clear my heart of some things. It's hard to think that anything could get more dangerous than it had been. But, when the eye of the public turns in your direction, it can bring with it other eyes and more implications. I was about to poke that eye out and finish this fucking war that had seemingly gotten sidetracked by a bunch of other bullshit. It was wild to think all this had transpired over my three idiot friends and the stupidity of the Kessler's to test me. I couldn't imagine anyone on the outside looking in trying to make sense of all this. It barely made sense to me.

As I was leaving, I wrapped my hand around Deedra's throat and pulled her to me. Kissing her deeply and passionately. "Later, I'll rearrange your insides and make you forget how to say anything but my name." I could feel her body quiver and almost go limp. The dazed look in her eyes made me smile as I told her I loved her and walked out the door.

As I drove across town, I started thinking about what it would mean to finish this. Times were changing, loyalty wasn't what it once was, and technology was growing at an exponential rate. What would all that mean for an old school raised crime family leader. How much longer was I going to get away with just killing people at will, and how much longer could I push the drug trade before it finally caught up to me. I really didn't even like pushing dope anymore. I had enough money for three lifetimes, why keep this up? I could see Devin and Pratt fading off into the sunset with their families and doing just fine. But what about Luka, Taska, and the Reapers? What life outside of this would make them happy? Could they even be happy living a normal life? I felt I had a responsibility to them. The fact was, if I didn't get away from this, I was going to lose myself in it completely. There was no guarantee after all this that life would ever be as we knew it. I had no doubt the Feds were investigating everything from the cartel hit to the gang elimination. Not to mention, what if Marcus' ace in the hole had been selling us all out to the Feds? At this point I couldn't discount anything as a possibility. It was stressful and I hate being stressed. It makes my bad side come out.

I spotted the SUV I was looking for as I pulled into the parking lot. This wasn't going to be a meeting anyone particularly wanted but was absolutely necessary to right the balance of things.

Kyl: *"I know I said I wouldn't ask this of you but in light of everything, I don't see any other way here."*

Driver: *"When I agreed to meet you out here, I knew what type of conversation we were going to be having. To be completely honest, I was going to make the call to you after what I just found. You just beat me to the punch. This has to happen and all I'm asking is that you let me do it my way."*

Kyl: *"Fair enough, I need it done by the end of the week. You got something else for me?"*

As he handed me the envelope, it hadn't occurred to me that whatever I was about to find in here would completely unravel everything I thought I knew about two people in my life and the depth of just how sick and fucked up they really were.

Driver: *"I'm warning you; you're going to want to go nuclear. But you have my word I'll take care of this."*

Now my heart was starting to race. What was in here and why was it going to have such a profound effect on me? I took a deep breath and slid the information out of the envelope. I was immediately sick to my stomach and the rage started to boil immediately. How the fuck could they do this? I opened my door and got out. I needed to walk around for a minute, catch my bearings, and not lose my shit in the process.

Kyl: *"Tell me this isn't fucking real?"*

Driver: *"It's fucking real. Tech pulled it straight off his hard drive. He tried to delete it, but we were able to restore it all. It's both of them Kyl, they've been doing it for a while. Sick fucks."*

Kyl: *"You're sure on that address?"*

Driver: *"One hundred percent, I've got Bird Dog watching him."*

Kyl: *"You make it fucking hurt. You understand me?"*

I slammed my door and white smoked the tires as I drove away. I was angry, no I was furious. Completely beside myself at what I had just seen, and I couldn't unsee it. How is it possible that these two had been doing this for so long? Even more importantly, how? How the fuck do you do that to your own flesh and blood. Two men I thought I had known so well were just a couple of backstabbing, lying, sick pieces of shit.

I pulled over abruptly. I had to clear my head, and I needed to look at the rest of what was in the envelope. I pushed the pictures aside and looked at the rest of the documents. This reporter had been taking payments from a shell company.

That shell company was attached to a Trust that was in turn fed by an LLC. That LLC was licensed to one Mitch Kessler as the primary and Marcus Stephon and the secondary. Son of bitch, he'd been working with them all along. At this point I wasn't that shocked. I was still reeling from the fact that both Marcus and William were pedophiles and had been selling pictures of their own daughters. How does any man, let alone a father do that? I still wanted to throw up. I wasn't in the mood to take any of the next steps that needed to be taken in any rational manner. In fact, I was going to take out my aggression on this lying reporter.

I pulled into the neighborhood and immediately knew what he'd been spending the money he got from Marcus on. These were half million-dollar homes. Certainly not what you'd be able to afford on a news reporters' salary. He hadn't even tried to hide the money. When I rounded the corner, I saw Bird Dog's undercover car. I pulled up alongside.

Bird Dog: *"I take it I should go get a sandwich or something huh."*

Kyl: *"This won't take long but sure, take a break. Grab a bite to eat. Not like he'll be going anywhere."*

He smirked and drove off. Bird Dog was an old school veteran beat cop and later a violent crimes detective. He'd seen more than his fair share of fucked up. He'd once told me that the only real justice was street justice. When a cop tells you that, it means he's seen the system get it wrong one too many times.

I parked in front of the house and grabbed the envelope as I got out. I wanted whoever found him to know he been a lying piece of shit. They could put that on the news. I stuffed the envelope in my back pocket and double checked that there was a round chambered. I rang the doorbell, took a deep breath, and waited.

To my surprise, the door opened probably less than a minute after I'd rung. As the door swung open, it was clear he'd been expecting someone else. His jaw dropped and before he could even say anything I raised my pistol and shot him directly in the face.

As his body hit the entryway floor, I fired three more times into his face and once in the chest. Just for good measure of course. I reached down and laid the envelope on his stomach and then walked back to my car. I had no doubt the whole neighborhood had heard every thunderous boom. I didn't care. Fuck him and fuck them too. When you want to make an example of someone, shoot them in the face. Say something, I dare you.

Chapter 30

A man should die for those he loves, doing what he loves.

As I drove away, I noticed that not a single person had come outside. I was the only who had a Viper like this, so it was no mystery who had just rolled up and executed the man in that house. I couldn't even tell him name. I didn't really care to know it. I suspected that anyone who had heard or even seen what had just happened, wouldn't be saying anything to anyone. At this point I didn't honestly care. Everyone else had come for me, fuck it, bring it on.

I made my way across town listening to Linkin Park. It was almost ironic that the song was called "In the end." These guys make great music, the whole album was good. I needed the mental distraction, and this helped. I was still jamming out hard as I turned down the road leading to the Mardechi compound. It looked as though Charlo had more than tripled the guard since Marcus had taken his daughter. Not a bad move at all considering all things of recent.

I approached the gate and was met by one of Charlo's long-time captains, Gino.

Gino: *"Kyl, you know I have to ask with the shit that happened. You come in peace or with other business?"*

Kyl: *"I'm here in peace to see my old friend and check on the family. The Mardechi family is my family, Gino."*

Gino: *"I meant no disrespect Kyl...Let me call the house."*

He was nervous and I could see him shaking in fear. You could almost always see the fear on a man no matter how hard they tried to hide it. Gino had been there the night we executed the two families.

He'd seen what I was capable of. That was enough to make any man question his bravery.

Gino: *"The boss welcomes you up to the house."*

I gave him the side eye and drove through the gate. I was low on patience of late and had to really put forth the effort not to be a raging asshole to everyone.

Charlo was waiting for me on the porch. My poor lifelong friend had seemingly aged more since all this had happened. He was a good man, a man who wasn't cut out for this life but had played the part well for so many years until I had pushed him to step back from the life. I couldn't imagine losing a child or the fear of what might happen to your child. How helpless it must've felt.

Charlo: *"Kyl...."*

Kyl: *"Don't. You owe me nothing and we're fine Charlo. Even if you had killed Diamond, I'd have forgiven you knowing what had happened."*

He nearly collapsed against me and began to sob. I just stood there and let him get it out. It's not often a man can break down. We're expected to be the pillars of our family and the strength of our business and for our loved ones. While I didn't know his exact pain, I understood pain. He'd held me the same way when I broke down over Gia's death.

He stood back and dried his eyes.

Charlo: *"My fucking daughter Kyl, Marcus took my fucking daughter. Fuck him, I'm glad he's dead and I'll piss on his grave. If Will feels disrespected, I'll fight him for honor."*

Kyl: *"Marcus isn't dead. He swapped places with the deputy mayor and skipped the country with the Columbians."*

He stood there with a blank stare for a minute before it turned to sheer anger.

Charlo: *"Are you fucking shitting me? That mother fucker is alive? Tell me how to fucking find him! I'll kill that mother fucker!"*

Kyl: *"I don't know where he is yet. His death sentence is set Charlo. William too. I have evidence they were both pedophiles. Both were selling pictures of their daughters. That's part of why I'm here Charlo."*

His eyes went wide and filled with tears and anger.

Charlo: *"Say it ain't so! You aren't telling me…You aren't saying that my Lucy was a part of that are you? Kyl, brother, please tell me it ain't so."*

Kyl: *"I'm sorry Charlo. She was a part of it too. The nights she stayed over there, ya know. He was taking pictures of her."*

The anguish on his face made my heart hurt and my gut twist in ways I hadn't felt before. He shook and then let out a soul wrenching scream and slammed his fist into the side of the house. I couldn't even begin to imagine what he was feeling.

Kyl: *"I thought you should know. I'm sorry."*

Charlo: *"You're going to kill them both right? You're going to make them pay, aren't you?"*

Kyl: *"It's already in motion and I'll scour the world to find Marcus. I promise you. But I need you to do something for me. I need you to take the family and leave the country, Charlo. You go and you don't come back until this is over."*

Charlo: *"Kyl…You need my help. I'm not bailing on you when you're about to take on Kessler. They have a fucking army."*

Kyl: *"This is my war Charlo. You're going to leave and when it's over, you're going to come back and you're going to out your bid in as the new mayor. You do as I tell you; do you understand? This city is going to be yours now. Fix it from what we made it."*

Charlo: *"Kyl, why are you talking like you're not going to be here? You're not going anywhere, right?"*

Kyl: *"I'm tired Charlo. I don't want to do this anymore. I'm going to war with the Kessler's to serve retribution and then I'm going after Marcus. The drug trade, the guns, all of it has always seemed like a victimless crime to me. But it's really not. I told myself that to justify my actions. Look at what it's done to all these people. Look how many have died or have been hurt by all of this. We finish this war and what was the cost? Peace came at the price of thousands of lives and just as many families left without their loved ones.*

I never wanted any of this. Not like this. It must end and that means I have to go. Dead or alive."

He just stood there staring at me. Completely dumbfounded and without a word. It was a lot to process and to be transparent, most of it had been on my mind but this was the first time I was speaking it aloud.

Charlo: *"I don't know what to say. My father said the greatest of men couldn't ever walk away from this life. Yet here you are ready to give your life to end it either way. You truly are the greatest Mafia Don that I've ever seen. You came to say goodbye, didn't you?"*

Kyl: *"I have to, I don't know that I'm ever going to get another chance. I have to speak my peace and go on my path from here. You do as I tell you. Go inside and pack your family up and go. Be gone tonight."*

He had tears rolling down his cheeks as he hugged me one last time.

Charlo: *"I love you brother; you're always going to be family. Fight hard, live fiercely, and if you must die, die with honor."*

Kyl: *"I love you too family. With honor it is."*

My heart was heavy as I walked away knowing I may never see the Mardechi family again. That this may be the last visit to her grave I may ever make. The weight of all of this had become so much.

I was strong and resilient but even at this point I felt weak in the knees.

I drove back down the cemetery road knowing I'd likely never be here again. I gathered myself, stepped out of the car, and headed to her grave site. As I neared it, a giant crow landed on her headstone. In some belief systems, the appearance of a crow is thought to be a message from the spiritual realm. Often it was interpreted as a sign that you are being called to pay attention to something important, or that you are being guided in some way. Either way, it gave me chills and even if purely a coincidence, I couldn't ignore the potential for it being a message. I just wish I knew what the message was. I knelt there and had a conversation with Gia as the crow watched silently. Eerie for sure.

The day was burning away, and I needed to meet with my Horsemen. It was a meeting I'd thought over thoroughly and I was confident in my decisions. I'm not certain how well received it would be, but I had to give it a shot. There were things I'd needed to accept for quite some time. They say all good things come to an end but really, all things come to an end, not just the good ones. The reality of it is, when you hold onto to something for too long, that ending could become extremely bad.

Unfortunately for me and everyone around me, I'd held on too long, and it had already begun to turn bad. This was my opportunity to change that course for some of those people and ultimately, myself.

I called Deedra and had her set out meeting at Natoli's. I felt like a good meal was in order and it could potentially be the last time I was able to dine there. Not that I was confident we'd overcome whatever Mitch Kessler had waiting for us, but the possibility was always there.

What I had to my advantage was that no one really knew the true number of Reapers that kept watch over the family. To anyone outside it appeared that there was only a dozen or so on hand. The true collection of them was in the hundreds. I'd spent years implanting them amongst the social construct around us. They train regularly but we're store owners, businessman, and even nine to five blue collar workers. Because of how they operated, no one could ever tell you one from the other. I rotated their ranks constantly so that everyone had their chance to serve the family. Nearly all of them were former assassins, guerilla soldiers, prior special forces, or mercenaries from around the world. All of them very dangerous and all extremely loyal to this family. All of them were about to be activated for duty to serve in this coming war.

I saw Luka and Taska when I was pulling in. They were wrestling around which was comical. Luka was no slouch in strength and skill, but Taska was over twice his size. It reminded me of a Chihuahua taking on the Great Pyrenees. I smiled to see them getting to enjoy life like it should be.

Kyl: *"Look at you too out here like a couple of high-school heathens in the parking lot."*

Luka: *"Hey boss, just trying to show this big lug that size and strength aren't always best."*

Taska: *"You couldn't even move me piss ant!"*

Luka: *"Ya but look at you panting like a dog over there!"*

They both erupted in laughter. I chuckled and headed for the door.

Most of the Natoli family were back in Italy right now. One of their founding family members had passed away, so everything was being run by their most trusted family friends and employees. They kept things in top shape and the food was as good as always. I was looking forward to that good meal.

We sat and told stories, laughed, picked on each other, and for the first time in a long time, we were just a family enjoying each other's time together. I wish it could just stay this way. I knew the reality was it never would though. I had to turn our time here into a serious conversation. I had laid out my future and the futures of Luka and the rest. We'd be growing old together one day but not where we were now.

Kyl: *"This has been great guys. Seeing us all here after all we've been through. It breaks my heart that not everyone is here, but all we can do is honor them and remember them as the warriors they were. We have some things we need to plan out, but first, I want to talk about a few things. I've decided that it's time for some of you to take your leave and go off into the sunset. More specifically, Devin, Pratt, you guys have done far more than I could've ever expected or asked. I brought you back from retirement and because of that, one of our brothers lost his life. I can't in good faith ask you to go any further than this with me. I want you to go home and pack up the family and leave for a nice long vacation."*

It was quiet, and everyone just sort of stared at me.

Pratt: *"You're serious about that? Boss we're at war."*

Kyl: *"Pratt, I know what's happening in your home. It's time you got out. You have a responsibility to be there."*

He looked almost sheepish and probably wondered how I'd found out. I wasn't as disconnected as most thought I was. I still had eyes and ears and I paid attention.

Pratt: *"Damn, nothing gets past you huh. Ya, the wife's prego, we're going to have a baby in about 5 months. A boy. I don't want to walk away from this, from you all, but I know my family would be happy if I did. I do owe it to them. If you're certain this is what you want, I'll take my leave boss."*

Kyl: *"I'm certain. I love all of you and I'm indebted to you for a lifetime. Go be with your families."*

Devin: *"I respect that and congratulations brother. However, I'm not in the same place and respectfully, sir, I'm not going anywhere. I'm going to see this through and then I'll take my leave. A man should die for those he loves, doing what he loves."*

I was tempted to tell him my orders stood, and he needed to go. Who was I to tell a man he couldn't do what he loved.

Kyl: *"You're sure that's what you want? You don't owe this family or me anything more. You are free to go."*

Devin: *"I'm not going anywhere."*

Kyl: *"Okay then, Luka and Taska I know you're in. Deedra, you can sit this out and no one will think any type of way about you."*

Deedra: *"Respectfully, fuck you. We had this talk, I'm at your side. Especially when it comes to the Kessler family."*

Everyone just looked at her, I think they were a little shocked when she spoke to me like that. I smiled and began to laugh, which brought on laughter from the whole group.

Luka: *"I'm starting think it's her we need to worry about taking out Kyl. Better watch yourself."*

Deedra: *"I'll whoop your ass too!"*

Everyone was laughing and having such a good time. The food was amazing as always and our drinks stayed full. It was good to see them smiling and relaxing. It felt forever since we'd been this relaxed. When this is all over, I think we all need a long vacation away from here, has to be somewhere tropical.

I was lost in the laughter and daydreaming that I hadn't noticed my phone had kept ringing. It was Horatio and chances are, this wasn't going to be a good call. *"Talk to me."*

Horatio: *"I need you at the West End ASAP and keep your head on a swivel."*

Kyl: *"On my way."*

Well, it was good while it lasted.

Kyl: *"Play times over. I just got a call from Horatio to get to the West End. He also gave a warning to be on alert. Let's roll."*

It was a very sobering thing when you're told to watch your ass like that. Looks like it's time to take this even more seriously. Someone was dead, and we were about to find out who.

Chapter 31

Proof it doesn't matter what side you're on.
No one was safe.

They say dead men tell no tales. The interesting thing about dead men is they in fact have a lot to say. If you look closely and listen carefully, they will tell you exactly who killed them. When you spend your lifetime experiencing murder and death, you get a deeper understanding of not only how to kill people, but how to read those who have been killed. Death's whisper is much more than a few words, it's a story. It was obvious with what just happened that Death and I needed to have a conversation. It was also clear I was going to have to start writing a lot more stories for Death to tell.

As soon as I pulled into the lot, my heart sank. I knew immediately who had met their demise and it was more than just a loss, it was a huge wrench in the process of everything. Someone knew exactly what I was after and just how much this would trip everything up. I parked and just sat there staring at that car. A lifetime of dreams and wishes granted just to end up being all extinguished in that dream reality. Yet another life lost at the cost of being involved with me. It didn't matter who you were. That shit bothers you at some point.

This had been the deadliest year for those around me. This was yet another example of that.

I sat there in thought staring at that car. My brain flashed back to the day I'd last seen him. How happy he'd been. I had to wonder if had he'd had the chance to realize he was dying in his dream car.

The knock on my window brought me back to reality. It was Horatio, he had a grim look on his face. I knew this wasn't good for any of us and he knew it too.

Horatio: *"Hey boss, this is going to draw some heat on us at some point. I'm going to report this as a John Doe, and I already had the car back filed as stolen. That also justifies you being here if anyone sees or is watching. I know you have a keen eye for this shit so I could really use your input."*

Kyl: *"Good call. Ya, I'll take a look. I suppose there's no working cameras nearby and I'm going to guess not one of the local businesses has outside cameras either."*

Horatio: *"You'd be correct. It's a literal dead zone. He clearly didn't know where he was and I'm going to guess he trusted who he was meeting."*

I walked up to the car and immediately knew this had been a hit. After years of being in the crime family and now being the head of the family, I knew a hit when I saw one. I'd ordered many such the same as this one.

Kyl: *"There were two people. Someone had his attention over here. There are smudge marks on the dirty mirror. They had gloves on, but the point had been to block the mirror. The second person approached from somewhere back here. The trajectory of the shot and the placement is purely professional to an execution hit. It's a tactic hit teams use for catching their target off guard. He told me he had a contact deep in the Feds he was going to contact. This was a Fed hit. They knew he'd gone rogue and rather than take a chance at him getting a message out to me, they just killed him."*

Horatio stared at me with a questioning look and a bit of confusion.

Horatio: *"How do you know this?"*

Kyl: *"You don't get where I am without having crossed paths with a few Feds before. There's a half dozen very well-off retired Feds out there that taught me a lot for a guarantee of a good life outside of their career. This was a hit. There's something they didn't want us to know, and they made sure we didn't find out."*

Horatio: *"So what now?"*

Kyl: *"We handle things as planned. We're all in at this point. We see this through."*

I turned and walked away, my anger welling up and the pain of another life lost weighing on me. Proof it doesn't matter what side you're on. No one is safe. You were a good man. Rest in peace Agent David Lewis.

Luka: *"You alright boss?"*

Kyl: *"It was Agent Lewis. It was a hit."*

Luka: *"Shit, what are dealing with here?"*

Kyl: *"It looks like a Fed hit. I'm not sure what we're up against but it's too late to turn back. We move forward immediately on Mitch Kessler. It's time to end this."*

Deedra: *"You sure it was a Fed hit? How do you know that? What did you see?"*

Kyl: *"Because I said so. I know what I saw back there and it's all the makings of Government hit."*

She looked as if she might continue to question me but decided to stop. I was annoyed when she questioned my analysis of the situation. Why the fuck did it even matter to her?

Kyl: *"We stick to the plan. How long until we're able to go mobile?"*

Devin: *"Twenty-four hours max. I'd like to be more prepared, but I can make it work."*

Kyl: *"Do it. Taska, I need you to call on our explosive techs that you pulled in before. You know what do right?"*

Taska: *"I got it covered boss."*

Kyl: *"Luka and Deedra, you're with me. Let's go pay some attention to the rest of the details."*

The gears of war had been set into motion and the war machine was fired up and ready to go. What would transpire in the next twenty-four hours would set this city on its side. Little did I know, those same twenty-four hours were about to change my life as I'd know it, forever. I couldn't help feeling that I'd done all this and come this far for nothing. The problem is, no crime family was ever built on the idea of a happy ending. It was always about money and power. In the beginning, that's all that had mattered to me.

Family had lost its appeal after everything that had happened. Through the years though, I'd grown to love and respect all those around me and had taken to them as family. It was my fault that those I loved had lost their lives. My complacency had made me blind to the fact that we weren't invincible. That at any given moment we could all be dead.

It was only due to my constant obsession with continuous training for my men that we'd been able to count on more than just luck. So, I hadn't gotten it all wrong. Wrong enough to get a dozen people close to me killed.

No matter how hard I was on myself or how much of the blame I felt I needed to take, the truth was, those who chose to stand against me were ultimately responsible for the state of all things currently. Historically, all who had ever crossed me ended up dead. This was no different.

Driving back to the Penthouse, I knew something was off. I didn't know exactly what, but I knew it was about to show itself. It was only a matter of time before it all came to light. The world is a lot smaller than you think, remember I said that. There was no running or hiding at this moment. I'd accepted my conviction to end this war. We were all the way in with no way out.

Chapter 32

May your last breath feel like all the pain you've caused.

You never know the true value of someone until they're gone. In the same regard, you never truly see how much peace someone being gone can bring.

No one would've ever thought we'd have been killers when we were younger. Many a man lost their lives thinking we didn't have what it took to take a life. The look in the eyes of a dying man as he realized he'd underestimated you was indescribable unless you'd seen it. The rumors swirled as word got out that a couple of kids leading a small army of killers had taken out two crime families including one that was his own family. I shot a couple people in the face before it finally sank in that I wasn't to be played with. Luka's level of violence became so scary it was legendary before he ever hit twenty years old. He killed on principal. There didn't have to be a good reason. It was because of that, people learned very quickly that they'd lose their lives for as little as a sideways look. When the Reapers came to be, that fear spread even more quickly. It was crazy how a few years of peace had emboldened so many to try and stand against me.

It was as if I'd made the mistake of not killing or having someone killed regularly just to make a point. I suppose this was why kings of old held frequent public executions. It kept it fresh on the minds of those in his kingdom that death was simply a mistake away. The kingdom was about to be reminded and those who questioned the order of things were all about to be put on notice.

There's a point where you hurt someone so badly that it changes them all the way to their core. Who they are what they're capable of is completely rewritten. It's quite possible that I put another checkmark on my card to hell with this one. But realistically, all I did was provide the opportunity and plant the seed that would grow into a tree of retribution. This wasn't about revenge. It was about freedom.

I sat down in the chair behind the desk. It was without a doubt the most comfortable office chair I'd ever sat in. It was the throne of comfort fit for a king. Marcus knew no limits on expensive and plush items of any sort. The extra income he had generated for years off the backs of my ventures could be seen in everything he touched. I could almost lean back and just go to sleep. That is if there weren't such pressing issues at hand. I didn't even have to be here for this, I simply wanted to be. I wanted to see this with my own eyes.

Besides, if it was going to get me closer to hell, I might as well enjoy it all.

I looked across the room at the other two. One seated and composed, the other pacing with a deteriorating sense of patience. I couldn't cast blame in this moment, nor would I even try to understand the feelings that had been festering for so many years. You couldn't find words that would ever suffice as comforting. I knew no matter what I said, it would change nothing. That's why we were here though.

After what felt like an eternity of waiting, the door finally opened, and a smiling William came in with a full-on swagger in his walk like he was king of the world.

William: *"I think you're in my chair there Kyl. That is the mayor's desk and I'm to be sworn in tomorrow. You know what, you enjoy it for a few. I'll have plenty of time in that seat."*

His smile faded as he realized I wasn't smiling, nor had I found anything he was saying cute or comical. He noticed we weren't alone either.

William: *"Horatio, I hadn't expected you to be here. Tisha? Pumpkin, what are you doing here? Kyl, what's this all about."*

She didn't flinch. She didn't say a word. She didn't even blink. She just stood there. I kept my composure and said nothing as well.

Horatio: *"William Stephon. I trusted you and followed you loyally for nearly a decade. I looked up to you as a leader. A mentor. Even though we made concessions for the crime families in this town, we kept an order to it that made me proud to wear this badge and work under your command. But now, I'm disgusted by the thought of it. After a thorough search and investigation, I have the truth about what you and your brother really are. You're fucking sick. I'm charging you with child abuse, child pornography, and the sale of child pornography. There will be no trial. No judge to make a decision. Today, we are here as your judge and jury. I find you guilty of all charges."*

William: *"You don't understand. He made me do it. This was his thing, not mine. I was scared of him! Pumpkin, Tisha, I'm so sorry baby. I never wanted any of this."*

She crossed the room and stood in front of her father. She wasn't shaking like I'd thought she would. She was calm. It was eerie how calm she was.

Tisha: *"You and Uncle Marcus have molested and sexually abused me my whole life. My pictures were sold to the world. I will never truly know peace because my body and the horrible things the two of you did to me are memorialized in pictures and films that are hidden away with who knows how many hundreds of people. You were supposed to protect me and love me."*

Before he could even respond his face took on a look of pure fear and sheer horror as he realized what was about to happen. He opened his mouth to speak and not a single word made it past his lips as she raised her arm and shot the man who had failed to be a father and had been nothing more than her abuser. She'd shot him in the mouth to stop any more lies from coming out. As he crumpled to the floor, she stood over him as he choked on his blood and watched as he struggled. She raised the gun and uttered the words "*May your last breath feel like all the pain you've caused.*" Then fired another shot right between his eyes. His lifeless body slumped to the floor, and it was over. She was finally free.

I'd only just learned the full truth of all this on the way over to the office. Her mother had known it was happening and never did anything to stop or prevent it. Tisha had also put a bullet in her mother's head. Horatio was going to spin it as a murder suicide.

The official report would notate the reason, but the case would be sealed, and all the details of the abuse locked away. I'd spoken to Charlo, and he'd agreed to take her in. He'd been like a father should've been to her and his daughter was her best friend. She could get away finally and start to heal.

With that done, it was time to prepare for war. The last stand against the only remaining rival family in this town. This wasn't like the previous cleansing of families. He knew we were coming, and he was going to be more than ready for us. I was either going to strike them down or be struck down. History would tell a story of my success or my defeat. I looked out over the city one last time then got in my car and headed to prepare to lead my army into battle.

Chapter 33

Death stood with us and against us, yet we marched on.

Driving across town knowing I was about to lead every person I loved and considered family into war wasn't easy on the mind nor on the soul. All I could do was embrace it and mentally prepare myself for what was to come. I popped my Skid Row CD out of the player and replaced it with Rage Against the Machine, Bulls on Parade, and cranked it up. I dropped a gear and lit the tires. My level of "fuck it" was maxed out and I wasn't going to back down now.

I had barely been at my house for months. I loved my neighborhood and my neighbors. They were all good people and after the shit show my former friends had caused, I felt it best I stay away as much as possible to keep the neighborhood safe.

I pulled into the driveway and sat there for a moment looking around. This urban lifestyle had really been all I had ever wanted. As lame as it sounds, I liked working in the yard and competing with the other neighbors for the best-looking yard. The simple pleasures of life. I could've walked away at any given point and yet I chose to stay in the life.

Here's what's really stupid about this all, how many mobsters have you ever heard of successfully retiring and living out a normal quiet life? This lifestyle was more addictive than any drug I'd ever sold. I was only just now realizing it as I watched the people in my quiet little neighborhood come and go. I only came here so I could get into the safe. Gia had given me a platinum gold chain and cross that she said would always protect me. I felt like I was going to need it today.

When I got out of the car, I noticed my neighbor Joe. He'd been sitting on the porch, likely watching me sit here like a weirdo. Joe had been a Navy Seal and had worked as a private contractor for years after his service. He was a man of many skills and tons of experiences. It didn't surprise me he had something to say at that moment.

Joe: *"I know the look of a man prepared to go to war. I'd say you were that man. Good to see you, Kyl. Anything I can do for you?"*

Kyl: *"Too smart for your own good Joe. I'm good, just needed to collect my thoughts for a moment."*

Joe: *"You know, we all know who and what you are. It's been very much appreciated the respect you showed in keeping your distance. You're a man of respect and honor Kyl. No matter what you do. Always remember that."*

Kyl: *"Thanks Joe, I appreciate that. I wish things were different today, but they're not."*

Joe: *"We all make choices in life that make us who we are. The key is to make enough good choices to counter the bad ones. You're a good man Kyl, you've done a lot of good for this city. I hope there's peace at the end of this next march. You've had enough battles my friend. It's time to end the war. I think you know that though."*

Kyl: *"I'll say it again, too smart for your own good Joe. Wise words though, I intend to do just that. End this war. Do me a favor and keep an eye on the place for me."*

He nodded and shook my hand. It's nice to have a good neighbor and friend. Not so great a feeling knowing you may never see them again. Reality was starting to set in. I'd been more than lucky more than a few times in this life. If I had nine lives, I was surely in debt at this point and owed a few more than I'd had to give. I think the balance was kept because of how many lives I'd offered up for Death take into the next life. He'd had his eye on me for a while though. I felt it more and more every time I drew too close to that line. Not yet my friend, I still had a few things to do.

I'd made all the preparations necessary for a quick escape and several back-up plans. You couldn't ever count on things like this going as planned. No matter how much time you'd put into preparing. Especially when your foe knew you were coming.

I stopped by the warehouse close to downtown so I could switch cars. The Viper wasn't going to be a good choice for this next part. It was a beautiful machine, but I needed something more war ready right now. I had bought this Ford Excursion and had it reworked with bullet proof glass and armored body. The motor made several hundred more horsepower than stock which made it ideal for the situation we were about to enter. I had another little surprise for them too, it was definitely going to blow them away.

If you didn't have a plan B, C, D, E, and F you weren't ready for whatever was to come. I wasn't nervous about dealing with Kessler, I just couldn't dismiss the feeling of something amiss. It had been bothering me since Agent Lewis' death. I was missing something, but I couldn't put my finger on it. I guess I'd figure it out if it came up. Not how I liked to operate but it was too late to back up or back out now. We'd know soon enough.

The last time I had gone through this, I'd taken down two families with just over fifty men. This wasn't the same scenario and from what I was being told, Kessler had around two hundred and twenty soldiers he'd recruited. I'm not sure how he managed to get so many people at this point with all the gangs having been eliminated and the cartel out of the picture.

Even with having pulled in all the Reapers and my whole crew, we were standing at around one hundred and twenty-five men total. I wasn't concerned by the numbers, whoever he'd pulled in wouldn't be as skilled as my Reapers or likely even my crew. That's not being cocky, I just was just that confident in my soldiers.

I pulled into the abandoned warehouse district and drove to where the mass of everyone was gathering. This is where we kept the bulk of our heavy arms, explosives, and armor. There was an old underground bunker that was never mapped so only a few people even knew it ever existed. It had been perfect for the purpose it had served all these years.

I had a feeling that we'd be up against a new heavily fortified compound with plenty of sniper positions. Within the Reapers, I had roughly a dozen military trained snipers from all over the world. There wasn't going to be an advantage for them like they were thinking. We had thoroughly scouted the area and had set up vantage points from every angle that they could use against us. This was going to be a war of skill and intelligence versus pure force.

It hadn't really set in yet that in the middle of all this, I'd fallen in love with Deedra and no matter what I said, she was insistent upon standing with me through all of this. To think, I'd finally learned to let go of Gia so that I could move on, and the woman who brought me new peace and love could potentially fall at my side in all of this. It made my heart heavy. It made my chest feel like it was weighed down, and I couldn't breathe right. If I lost her in this, I'd never forgive myself. I had to protect her at all costs. Even if that meant giving my life for hers.

I stood there looking out at all these men, these warriors ready to go to war for me. For this family. I'd given plenty of speeches over the years, there just wasn't one that could possibly equate to anything sufficient in this moment. I simply said "We all know our place and our role. Don't die."

And with that, the war machine was on the move. There was no turning back. No changing my mind. Death stood with us and against us, yet we marched on.

Chapter 34

The blood will stain more than the ground on this day.

It had been eerily quiet amongst us. Deedra held my hand in hers. She sat there looking at it like there was something she was expecting to see. She's held whatever emotions she'd been feeling inside without showing anything but a stone-cold stare. I reached up to touch her face and she turned towards me. The look in her eyes said so much, it pulled at my heart.

Kyl: *"I love you; it's going to be okay. We've got this."*

She immediately melted and that stone cold look turned into tears as she buried her face into my shoulder.

Deedra: *"Fuck you, Kyl. Dammit. I was trying to keep my shit together. I love you too. Don't you dare fucking die today. I've never felt the way I feel with you. I feel you in every breath and I'm never complete when you're not near me. I miss you when you're in the next room. I want to crawl inside of you when I'm close so I can be closer. You make me who I want to be."*

I was a little taken back. I didn't know she felt like I hadn't been able to explain. She had hit it perfectly. This woman. God, I don't know if we're good or not, but if I can ask just one thing from you, please protect this woman.

Kyl: *"You're everything to me, I thought I'd never feel my heart again. Now, it beats every beat for you. I breathe you in and exhale us. Life has a real meaning with you as a part of me."*

She pressed her forehead against mine and kissed me like it was the last kiss we'd ever feel together.

The people in this truck were my life. Every one of them loved as much as I could ever love anyone. Luka, Taska, Devin, and now Deedra. I felt like a broken record in my own head but in light of everything lately, I think I've been reflecting on the things we often take for granted until they're either gone or we're at risk of losing them. I was glad Pratt had taken his leave. I'm grateful for Devin being here but I do wish he'd have done the same. He's given so much, so many times for me and this family. He will never want anything after this is over. I'd make sure of it.

According to the scouts and Reaper snipers, they're fortified the Kessler compound with everything from razor wire to flood lights, and even mini towers to overlook the grounds.

The compound itself sat on around ten acres. It wasn't going to be a stroll in the park to get to the house itself. But, when you create chaos, you create opportunity. That's exactly what was about to happen.

Fireworks make for a great distraction as much as smoke does. I'd acquired around 50 military M18 smoke grenades. Each one lasted a little over a minute. Combined with the commercial grade artillery shell fireworks, they were going to be quite confused about what was happening. This would give me ample opportunity to get the semi surprise through the gates and as close to the house as possible. My Trojan horse.

It looked like something out of Mad Max. I was quite proud of the work they'd done getting it prepared. As we approached the rendezvous point, the titan pulled out and began its acceleration towards the compound. It was going to require a speed of nearly eighty miles per hour to bust through those heavy iron gates.

I glanced at my watch and gave the next set of signals. Lights were starting to go out as the snipers went to work. The smoke and fireworks started, followed by the explosions one after the other breaching the walls around the compound. They knew we were coming now.

Luka called out over the radio for the ground forces to start moving. The Reaper snipers were fast at work neutralizing anything that moved outside of the building. The calls were coming back as they dropped sniper positions within the compound. What came next shook me at my core, but it was too late to stop.

There were multiple calls coming across the radio that several of the targets that had been taken out, were in fact FBI agents. Fuck. Not something I wanted to hear. Let alone anything I thought I'd be hearing. Luka and Devin looked at me with wide eyes.

Luka: *"What the fuck are the Feds doing here?!"*

Devin: *"This can't be happening right? The Feds teamed up with Kessler?"*

Kyl: *"I had a feeling something was off. I guess I wasn't wrong. Makes sense for why they took out Agent Lewis. He must've figured out what was going on and they shut him up."*

Luka: *"Well what the fuck do we do now? Now we're killing Feds too?"*

The smug look of disgust on Luka's face made me laugh.

Kyl: *"Fuck it, we're all going to hell anyways and you know damn well there's something dirty going on here. Looks like we're killing Feds too boys."*

Luka smiled and began to chuckle.

Luka: *"Fuck it. Let's do this."*

Devin: *"Until the wheels fall off brothers."*

Deedra just nodded. She was quiet, almost like she was on autopilot.

I didn't ask what she was thinking. It didn't seem like the appropriate moment to delve into that. There was something in her eyes I hadn't seen before. Almost a different type of worry. I wasn't exactly sure.

We were in this now, there was no turning back. This had gone from complicated to complete cluster fuck. Killing a bunch of Feds hadn't been a part of the plan. On the other side of it all, no one could've predicted Mitch Kessler would be teaming up with the FBI. The fact they had killed Agent Lewis told me this operation wasn't exactly sanctioned.

Sixty seconds to impact. I closed my eyes; this would be my last minute of peace, possibly forever. I might not make it out this time. I took a deep breath and steadied my hands on my M4. Ten seconds. Here it comes. Five seconds. This is it, here we go. The impact of my titan semi hitting the reinforced gates shook the road hard enough we felt it in the armored Excursion. Automatic gun fire erupted Immediately. I could already hear the rounds bouncing off the truck as we blew through the gates. Death's icy hands were already busy plucking the souls from those being dispatched from this life.

I knew there was no direct path to the main house. We'd have been foolish to get that close yet. But getting the titan semi deep into the compound had been vital to the plan. The driver had done a good job of that but upon exiting the truck, had expired in a flurry of bullets. Unfortunately, he'd done his job.

As we all exited the vehicle, the fire fight seemed to get even more intense. With the truck as a shield and the wall at our backs, we began to drop our adversaries with strict precision. There was no way to advance yet, we were taking heavy fire from several directions. My ground troops were expelling targets but were also pinned down at the moment.

The whole dynamic of this had changed with the presence of the Feds. They were far more adequately trained and more well organized than anything Kessler could've planned on his own. It added an air of difficulty and definitely slowed things down for us. It wasn't impossible but it certainly wasn't going to be easy now.

As he began to advance, I kept Deedra just behind me and to my right. She was a hell of a shot surprisingly and she seemed oddly able to predict any movements the FBI were going to make. She was picking apart their tactical movements before they were even able execute. That type of tactical skill isn't just acquired, it takes years of study and practice. I had questions but right now wasn't the time. She was getting us closer to the main house a lot more quickly.

A sudden burst of warm liquid covered my face. Had I been hit? Devin had been at my left, I reached for him to steady myself as I wiped the blood from eye. But my hand fell on empty air. As my vision cleared, I looked down, my heart sank, and I dropped to one knee. He was gone, shot in the head. My long-time friend, confidant, General, and fabled member of the Four Horsemen lie dead at my side. I wanted to scream but it was caught. The lump in throat wouldn't let me. The tears welled up in my eyes as I stood and struck down the man who'd taken his life. I surged forward into the hail of gunfire as if I were invisible. I dropped three more before I realized I'd taken a few hits in the vest and couldn't breathe. I was suddenly lifted off of my feet. Taska had grabbed me and pulled me back into cover. Deedra and Luka rushed to my side as I tried to catch my breath. The vest had done its job, I was alive.

Deedra was in my face immediately.

Deedra: *"Don't fucking do that again! I'm sorry about Devin, I am. But we need you, this all falls apart and is pointless if you're dead Kyl!"*

Luka: *"Agreed. We will get our revenge. You can't lose your shit now. We need you."*

I took several deep breaths and closed my eyes for a few seconds to collect myself. As I opened my eyes, I looked around and noticed more than two dozen of my men strewn out across the compound dead. Fuck. Dammit Devin.

We'd pushed the mass of Kessler's army and the Feds back into the main house. I'd have much rather kept most of the fighting on the outside grounds, but I knew at some point it would come to this. Deedra had given us a very detailed map of the inside so at least we weren't going in blind.

Kyl: *"Taska, have a couple men take Devin's body out of here."*

Taska: *"Yes sir."*

We were fifty yards from the main house. It was an impressive building in size. Had to be nearly ten thousand square feet. With most of the fighting centralized in the main house, I had to tip the scales here into our favor. It was time for my Trojan horse to be revealed and we most certainly did not want to be any closer than we are now.

The titan semi had been modified to take heavy fire and be strong enough to bust through the gates. It had been important that the rig itself took the brunt of the force and impact to keep the tanker trailer it was hauling safe. The tanker itself didn't look like anything special beyond a regular tanker. It was on the inside that all the work had been done. The interior of the trailer had been fitted to accommodate an extremely volatile mixture of explosives. I leaned back against the building we were behind, plugged my ears, and pressed the detonator.

Surprise mother fuckers.

Chapter 35

Death, love, loathing, and betrayal

As someone who's never overdone anything, especially explosives, I may have overdone it here just a tad bit. I was surprised right along with all the mother fuckers that were supposed to be surprised.

Aside from the absolute deafening percussion of the explosion, the damage it caused was well into excessive. Most of the building we'd been hiding behind had been obliterated. Some of the closer buildings had literally been vaporized. I know that sounds ridiculous but it's certainly not. They were completely gone. A rubble littered foundation was the last remaining clue to the fact there'd ever been a building there. The truck itself was just gone and all that remained was a thirty-foot-wide crater probably five or six feet deep.

The West wing was completely gone and a substantial portion of the front of the house had been wiped out. The gun fire had already resumed, and small fire fights were breaking out around the complex. Mostly the east and south sides of the house had largely been unaffected by the explosion.

At this point, I had no idea who was still in this. I was certain we'd taken out a large portion of the Feds that had been involved. Judging by the fact they had no backup coming to bail them out, I had to believe at this point they'd been all bought and paid for. I'm sure there were likely some upper rank involved that had been paid well also. Who of course would take all the credit for taking me down in his top-secret investigation, or more accurately at this point, would assume no knowledge of any of this and all those included would have acted on their own as a rogue group. Fucking Federal agencies couldn't be trusted in any capacity.

Kyl: *"Everyone still in one piece?"*

Luka: *"Still fucking here. You're fired from explosives duty from now on though. Holy shit."*

Deedra: *"No joke, we're lucky it didn't bury us. For fucks sake Kyl."*

Taska: *"Lighten up guys, that was a blast."*

Everyone stared at him. No one had ever heard Taska crack a joke. I couldn't help myself, I burst into laughter. Taska smiled and everyone else chuckled along with me.

Kyl: *"Let's finish this shit and go get a drink."*

There was still so much dust in the air it made moving towards the main house easier. We were met by practically no resistance at all. Once we were inside, it was a whole different story. We immediately came under heavy fire, and it wasn't easy to move forward at all. We'd taken heavy casualties already, the bodies of my men laid out across the entryway and adjoining rooms. I watched Luka's face turn from pain to anger as he began to recognize many of those who had fallen. He knew most of them better than I ever had and several amongst the dead were Reapers. He let out a war cry and lunged forward, firing wildly. In his anger and haste, he hadn't noticed the partially crumbled wall that was hiding several guys from the opposing side. Taska leaped into action before I could say anything. He immediately absorbed the initial burst of rounds that had been headed for Luka. As soon as he realized what was happening, Luka turned to return fire but was at a bad angle that exposed him again. Taska laid down round after round, again moving in front of Luka. He swept Luka to the side as if he'd been weightless. I was able to slip through the door and blindside them, but it had been too late. Taska had taken more than a dozen hits and the vest hadn't stopped them all. I rushed to Taska's side and dropped to my knees. I immediately tried to apply pressure to the worst of the wounds.

He reached up and grabbed my hand.

Taska: *"It's okay boss, I had to protect him."*

Kyl: *"You did good Taska, you did real good. It's going to be okay; we're going to get you out of here. Just hang on."*

He squeezed my hand and began to speak again.

Taska: *"When worlds collide, you're going to lose those you love most. It's part of it sometimes. It's been the greatest honor to serve under your command and guard you all these years. I'm proud of the life I lived next to you sir. You guys are my family and I love you all."*

His giant hand felt as if he was still holding on, but he wasn't. He was gone. I couldn't hear the gunfire anymore. There was no noise at all. I sat there with his hand on mine, just looking at him. "I love you too brother, the honor was all mine."

My head started to spin. I was dizzy with fury, and I could feel the anger starting to spill over from deep within. They were all going to die. I was going to kill every single one of these bastards until their blood filled the street leading up to the compound.

I stood and yelled at the top of my lungs.

Kyl: *"Kessler I'm fucking coming for you. I'm going to fucking kill you!"*

Luka stood, the tears streaming down his face. His eyes had turned black, it seemed. He looked at me, checked his weapon, bit back the sob I knew he was holding in.

Luka: *"We end this now boss. For Devin and for Taska. For all these fallen men. We owe them that."*

Deedra: *"If I had to guess, Kessler is likely held up in the southeast corner. That's where the safe room is. It's inside of his bar and billiards room. This way."*

With that, we started moving with even more purpose. We were possessed by rage and driven by revenge. They had started this war, but I was going to end it.

Just so you know, sheer will, and determination does not mean it just automatically gets easier. As we moved through the house, clearing room by room. It was nothing short of seemingly impossible to make our way to where we were going. Kessler had concentrated the majority of his remaining forces in the east wing. Our only real saving grace had been that none of them were a good shot. It was the volume of bullets coming in our direction nearly constantly that made it feel like we weren't going to make it.

Then, as if fate decided we needed a break. Someone on the other side had a whole full blown retard moment. They had lobbed a grenade at us but hadn't pulled the pin. I picked it up, pulled the pin, and tossed it right back at them.

After it went off, the gun fire stopped. I waited for what felt like an eternity. Nothing. I leaned to my right and looked down the hall. Luka and Deedra both looking from their vantage point. I slowly stood and began to make my way cautiously towards the makeshift blockage in the hallway. The blast had killed the remaining four that had been huddled up here. Thanks for the extra hand there fellas.

Directly in front of me was the door to where I had to assume Kessler was holed up. The doors had taken the majority of our return fire so there wasn't much to get them open. Luka gave it one swift kick and just like that, we were in.

It was oddly quiet. There were a few sporadic bursts of gunfire here and there. The safe room door hadn't been closed all the way. Strange. I carefully slid the barrel of my M4 into the opening and wedged it open a little further. I could see a body lying on the floor. I opened the door and stepped the rest of the way in. There in the center of the room, was Mitch Kessler dead on the floor in a pool of blood. Someone had shot him directly in the face. I was really fucking angry that he was dead.

I wanted to kill him. I needed to watch him die. Someone had taken that from me.

Luka looked every bit as disappointed as I was. He pulled out his pistol and shot Kessler in the dick. He just looked at me and shrugged.

Luka: *"I needed to feel like I took something from him. Now they can bury him with no dick."*

I nodded. Fair enough, I wanted to shoot him too, but something was bothering me. Who had shot him? He wasn't even armed. He trusted whoever had killed him. Something was off. The air even felt wrong.

Kyl: *"We have to move now. Deedra, fastest way out of here not the way we came in."*

As she began to answer, a heavy presence of footsteps rushed towards us.

"FBI! Drop your weapons!"

They had to know that wasn't going to happen and they recognized it almost immediately and without much warning opened fire. Luka stepped in front of me and opened fire as he took several rounds in the vest knocking him down. I grabbed him and drug him behind the bar. Whatever misconception you might have about getting hit in a bullet proof vest not hurting, we're absolutely wrong.

It hurt like a mother fucker. It was comparable to getting hit in the chest with a baseball bat.

Luka gasped for air trying to catch his breath after being hit. Deedra laid down cover fire while I tried to figure out how we were getting out of this room. There were no windows, the only way out was through that door. I looked around quickly. There were dozens of bottles of liquor back here. Anything over forty percent alcohol would burn and almost all of these were. I started tossing bottles at the hallway, it was a long shot, but if I could get them to back up far enough, we could bolt for the room across the hall. I stuffed a rag into one of the bottles and made my own Molotov cocktail. Just as I was about to throw it, gunfire erupted from the other end of the hall. The Reapers had made their way through the house. This was our one shot.

I lit the rag and flung the bottle into the hallway igniting all the other liquor I'd tossed out.

Kyl: *"Move now, the room across the hall. Go!"*

They hadn't been so distracted that they'd forgotten us. Shots rang out and I could hear the bullets whizzing by as we made our way into the next room. Fortunately, a lot of these rooms were connected so we were able to continue moving. The more distance we could put between us and them, the better off we'd be.

I grabbed anything not bolted down and began throwing it into the hall. I wanted to barricade the way and provide enough cover to shoot from.

Deedra slid across the hall and started to pick off anyone in the open. I saw two drop as I dropped two others. Luka was propped against the doorframe taking his shots as I was reloading.

I noticed there was blood on the door and when I looked down, I could see more dripping from Luka's arm.

Kyl: *"Shit, are you hit?"*

Luka: *"Ya, I caught one crossing into the other room. Slipped past the vest around my side. I'll live, no worries."*

Deedra flashed me a worried look.

Kyl: *"We've got to get out of here."*

Deedra: *"There's too many outside over here... I've only got two mags left."*

Luka: *"Same."*

Kyl: *"I have three. We're just going to have to press through the house back towards the west end. If we can get to the Excursion, we're out of here."*

As I readied myself to move, a voice yelled out from down the hallway.

FBI Agent: *"This is Agent Timothy Hague with the FBI. You killed my brother. I'm going to take you down, you piece of shit. Dead or alive doesn't matter to me"*

You have got to be shitting me. There's another Agent Gag. I started laughing almost hysterically.

Kyl: *"Check it out, your brother was a real douchebag. But I didn't kill him or order him killed. His ATF partner took him out on his own and you took him out already. So, what do you say we call things square, and we go our separate ways. You can take credit for taking down the Kessler family and I'll disappear."*

Agent Hague: *"Nice try, but I'm taking credit for taking all of you down. But if you put down your weapons and surrender, I'll let you live out your life in Federal prison."*

As he'd been talking away, I had been able to draw a clean line of fire on the agent next to him. I squeezed the trigger and watched the red mist followed by his body slumping to the ground.

Kyl: *"Was that a clear enough fuck you? Not happening shit sack. I'm walking out of here and if that means I have to kill you first, then so be it."*

I could hear the anger in his voice as he gave the order to open fire. Fuck him. I couldn't believe this was all over the stupid pain in the ass Agent Gag. Now I wished I had killed him. I wouldn't miss my opportunity this time around.

With the Reapers behind them and us still throwing shot after shot towards them, we were at an advantage to be able to put some ground between us. I sent a few more rounds down the hallway as Deedra and Luka made a break for it.

As we made our way into a large living room, we were blindsided by another small group of Feds. There were at least six of them and they had all opened fire on us. I saw Deedra go down first and then I felt a round dig into the back of my vest. I slid to Deedra's side and laid my body over hers as two more rounds found a home in my vest. I felt a hot burning sensation in my side. One had clearly slid past the armor and sunk into my flesh. Another one ricocheted off something close and then glanced off the side of my head. Everything suddenly slowed down as I scrambled to get Deedra up and moving. I turned to grab Luka, but he had stepped out of my reach. He was firing wildly at the group bearing down on us. He'd already taken several hits.

I started towards him as Hague and his group turned the corner in the room. I had already had my rifle raised and without hesitation, I shot and killed him. One well placed shot in the forehead,

As soon as he hit the floor, they all opened fire. Luka was screaming at them to die, and I was screaming at him to come on.

He'd backed up just enough to grab cover for a moment behind one of the large pillars in the room. He turned and looked at me and my heart sank as I saw all the blood pouring from him. I could feel the tears streaming down my face.

Kyl: *"Luka we got to go now. Come on, we've got to get you to a doctor. Move it."*

Luka: *"Not this time Kyl. You have to go, brother. I'm going to cover your exit, but you have to go."*

Kyl: *"Man don't do this to me, let's go now!"*

Luka: *"I love you brother; you were the only real family I've had here. It's time for me to repay my debt to you giving me a life I've loved. Go, I'm right behind you."*

He looked at Deedra and she grabbed my arm and was screaming at me. I couldn't hear anything as the gunfire erupted from the other side of the room. Three Reapers opened fire as Luka began to slide out from behind the pillar.

There were so many bullets flying in all directions. I couldn't get to him. I couldn't save him. I fired until there was nothing left in the mag while Deedra pulled me towards the door. I watched as Luka stood his ground and took round after round trying to give us cover to get out. He turned one last time and looked at me, smiled, and fell to the ground dead.

I couldn't feel anything anymore. My body had gone numb from losing blood. I was screaming but I couldn't even hear myself scream. I'd just watched the only person I'd ever considered my best, closest, and most trusted friend die. We'd had so much history and so many close calls. He was my brother.

Deedra had been pulling on me and screaming to move. I hadn't even noticed she was still there. My legs were jello and my arms felt so heavy as she led me down another hall and into a room. She was bleeding too. I couldn't stand anymore and just collapsed against the wall and slid down.

I began to sob as she tried to console me while working to get pressure on my open wound. She kept telling me how much she loved me and that we were going to be alright. She was all I had left. Everyone was dead.

She was leaning in, looking me in the eyes and kissing my forehead. I pulled out my pistol because my rifle was out of ammo. My timing couldn't have been any better either. Just then, the door burst open and before the agent could raise his weapon, I fired, hitting him in the left eye. The one behind him got a round off as I pushed Deedra out of the way. The bullet struck me in a weak spot and penetrated the vest. Deedra spun to fire, but she hesitated.

FBI Agent: *Agent Symonds? Holy shit! We've been looking for you everywhere!"*

The agent didn't get another word out before Deedra fired and killed her on the spot.

My heart was racing. I was sitting there bleeding out. My head was so fuzzy from everything, but I had heard and seen exactly what had just been said. I was suddenly overcome by a deep sense of anger and betrayal. I'd promised myself no one would ever betray me again and live to tell about it. So much death, love, loathing, and betrayal. I raised my pistol in her direction. My ears were ringing, and my vision was fading.

Deedra: "Kyl, please baby I can explain everything. Let's just get out of here and..."

Before she could even finish her sentence, I closed my eyes one last time and squeezed the trigger. Click. Boom.

About the Author

Kyle A. Medlam – Kyle was raised on a small farm in Kansas but found his way to Oklahoma in search of a fresh view on life. He owns and operates a small professional consulting and life coaching firm as well as being a full-time single parent. The gym and healthy living are a way of life, but nothing is more important than being a good dad! Together they enjoy fast cars, anime, and gaming. If you'd like to learn more, follow on TikTok: @kylemedlam and Instagram: @kylemedlam.

www.ingramcontent.com/pod-product-compliance
Lightning Source LLC
Chambersburg PA
CBHW070849260626
47170CB00007B/2552